TRUTH ENDURES

Je Anne Boleyn
Book Two

Sandra Vasoli

As Anne loved Elizabeth…
For Stacey

TRUTH ENDURES
Je Anne Boleyn
Book 2

ISBN-13: 978-84-944893-7-2

M

MadeGlobal Publishing

For more information on
MadeGlobal Publishing, visit our website:
www.madeglobal.com

Anne Boleyn illustrated by Dmitry Yakhovsky, based on the "Hever Rose" portrait of Anne Boleyn.

DRAMATIS PERSONAE

Anne Boleyn (c.1501 – 1536): Marquess of Pembroke, Queen of England from 1533 – 1536

Anne Brooke, Baroness Cobham (1501 – 1558): wife of Sir George Brooke, 9th Baron Cobham. Attendant horsewoman at Anne Boleyn's coronation; possibly an accuser of Anne in 1536

Anne Gainsford Zouche (1495/1500? – 1545?): Anne Boleyn's lady-in-waiting and close companion

Anne Savage (c.1496 – c. 1546): Baroness Berkeley; lady-in-waiting and friend Anne Boleyn; one of the few documented witnesses to the wedding of Anne Boleyn and Henry VIII on 25 January 1533

Anne (Nan) Saville – mentioned in primary documents as lady-in-waiting to Anne Boleyn; very little known of her

Bess Holland (d.1548): mistress of Duke of Norfolk from 1526; daughter of Norfolk's chief steward; maid of honour to Anne Boleyn

Cardinal Thomas Wolsey (1473 – 1530): Henry VIII's Lord Chancellor, and Archbishop of York

Charles Brandon (c.1484 – 1545): KG; 1st Duke of Suffolk, 1st Viscount Lisle; married to Mary Tudor, sister of Henry VIII

Dowager Duchess of Norfolk - Agnes Howard (c.1477 – May 1545): second wife of Thomas Howard, 2nd Duke of Norfolk. Anne Boleyn was her step-granddaughter

Elizabeth Barton (1506? – 1534): known as The Nun of Kent; executed as a result of prophecies against the marriage of King Henry VIII of England to Anne Boleyn

Elizabeth Howard, Lady Boleyn (1480 – 1538): Countess of Wiltshire; wife of Thomas Boleyn, Earl of Wiltshire; mother of Anne, Mary and George Boleyn; mistress of Hever Manor

Elizabeth Howard Lady Norfolk (d.18 September, 1534): daughter of Thomas Howard and one of six ladies who accompanied Anne Boleyn to Calais in 1532

Emporer Charles V (1500 – 1558): ruler of Spain; crowned Emperor of Holy Roman Empire by Pope Clement VII in 1530; nephew of Katherine of Aragon

Eustace Chapuys (c.1490/2 – 1556): the Imperial ambassador to England from 1529 to 1545; wrote detailed letters to Charles V about the politics of Henry VIII's court; supporter of Katherine of Aragon and enemy of Anne Boleyn

Francis Bryan (1490? – 1550): courtier and diplomat; became Chief Gentleman of the Privy Chamber to Henry VIII; cousin to Anne Boleyn

Francis Weston (1511 – 1536): Knight of the Bath; a gentleman of the Privy Chamber at the court of King Henry VIII of England; accused of adultery with Queen Anne Boleyn, tried and executed on 17 May 1536

François I (1494 – 1547): monarch of the House of Valois; King of France from 1515 until 1547

George Boleyn (1503 – 1536): 2nd Viscount Rochford; brother and confidante to Anne Boleyn; married to Jane Parker; statesman and diplomat; accused of adultery with Queen Anne Boleyn, tried and executed on 17 May 1536

Gregorio Casale (c.1500 – 1536): Italian diplomat; Henry VIII's representative in Rome and at the Vatican

Henry Fitzroy (1519 – 1536): Knight of the Garter; 1st Duke of Richmond and Somerset; illegitimate son of Henry VIII of England and Elizabeth Blount; married Lady Mary Howard, daughter of Thomas Howard, Duke of Norfolk

Henry Norreys (c. 1482 – 1536): courtier and Groom of the Stool to Henry VIII; accused of adultery with Queen Anne Boleyn; tried and executed on 17 May 1536

Henry VIII (1491 – 1547): King of England from 1509 - 1547

Honor Grenville (1493/4 – 1566): Viscountess Lisle; friend to Anne Boleyn; married first to Sir John Bassett, then to Arthur Plantagenet, 1st Viscount Lisle

Jane Seymour (c.1508 – 1537): Queen of England from 1536 to 1537, succeeded Anne Boleyn as queen consort to Henry VIII. Seymour's family estate was Wulfhall, Savernake Forest, Wiltshire. Jane was not as well educated as Anne, had some ability to read and write; was trained in household management and sewing

Jean de Dinteville (1504 – 1555): French diplomat; associate of French humanists, most notably Lefèvre d'Etaples; the figure on the left in Holbein's painting *The Ambassadors*

John Robyns - educated at Oxford; advisor to Henry VIII on astrological matters

John Skut - royal tailor during the reign of Henry VIII of England; served all of the King's six wives

John and Lady Anne Walshe - Owners of Little Sodbury, the estate where William Tyndale worked for two years (circa 1521) after leaving Cambridge, probably as a tutor to their two young sons; known in the region for hospitality to nobility and clergy; and received a visit from King Henry VIII and Queen Anne Boleyn in 1535

Katherine of Aragon (1485 – 1536): Princess of Spain; first wife of Henry VIII; Queen of England from 1509 – 1533

Margaret Bryan (1468 – c. 1551/52): Lady Governess to Elizabeth, also all of Henry VIII's children - Mary, Elizabeth, Henry FitzRoy and Edward

Margaret Wyatt, Lady Lee (1506 – 1561): sister of poet Thomas Wyatt; wife of Sir Anthony Lee; close friend and lady-in-waiting to Anne Boleyn

Margery Horsman (died c. 1547): maid of honour in the household of Katherine of Aragon and Anne Boleyn, possibly to Jane Seymour as well

Marguerite d'Angoulême (1492 – 1549): sister of François I; Princess of France; Queen of Navarre; French mentor to Anne Boleyn

Mark Smeaton (c.1512 – 1536): musician at the court of Henry VIII; served in the household of Anne Boleyn; accused of adultery with Queen Anne Boleyn, tried and executed on 17 May 1536

Mary Boleyn/Mary Carey (c.1499 – 1543): sister of Anne Boleyn; mistress to Henry VIII; wife of William Carey and, after his death, of William Stafford

Mary Scrope (d. 1548): said to have been in the service at court of King Henry VIII's first four wives; wife of Sir William Kingston, Constable of the Tower of London, in attendance on Anne Boleyn during her imprisonment in the Tower in May 1536; she and her husband were among those who accompanied Anne to the scaffold.

Mary Tudor (1516 – 1558): daughter of Henry VIII and Katherine of Aragon; Queen of England and Ireland from July 1553 until her death

Matthew Parker (1504 – 1575): influential theologian; Queen Anne Boleyn's chaplain; before Anne Boleyn's death in 1536, she commended her daughter Elizabeth to his care

Pope Clement VII (1478 – 1534): Giulio di Giuliano de' Medici, elected Pope on 19 November 1523 and served until his death; opposed the annulment of the marriage of Henry VIII and Katherine of Aragon

Rowland Lee (c.1487 – 1543): Bishop of Coventry and Lichfield; supporter of Henry VIII's annulment; possible officiant at the marriage of Henry VIII and Anne Boleyn

Thomas Audley (c.1488 – 30 April 1544): Knight of the Garter; Lord Chancellor of England from 1533 to 1544. Succeeded Sir Thomas More as Lord Keeper of the Great Seal

Thomas Boleyn (c.1477 – 1539): Knight of the Garter; Earl of Wiltshire; father of Anne, Mary and George Boleyn; statesman and diplomat for Henry VIII

Thomas Cranmer (1489 – 1556): Fellow of Cambridge University; humanist and leader of the Reformation; appointed Archbishop of Canterbury in 1532 by Henry VIII

Thomas Cromwell (c.1485 – 1540): Knight of the Garter; 1st Earl of Essex; advisor to Cardinal Wolsey; member of Henry VIII's Privy Council and chief minister from 1532 to 1540

Thomas Howard (1473 – 1554): Knight of the Garter; 3rd Duke of Norfolk; married to Elizabeth Stafford; uncle of Anne Boleyn

Thomas More (1478 – 1535): Henry VIII's councillor and Lord Chancellor from 1529 to 1532; lawyer, humanist and statesman

William Brereton (c.1487 – 1536: Groom of Henry VIII's Privy Chamber; accused of adultery with Queen Anne Boleyn, tried and executed on 17 May 1536

William Kingston (c. 1476 – 1540): Knight of the Garter, Member of Parliament; English courtier, soldier and administrator and Constable of the Tower of London during much of the reign of Henry VIII

William Sandys (1470 – 1540): Knight of the Garter; 1st Baron Sandys of the Vyne; diplomat; appointed Lord Chamberlain in 1526; favourite courtier of Henry VIII

William Tyndale (1494–1536): born in Gloucestershire, a scholar who was a primary figure in Protestant reform. Known for translating the Bible into English

Jane Ashley; Margaret Gamage, Mary Norreys, Grace Newport; Eleanor Paston, Mistress Frances de Vere Elizabeth Browne – all notated as ladies in waiting to Anne when she was Queen

The Palace of Whitehall
February 1533

LO, HE WAS something to observe - as observe I did, with pride and pleasure: my royal consort in resplendent authority, impeccably groomed and luxuriously draped in burnished sable, his broad chest weighted with a golden, gem-studded collar. He was radiant! Flush with health, his resonant voice echoing as he paced the length of the new gallery in Whitehall with his councillors. The events of recent weeks had steeped him in vigour and confidence.

No one wore an air of aplomb as well as did my husband, Henry VIII of England.

Unconsciously I placed my hands on my gently swelling belly. The gesture had become a habit for me of late. With a contented smile I reflected over the months since late autumn, when Henry and I had travelled to Calais to meet with the French king, François I. It had been a triumphant visit for me - Anne Boleyn - the girl who had spent her youth at the royal court of France, being groomed in the ways of royal demeanor, Christian humanism, and womanhood. Now I returned in splendour as a Marquess in my own right, accompanied by my betrothed, His Grace the King. We enjoyed a most pleasing and very successful stay, and an even more romantic trip homeward, taking our time crossing the English countryside, revelling in each other's company before – very reluctantly on my part - returning to London just before Christmastide. Even that sojourn had been an unexpected pleasure. The winter season spent at Greenwich was jubilant despite our increased disillusionment with the Pope and his obstinate refusal to align with Henry in granting him his rightful divorce from Katherine of Aragon. Regardless of that cumbrance, I basked in the adoration of a man with whom I now lived as if we were husband and wife. Yes, I had decided before we departed for Calais to abandon my dogged stance to remain chaste before we wed. The resulting fulfilment of living as a couple was rewarding and we were happy and content with one another. Indeed, it was a Christmas to be remembered.

During that halcyon period, I did admittedly experience one cause for anxiety - it seemed I had the beginnings of a nagging illness which I could not identify. I had eaten less and less yet remained nauseous throughout the day while feeling overbearingly tired in the afternoons. Only when my maid, Lucy, tried valiantly to lace me into the bodice of a new gown, resulting in the spillage of an unusually ample bosom from its neckline, did I finally perceive the exultant truth - I was pregnant with Henry's child! Please be to God, with his *son*? Never again will there be such a gift for the New Year as was that realization. The tender scene between us when I told him the news will be forever etched in my mind's eye. Occasionally I had allowed myself the luxury of imagining a time when I might announce a pregnancy to the King – I would create a gorgeous, elaborate tableau in which to unveil the news. The moment came, however, when Henry's exhaustion and melancholy over years of thwarted effort to gain his freedom to marry me were etched deep in the lines on his face. In truth, at times, I had wondered why he persisted in his intent to have me – to marry me. Was it not possible with the very next obstacle thrown in his path - one more denial from the Pope - he might just give up, even though we loved one another? But then! *Sweet Jesu*! The pregnancy I had suspected became certain, and while we dined together alone one evening, I tenderly turned his tired face to mine, and in a voice thick with emotion, told him, simple and plain. At first, he was devoid of expression, and I held my breath, fearing he had already determined to abandon me and our hopeless suit. But then his face crumpled, and he had clung to me, weeping into my shoulder. I held my strong and powerful King and felt his shoulders heave with quiet sobs, overcome with relief and joy at the news he so desperately wanted: had waited an eternity to hear.

The next day and those that followed were imbued with the exhilaration of an expected prince.

In late January, then, urged on by the great blessing the Almighty had bestowed upon us, His Grace the King had taken decisive action by designating Dr Thomas Cranmer, our staunch supporter and friend, as his choice for the vacant position of Archbishop of Canterbury. This step placed in Cranmer's capable hands the task of acquiring licenses necessary for our very secret marriage. So in the dark pre-dawn of 25 January 1533, Henry and I were wed in the northern tower of Whitehall Palace. While snow softly cloaked London's rooftops, we had stood in the fire-lit chamber with only the fewest witnesses, looked into each other's eyes and, prompted by the Reverend Rowland Lee, stated our vows to remain together 'til death us depart'.

And thus did I find myself impervious to all previous misgivings. No less powerful a man than the King of England had promised, even before God, to become my sworn protector.

Pregnant, married at last, with a husband who doted on me?Life could not be more blissful. More secure.

•

Here were now three highly competent men operating from the leading positions of power in Henry's Council, all of them motivated to present His Highness as the ultimate determiner of all matters, political and theological, pertaining to his realm. His word would thus be supreme, and the dependency on the Church of Rome and those decisions previously considered the prerogative of Pope Clement VII conclusively broken.

I observed with satisfaction the culmination of what had been a long and arduous campaign to gain Clement's agreement to annul Henry's marriage to Katherine of Aragon. Despite many setbacks, a combination of brilliant logic, practiced crusading and, ultimately, sheer force of will, had brought us to the present status: Henry firmly in control, and me a married woman, expecting a fully legitimate prince, heir to the throne of England.

Before me strode the ingenious lawyer Thomas Cromwell, who, by demonstrating cunning and dedication to the King's service, now held several illustrious titles including Master of the Jewels and Chancellor of the Exchequer. Beside him walked Thomas Cranmer, Henry's personal nominee as the new Archbishop of Canterbury, and - of no lesser stature - His Grace's recently installed Lord Chancellor, Thomas Audley. They, along with Henry, would appear before the House, make their case and subsequently, following negotiation, payments, and politicking would confidently await an acknowledgement from Rome on Cranmer's appointment to the highest clerical office in the land.

Undeniably, the tactics this trio had devised to gain victory were worthy of the master manipulator and Florentine statesman Niccolò di Bernardo dei Machiavelli himself. We had heard much of Machiavelli and the crafty principles he espoused. Cromwell was an enthusiast of Machiavelli, and for that matter, all things Italian; especially the barbed offensives so aptly utilized by the powerful families who ruled the principal city-states. And of course, Henry had long been an admirer of the great Lorenzo de Medici and a student of the humanism flourishing in Florence. I was aware that the Florentine principles of leadership were exacting a great influence on Henry's newfound determination to grasp and direct his destiny.

Once formally sanctioned by the Church in Rome, it was intended that Cranmer would immediately use his newly appointed authority to exercise the conviction that the King of England was now Supreme Authority of the Church in England and that his previously held jurisdiction was no longer the privilege of the Pope. The premier directive? To officially pronounce Henry's long marriage to Katherine of Aragon null and void, and let the Pope be damned!

With that act of defiance, we would be sure to hear the bell toll for the Church of Rome in England.

Until Dr Cranmer's new position was confirmed, which would then allow him to create the necessary official documents for certification of our marriage, I was obliged to keep my two 'secrets', albeit there were a few in my closest circle who did know the truth ... that I was the wife of the King - his new Queen - and I carried his child. Oh, how difficult it was to remain circumspect when I wanted to shout the news from the Palace towers!

I resigned myself to maintaining the privacy of my condition, but at least felt able to share the joy with my family. My mother and my sister Mary proved great sources of comfort and advice as I became accustomed to life as a pregnant woman. It proved helpful, being able to discuss the peculiarities and subtleties of what I experienced as the early days of sickness began to wane, and other cravings took precedence. Particularly I delighted in being included in that special clan of women who smiled knowingly when pregnancy was discussed.

My queasiness did subside, and in its place, I found I had little tolerance for meats but had a great urge to eat fruit, especially apples. I delighted in how my belly had become firm and had begun to swell as the babe within me grew and flourished.

Admittedly there were times when my resolve to remain discreet faltered. Rapturous over my new and treasured position as the King's pregnant wife, and simply itching for some jovial mischief, one wintry and bleak February afternoon I mingled with the usual groups of courtiers clustered, talking and passing time in the Presence Chamber. While conversing with Thomas Wyatt and the newly married Anne Gainsford Zouche I'd first looked artfully about to assess the crowd within earshot, then, during a lull in our discussion, had selected an apple from a porcelain bowlful which sat upon the sideboard before calling loudly and playfully, "These apples look delicious, don't you think, Thomas? It is quite strange because, of late, I find I have an insatiable hankering to eat apples such as I have never experienced before."

I waited for my words to register, and then widened my eyes in mock disbelief. "The King tells me it must be a sign that I am pregnant. But I have told him I think he *certainly* must be wrong ...!"

Then I laughed loudly, thinking this little scene terribly humorous, prompting heads to turn and everyone within range of hearing to stare. Gratified with the reaction thus generated, I stood, gathered my skirt with a flourish and swept coquettishly from the room, leaving all in my wake wondering what had just taken place.

Not that Henry, either, could contain our joyful secret entirely. He was giddy with unbridled elation at being a new husband and father-to-be. And although no official royal announcement had yet been made concerning our matrimony or my condition, he became less and less concerned with guarding the news. And how rightfully he deserved to proclaim the reasons for his exuberance for, I thought, no man had ever shown such patience, such loyalty, such *dedication* to any woman as did my Henry to me.

To provide him with just the smallest demonstration of my gratitude and devotion, I planned an elegant banquet in his honour, which was to be held in my beautiful new apartments in Whitehall on 24 February; the Feast of St Mathias. I invited all of the great personages of the court, and personally attended to every detail, as was my wont, to ensure the room looked its grandest. With fine arras lining the walls, masses of glowing gold plate on display, and spectacular dishes presented in elaborate style, my position and wealth were now evident to all. The ladies whom I had assembled as members of my household were all present, gaily bedecked, looking stunning, and in high humour. On that evening, Henry had chosen to partake of *aqua vitae*, or as its distillers called it - *uisge beatha* - the wickedly potent spirit produced by Scottish monks. He quickly became flush with the drink, jesting and flirting madly with me and my ravishing companions. I found his boisterous, ribald jokes and silly levity to be completely endearing, thinking how much he deserved an evening of release after the tensions he had endured. At one point he gave me a staged wink so noticeable that anyone in view would have wondered what was to come, then moved close - *much* too close - to the very proper Dowager Duchess of Norfolk before blurting loudly, with a noticeable slurring of the tongue, "Your Ladyship! Doth you not think that Madame the Marquess, seated right here next to me, has an exceptionally fine dowry and a rich marriage portion as we can all see from her luxurious apartment?"

He gesticulated wildly with his arms to indicate the scope of my possessions, nearly knocking the goblets from the table. "Does that not make her an excellent marriage prospect, hey?" Then, as I had done just a few days prior, he exploded in raucous laughter at his drink-fueled sense of comedy. The Duchess, stony-faced, leaned as far back in her seat as was possible in an attempt to escape Henry's liquored breath while those observing tittered behind their hands. Watching my beloved sway while he roared with amusement, I couldn't help but enjoy my own hearty chuckle.

The celebration did not conclude till early the morning next. From the room littered with the debris of gaiety, I saw the King off. Henry Norreys, his Groom of the Stool, had his arm firmly about the shoulders of His Majesty as he guided him, staggering amiably, toward his chambers. I suspected I would not see Henry at all on the morrow since there was little doubt he would remain abed till he could recover from the effects of the *uisge*. Smiling happily as I took myself to bed, I reflected on the entertaining moments of the evening, and mostly on what an irresistible drunk my husband had been.

•

Maggie Wyatt, Anne Zouche, Nan Saville and I sat at a polished table in the well-appointed Queen's Presence Chamber at Whitehall. Sipping small ale, piles of letters and personal references strewn before us, we reviewed the lists of maids and ladies who had been proposed to make up my retinue: potential appointees to the household of the Queen. Glancing up from a sheet of parchment, Maggie looked at me inquiringly. "How well do you know Lady Cobham, Anne?"

"I know her scarcely. I have met her on several occasions but can't say I have ever had a conversation of any depth with her. Do you know her, Maggie? How is her temperament? I daresay I am not keen on having those unknown to me as a part of my close personal circle. But then, I am not permitted to make strictly my own selections." Eyeing the stacks of letters from noble families all imploring for a position for a daughter or niece, I added, "His Grace the King owes many a favour, and I conveniently provide a solution by taking daughters of those so favoured into my household." I paused then, sniffing, "… even though it is of considerable concern to have someone unfamiliar serving in such proximity."

Indeed, I believed I was well justified in feeling irritated by this requirement. With a sharp stab of anguish, I remembered the incident of my stolen love letters. I recalled, as if it had happened only yesterday, my panic at the discovery and resulting despair which flooded me when I'd realized that someone – a spy; a secret enemy within my closest personal space! – had stolen the locked casket which concealed the letters which I had carefully kept together, and out of sight, over the years. I believed the miscreant was a maid employed to serve me in my privy chambers. She was recommended by my Uncle Norfolk's wife, but at the time I was unaware of the extent of Elizabeth Howard, Lady Norfolk's animosity toward me. So I fell into the Duchess's vicious trap and naively exposed my greatest treasure to an individual who had been hired by a detractor to steal evidence of Henry's love for me. They were intimate and immensely personal: gorgeous letters full of the romantic expression of a man deeply in love - missives composed by Henry throughout the beginning years of our courtship, mostly while we were apart, I having been at Hever while Henry remained at court. Every scratch of the quill, each splotch of ink smeared by his big hand had drawn me closer to him. He had revealed his wit using clever wordplay, and his bawdy, waggish self when he described a beautiful gown he had had made for me – one that he longed to see me in – and out of! Mostly, I ached to see once again those sweet and wistful drawings of a small heart, etched around my initials at the close of an especially endearing letter. I pored over them often, running my fingers over his writing, knowing he had meant them for my eyes only. And then, in a trice, they were gone, never to be returned or seen by me again. My heart broke every time I thought of it.

I was pulled back to the business at hand as Maggie shrugged, "I too, know her only superficially even though she is sister-in-law to my brother Thomas … or *was* when Thomas was married to that little scandal, Elizabeth Brooke. But the few times I have been in her company, she seemed quiet. Or perhaps simply exhausted, seeing as she has seven children!"

"That I cannot even imagine," I rejoined, wryly patting my stomach. "I am happy to be working on just one."

Anne smiled indulgently at me. My dear, close friends were treating me with such loving care. Then, narrowing her eyes and peering again at the list, she questioned, "And what of Mistress Seymour? Do either of you know much of her? She has been at court off and on for years since she served Katherine yet still I have never talked to her about anything of consequence."

I could not resist the temptation to be waspish about a woman of questionable allegiance, for whom I cared little anyway. Arching one groomed brow, I sneered "Why, is that not simply characteristic of Mistress Seymour? And the reason is that she appears to hold naught in that empty little head of hers which *is* of any importance …"

Hearing myself, I ruefully observed that my pregnancy had somehow stripped away a goodly layer of the discernment needed to avoid saying whatever came to my mind, no matter how cutting. But I didn't care so I added smugly, "Forsooth, ladies, her intelligence mirrors her looks - quite common!"

Anne and Maggie looked at each other and pressed their lips tightly in an attempt to suppress their laughter. Apparently they found my unchecked outbursts entertaining.

"WELL … Am I wrong?" I demanded with mock severity, my probing glance shifting between the two. "Speak out - what *do* you both think of her?"

"You are by no means in the wrong, Anne," Maggie hastily allowed. "She is quiet and dull as a tiny titmouse. She will offer no hardship as a member of your household because she will provide no opinions, and no one will even notice her."

Mollified, I grumbled, "Well then, that should be acceptable to me," and continued to peruse the lists.

The assembling of ladies who would make up my household neared completion, with many well-liked appointees and some about whom I was indifferent but whose appointments served their purpose. My closest confidantes had already been included, and then we added to the total number Nan Cobham and, somewhat grudgingly on my part, Mistress Seymour. It only remained, then, to confirm positions with Jane Ashley; Margaret Gamage, who was betrothed and set to marry William Howard in the spring; young Mary Norreys, who was the daughter of Henry's Groom of the Stool; the very pretty Grace Newport; Eleanor Paston, Countess of Rutland and a mother of six; Mistress Frances de Vere – at sixteen already wed to Henry Howard, Earl of Surrey. There then followed Elizabeth

Browne, Lady Worcester, and my sister-in-law Jane Parker, Lady Rochford. All were possessed of a singular degree of beauty - apart from Seymour. It was important to me that my ladies present an exceptional appearance and, furthermore, conduct themselves with unblemished gentility, and I fully intended to duly instruct them once they were all in place.

As for the men of my royal household, there were to be numerous trusted advisers. Thomas Cromwell, already indispensable to the King, was among those whom I considered beneficial, and he would serve an important place in my retinue once I was Queen. George Taylor would continue his good work as my Receiver-General. William Coffin, long in the King's service, would assume the position of my Master of the Horse; Thomas Burgh as Lord Chamberlain; and Sir Edward Baynton as Vice Chamberlain. Perhaps most important to me were those selected to be my personal chaplains. These brilliant men would confer with me and preach on our shared reformist views, a mission which would demand keen intelligence, a broad knowledge of theology and, perhaps above all, courage. We selected Hugh Latimer, a Cambridge scholar; Matthew Parker, another Cambridge theologian whom I had liked and trusted from the first time I met him; William Betts, who had already proved his mettle several years prior when found to be one of a group of scholars boldly circulating books deemed by our opponents to be heretical; and the redoubtable John Skypp. Skypp could be almost too resolute in the expression of his views, but I admired that about him. All in all, I intended to surround myself with a strong, outspoken assembly who would advance the cause of reform and unfailingly support Henry's right to supremacy.

Yet there were many in and around court who remained sources of great frustration to me. My abiding perception that Henry's chosen ambassador in Rome, Sir Gregory Casale, was apathetic had proved all too true when, late in January, we were given letters he had written boasting his self-described 'advancement' of Henry's cause. After years of fruitless negotiation on the Great Matter, Casale still considered it acceptable to present letters to the King that laid out numerous additional conditions demanded by the Pope to pronounce in Henry's favour. First, Henry must send a mandate for the remission of the cause, along with a newly appointed legate and two auditors. Then, he must persuade François to accept a general truce for three or four years, even amongst other ridiculous requirements. This contrivance was in complete opposition with Henry's instructions to Casale and did the Ambassador's credentials no service in my view. Henry however, always the gracious Sovereign, still responded politely to his man in Rome, advising him to thank the Pope, and discreetly tell his Holiness that the overtures were taken in good part, and trusting the Pope would concur, only by 'will and unkind stubbornness, with oblivion of former kindness, which be occasions of the let of the speedy finishing of our cause'.

I had looked on Henry's temperate reply in amazement, and with no small measure of cynical admiration. It made me realize I needed to learn all I could from him, seeing that soon I was to be Queen, and would often be required to respond well and fairly to vexing situations. Learn I must, because had this particular matter been left to me, I would have delivered a tongue-lashing to Signore Casale that he would not soon have forgotten!

On occasion, I would think back - oh, not so many years - to my life in France followed by my early time in the court of Henry and Katherine, and marvel at how my existence had changed so dramatically. Upon reflection, those days were so easy and light-hearted in their simple pursuits: maintaining a young lady's proper demeanor; hunting, dancing, playing at witty pastimes, dallying with the most handsome men and adorning oneself to play the coquette ... the threads weaving my life's tapestry had long since become much more intricate indeed.

•

Ever conscious of the new life – the all-important life – growing within me, I was engaged from morn 'til night. Details concerning the establishment of my household called for my attention; audiences were requested by those who sought my support in pleading matters to the King's Grace; there was constant worry about the increasingly intense skirmishes between Scotland and England while the tentative relationship with France was always of concern. Above all hung the palpable hostility of my opposers. Those critics – I had begun to think of them as enemies – were becoming ever more brazen, and openly included some who had been previously close to Henry and me: his sister Mary chief amongst them, with her husband Charles Brandon, Duke of Suffolk, who precariously balanced between the opinions of his wife and his King ... even my Uncle Norfolk, surprisingly – whose position could only be strengthened by the Howard bloodline on the throne, yet who openly disapproved of the dire measures being taken with the Church to achieve that goal.

At times I did wish for a reprieve, just a simple moment in time when I might revert to being Anne from Hever – but, of course, it was not to be had.

I could do naught but rejoice, however, when, in March, Cromwell delivered his carefully crafted *Act in Restraint of Appeals* to the Commons in Parliament, urging them to approve the statute which would enforce Henry's supremacy in all things pertaining to his realm. Both Houses approved the Act, and on 10 April, just before Easter, a definitive blow was delivered to Katherine. She was informed by a deputation comprising Norfolk, Suffolk, Exeter, Oxford, and the royal chamberlains that we had been married and, on direct orders of Henry the King, she was no longer Queen but would henceforth be referred to as the Dowager Princess of Wales. Her daughter Mary, whom I had not seen – or frankly, even given much thought to - in many months, remained apart from her mother with a diminished household.

True, the mere fact of their continued existence presented me with a vexation - but how good it was to think no longer of Katherine, or the former Princess, now known simply as Lady Mary - as active threats to the happiness I shared with Henry!

And happy we truly were.

Whitehall
Late March 1533

I WAS EXTREMELY APPREHENSIVE but nevertheless managed to paste a forced smile when Henry excitedly bid me take my seat at the table. He had invited his favoured astrologer, Master John Robyns, a Fellow of All Souls, Oxford, and thereby most accomplished, to a private supper with us for the purpose of receiving Robyns' prognostications on the impending birth of our child.

Now well into my fourth month of pregnancy and with my health seemingly superb, I was nevertheless unaccustomed to being in the presence of soothsayers and felt uneasy about what he might have to impart. Henry, on the other hand, positively throbbed with anticipation, and so we readied ourselves for what the esteemed astrologer would reveal.

I watched Henry as he and Robyns became thoroughly absorbed in studying the astrolabe set upon the long table in the library. I could not pay mind to what they discussed, however, as I was distracted by a peculiar sensation in my stomach, so much so that while they were engrossed in conversation I rose to walk about, then found a place to sit somewhat apart on a more comfortable chair, willing my supper to digest. Though I had not eaten overmuch, still I felt the food quivering in my gut. I thought it unusual because I was not nauseous or in pain, just feeling a constant fluttering … and of a sudden it all came clear! I sat bolt upright, placing my hands on my belly. It was not indigestion; it was the quickening of my child – my *babe* – within my womb! I could not stem the tears which filled my eyes, and fought to keep myself in check for, in truth, I did not wish to share such a very special moment with Master Robyns present. Though I did want to hear what he had to say, I could not wait 'til he had gone and I could share this wondrous event with my husband.

"Your Highnesses," Robyns half turned to address me while he and Henry continued to sit at the table strewn with parchments inscribed with celestial charts and figures. "I have excellent news. After much study and great deliberation, I am happy to inform you that your child, the Royal Child, will be born under the sixth astrological sign – indeed the most auspicious sign. That of Virgo ..."

"In what manner auspicious, Robyns?" Henry interjected tensely, betraying the depth of his anxiety. But the astrologer, tone deep and throaty, long white academic beard swaying with practiced gravitas, was not to be deflected from his ponderous delivery by a mere monarch.

"Virgo is a mutable sign, Your Grace, and gives rise to individuals who are appliant, thrive on changeability, and who possess a highly developed sense of social order. Virgoans are rooted to the earth, and those born to its coordinates are refined and precise. They are observant, keenly intelligent and have a great love of knowledge. And, most important for the future King of England, your son …"

My heart leaped. So I *was* to have a son …! John Robyns, the most highly esteemed soothsayer in the Kingdom, was confidently predicting I would bear a BOY-child!

"... will be ingenious, easily able to make swift and accurate decisions concerning the most complex of issues. He will be a most learned – a most *capable* - king who shall, I predict, prove a ruler equaled by none other than, perhaps, the legendary King Arthur ..."

Robyns interpreted the change in Henry's expression and hurriedly supplemented, "... and, of course, your *own* Majesty - a matter of fact that goes without saying, Sire."

The King cleared his throat, placated. The astrologer continued. "The signs foretell that his birth should occur in the earliest days of September, Your Highnesses ..." Robyns began to rise stiffly while offering a sage nod, "His reign will certainly mark a golden age for England."

I exhaled with immense relief as he, at a gracious expression of thanks from his Sovereign, concluded the audience. Despite the man's venerable bones, he offered a sweeping bow, that fascinating beard near brushing the silken carpet.

"Thank you, Master Robyns, this is wonderful news indeed," I heard myself call before feeling compelled to seek his further reassurance. "And this special Virgoan child ... he *will* be a boy, you say?"

"Beyond any doubt, Madame."

I smiled at him gratefully as he backed from the room.

Once Robyns had taken his leave I called Henry to me whence, placing his hand on my stomach, I delivered the marvellous report that his son was thriving and active. How I wished he, too, could feel the still flitting babe, but its movements were as yet too subtle, so I assured him that soon he would and we should both exult at the excellent signals we had received on this night. A healthy, kicking child - a *male* child - and with a birthright of such bright promise? How wonderful, and how grateful I was as I grasped Henry's hand and implored him to send pages in search of our closest friends, bidding them share in our delight and celebrate with us.

I travelled the torch lit halls of the royal apartments to return to my chambers. The movement of the baby had settled, and as I walked, I thought about Master Robyns, his maps and globes and pronouncements. Although his news had been delivered with the assurance of a man who had spent many years in the study of his craft and many of his prophecies had proved accurate, I could not help feeling a sense of unease. Above us loomed God's firmament: infinite and brooding. In truth, could any mortal man, no matter how wise, how gifted, possibly foretell Our Lord's intentions? I hesitated, moved to seek Henry's library instead of continuing on my way back to my chambers. I hoped to find some verification that Robyns' prophecies were valid. Once within the panelled walls, surrounded by the many cases bearing books, I searched and paged through numerous works until I found the volume I desired. Written entirely in German, it was the *Schürstab Codex*, a beautifully illuminated text which guides the reader throughout the year, with instructive tables and charts designated for each month and day. I had perused this book before, and knew it to give sage advice concerning household requirements, medical problems, and divinations plotted by the heavenly constellations. I flipped through its leaves of smooth vellum, inspecting the miniatures which depicted the signs of the zodiac until I came to rest on the pages allocated to August and September. On my left was an illustration of a man with cattle tethered to a plow, scything the harvest. I looked to the right and sat stock-still. Symbolically representing the exact time predicted by Master Robyns for the birth of our child was a maiden - the Virgin Maiden. It was a *maiden* who characterized the sign of Virgo, the sign under which our child would be born.

After a few reflective minutes, I slowly and carefully closed the book and replaced it on its shelf. I remained motionless, standing between the looming stacks. After a few moments, I squared my shoulders, drew a deep breath, and set off to ready myself for a supper with Henry and our closest friends, at which we were to share joyfully our good news.

Greenwich
Holy Week
April 1533

CAREFULLY, TENTATIVELY, I lowered my pregnant body until only my hands and knees bore contact with the cold tiled floor.

In the paling light, the ceremonial cloth stretched away and across the chequered, echoing reaches of the Chapel Royal. With my ladies around me, I began the slow process of creeping, measure by measure, toward the easternmost altar upon which lay the Holy Cross. From a bay window in the Queen's closet, I had earlier watched the King and his nobles do the same on this Good Friday evening. Henry had mandated we must follow the reverential tradition of creeping to the Cross, '*Signifying a humbling of ourselves to Christ before the Cross, and kissing it in memory of our redemption*.' He might be locked in a battle of wills with the Pope, but his piety remained unwavering, and he would so demonstrate for his subjects to see.

The babe in my womb stirred and became restless at the unaccustomed gait of its mother. After what seemed an eternity I reached the high altar and gratefully clambered forward to kneel upon the soft cushion placed before the crucifix. Stooping to kiss the roughhewn wood I raised my head to find that Henry had extended his strong hand to help me to my feet. I then stood with him while my ladies followed suit.

Now we were all assembled at the high altar, its golden crucifix hidden under a cloth of purple in observance of Good Friday. Master Cromwell, Keeper of the Jewel House, stepped forward with a silver basin containing the crampe-rings. These specially forged silver and gold rings, once blessed, were to be distributed amongst select subjects who were afflicted with the palsy every year on Good Friday. The Clerke of the Closet and the Chief Almoner stood beside Henry with a missal containing prayers for the hallowing of the crampe-rings. Henry led the invocation over them, asking that they may have the power to restore the painfully contracted limbs of those who suffer. The basin was held before me, and in the tradition of Queens, I rubbed the rings between my hands, asking God that our appeal be granted. Finally, holy water was poured into the basin, washing the rings and readying them for distribution to members of the nobility and common folk.

The Good Friday service concluded to my silent relief, and I processed with Henry from the Chapel into the chill, river-damp evening air. Despite its inclement bite, I felt elated. Though my coronation was as yet more than a month away, I had just fulfilled my first duty as Queen of England.

I was grateful to be seated on a cushioned chair near the warming fire, anticipating our meagre meal. We broke only rough, brown bread with butter and drank small ale on this solemn day of fasting. While I ate with unseemly enthusiasm – I was hungry and needed to feed myself and my child - Henry recounted to me the inconceivable conversation he had with the Spanish ambassador, Chapuys, on the previous afternoon. A sleek and catlike diplomat, Eustace Chapuys assiduously pursued his commitment as the representative of Charles I of Spain - Katherine's nephew - to advocate on her behalf. As did Katherine herself, Chapuys refused to employ her new title appointed by the King: the Dowager Princess of Wales. He maintained a dogmatic view that she was Queen of England, contrary to the King's command, and he was altogether dedicated to her defense. As I laboriously chewed the tough bread while listening to Henry's account, I thought Chapuys ever so reckless in assailing the King with his contrary opinions. According to Henry, Chapuys had flagrantly challenged the extent of the King's devotion to God. The brazen man had spoken heedlessly, disclosing that he could not believe Henry would be so careless in setting a pitiful example to the world by wanting to leave his wife of *twenty-five* years!

Henry had replied that he and his God were on very good terms indeed, and in fact, the marriage had not been one of twenty-five years, but less. Indignant, Henry retorted that if the world thought this divorce extraordinary, still more it must be considered exceedingly strange that the Pope should have dispensed with the case without having the rightful power to do so.

In disbelief, I listened as the narrative continued. Chapuys had perversely insisted upon detailing each and every name of those Sorbonne theologians not in agreement with Henry's argument for a divorce. I was confounded as to how little this foolish consul must regard his well-being by provoking the King so! Henry, quite indulgently, I considered, explained that his wish was to leave a successor for his kingdom. In reply, Chapuys had the audacity to remind Henry that he already *had* a daughter endowed with all imaginable goodness and virtue, and of an age to bear children herself. At this juncture, I ceased chewing altogether, slack-jawed at what I was being told. *Still* the hapless Ambassador had forged on, admonishing Henry that he had received his title to the realm through Elizabeth of York, his lady mother; therefore, he should surely be obliged to restore the same privilege to his daughter, the Princess Mary.

And it seems that particular comment had finally marked an impertinence too far. Henry - by then furious and altogether done with the encounter - had rebuked Chapuys, shouting that it was his rightful choice to desire better than a daughter and that HE intended to have a son! I was staggered when Henry told me how the ambassador, apparently unaware of my condition, had hissed that the King could not be certain he would even *father* another child!

Enraged by this transgression – an unmistakable slur on his virility - Henry had spat at him, '*Si nestoit point home comme les autres? Si NESTOIT*'? 'Am I not a man like *other* men? Am I NOT?'

And with that, Chapuys had been banished from Henry's sight. I took another sip of ale while wondering if the witless fool knew how perilously close he had come to being murdered in cold blood!

On Saturday, the eve of Easter, my lodgings were a clamour of commotion as my ladies and I were being readied for a significant event: the first official ceremony at which I was to be known as 'Anne the Queen' and no longer the Marchioness. It was convention that the Queen and her court would attend Saturday evening Mass. For this special occasion, I was to be adorned in royal splendour, dressed in a flowing gown of purple overlaid by a robe of cloth of gold frieze. My ladies assisted me by fastening the jewels which embellished my attire from head to toe. The weight of such apparel was alarming and, ever more conscious of my condition, I was glad I would not have to stagger far while supporting it.

Once all was in place, we assembled in order – sixty of my ladies, with my cousin Mary Howard, now proudly betrothed to young Henry Fitzroy, as trainbearer. Solemnly we processed to the Chapel where, during Mass, I was referred to, for the very first time in a public utterance, as Her Royal Highness, the Queen. The congregants were asked to pray for me. All the while, Henry could barely draw his eyes from me, his beautiful face aglow with pride and attainment.

•

It was late in the afternoon on Easter Sunday. Following the conclusion of an enormous dinner for the King and his court, I rested awhile in my privy chamber with my lady mother and Maggie Wyatt - whom I should now more correctly refer to as Lady Margaret Lee, considering she had married Lord Anthony Lee several years ago. To me, though, the friend I had grown up with – the daughter of the Wyatts of Allington, a neighboring estate to my family home at Hever - would always be known by her girlhood name.

Reclining in a plush chair, my tired feet propped on a low padded stool, I shook my head in frustration. "I am stumped, Maggie. I just can't seem to create anything inventive enough. I have thought and thought on it, but every time I have an idea, it seems laughable by the morrow. I fear I will blunder into something which will make me out to be a buffoon, just as I did before."

In preparation for my coronation, I was required to invent a personal motto; the one which would identify me as Queen. The task was proving a surprisingly heavy burden, knowing that whatever I adopted must maintain its relevance regardless of what transpired during my reign. I had already experienced one mistake with a device I had rashly chosen in the late autumn just over two years ago. Irked by the lack of progress in the dissolution of Henry's marriage, and stung by underhanded and malicious remarks made by certain sneering individuals, I had impulsively decided to have a particular phrase emblazoned on the livery of my servants. At the time I felt it to be fitting; after all, I'd recalled a similar saying from the court of the erudite Margaret of Austria when I was in her service as a girl. The phrase had struck a chord with me then, and foolishly I'd determined it was just what I needed to counter my adversaries:

'Ainsi sera, groigne qui groigne' quoth the embroidery. 'Let them grumble; that is how it is going to be'.

Needless to say, no one but I thought it diplomatically constructive, least of all Henry. So I promptly had it removed, mortally embarrassed by the indiscretion and, since then, had not dared to give thought to what might be a more fitting motto.

"I cannot offer any worthwhile suggestions, Anne," responded Maggie, relaxed against pillows lining the deep window seat. "This kind of thing is usually within the purview of my brother, Thomas, as he is the accomplished linguist in our family."

Then I heard a gentle voice; that of my beloved compass, somehow knowing when her direction was needed: "Well … since you must use a phrase that reveals something of yourself, Nan, you might consider that you have so much to be thankful for right now. Why not reflect that in your motto?"

I looked at my mother appreciatively. Leave it to her to provide just the right guidance. "Of course, you are right, Mother. It makes perfect sense. And perhaps, this time, I can manage something more graceful than the pig's breakfast I offered before."

I knitted my brow, still struggling to devise something meaningful and clever. Again, my lady mother provided a stroke of brilliance. "Nan, remember so long ago when you and I walked together in the gardens at Hever? When we talked about your desire to marry for love, and I told you to abandon such a romantic notion and resign yourself to an arranged marriage?"

I thought back and instantly knew what she intended. "I do Mother. I'd said, '*What if my marriage happened to be both one of love and advantage*?' whereupon you replied, '*Well then you would be a most happy woman.*' I have never forgotten it."

"And now, remarkably, it has come to pass," Mother smiled. "You *have* married for love, Nan, and I doubt that even your father could ask for a better family position."

"… thus, I am both happy, and very advantaged indeed, Mother," I finished for her while clapping my hands with relief and delight. "And so therein should lie my motto: '*La Plus Heureuse* - The Most Happy'! What think you both of this choice?"

Mother nodded sagely while Maggie chirped, "It is perfect, Anne. And I suspect the King's Grace will heartily approve."

Thus, it was in that most marvellous of springs as my pregnancy progressed and my coronation was being planned that those words were emblazoned just so on my badges:

The Moost Happi.

Greenwich
Tower of London
Westminster
May and June 1533

MY FAVOURITE CHAMBERMAIDS, Lucy Holbrook and Emma Potter, had fussed over me for the past hour. Anne Zouche had just departed for her chamber, and Bridget, Lady Wingfield, remained in one of my outer chambers where she would spend the night.

Emma purposefully pried from my hands the book I had been reading, closed it with a resounding clap, and shooed me toward my bed which had been invitingly turned down, exposing crisp white sheets beneath its silken coverlets.

"Your Grace, you simply *must* get into bed. Please do not give me cause to rail at you! You have an exhausting four days ahead: indeed, I worry myself sick thinking about how you, in your delicate condition, will ever endure all that you need do, as wonderful as it promises to be. But the pageantry concerns me not: my job is to look after you, and I will not shirk my duties ... To *BED*!"

The daylight was just fading, and it was earlier than I typically retired, but I conceded that Emma was right. On the morrow, I was to be collected from Placentia Palace at Greenwich and conveyed by barge, in the van of a mighty waterborne procession, to the Tower, where I would reside in preparation for my coronation as Queen of England. I had once again that strange sense of feeling as if all of the preparation and all the pomp and celebration to come was for someone else and I would be but a spectator. Still, heeding Emma's affectionate protests, I allowed her to remove my dressing gown and, in my chemise, clambered between the sheets. I wondered if I would be able to sleep, but by the time Lucy had snuffed the candles and stepped from the room, gently drawing the door behind her till it stood barely ajar, I had drifted off.

I arose refreshed on the following morning, Thursday 29 May. The skies were blue with wispy, high clouds. I gave thanks that, on this day at least, there would be no rain.

It was the oddest thing. One would think that my day would have been a whirlwind of continuous activity. Instead, there were so many women serving me, each with her assigned task, that I had little to do but obediently turn this way and that, sit and stand as instructed, step into layers of silk, satin, and tissue, and allow myself to be ministered to. I had become used to being served, but the degree to which my ladies handled everything about me only increased my ethereal sense of displacement. While eager for the ceremonies to come, I nevertheless struggled to feel aware, in every aspect, of what was happening and desperately hoped the strange fog would lift.

At just after three of the clock in the afternoon, Henry met me and escorted me to the wharf, whereupon a number of my ladies and I boarded a barque – the Queen's barge, gaily painted and decorated with my colours, which set off and took its place amongst the most marvellous parade of watercraft one could have imagined. Most fantastic was the leading vessel, a many-oared galley from whose decks writhed a huge dragon, twisting, turning and spitting flame! Surrounding this ship were other vessels, each supporting gargoyles and monsters breathing fire and emitting fearsome noise. They led the way, and following came the Mayor's barge and the Bachelors' barge. From each ship drifted lovely music played by minstrels on board, although the musicians themselves were fairly hidden by swathes of gold tissue and bright shining silks draping the decks.

I sat on the deck of my barge and gazed about me, giggling with delight. Scores of craft - all sizes and shapes – bobbed on the sparkling river with standards and flags waving gaily, bells tinkling from the rigging, musicians on most of them, playing and singing, and everywhere a gleaming profusion of golden tissue, flags, and other adornments, flashing gloriously in the afternoon sun. It was a breathtaking sight – splendidly colourful and, I thought, a perfect foil to the formality to come. As we rowed past bankside landmarks, mighty gunfire discharged in salute while I could see the crowds ashore waving gaily as we sailed by, no doubt enchanted by the exotic water pageant. The fair beauty of the day allowed the sides of the vessels, lined with beaten gold, to appear as if they were on fire, and from the riverbanks, we must have presented a spectacular sight. As my barge drew near to Wapping Mills, a four gun salute gave notice to the Tower that we approached. Thoroughly captivated by the river journey, my ladies and I clasped our hands, squealing in mock terror when the guns fired nearby. Gone was my fog. At last, I felt fully alive, thrilled with the excitement of the scene.

Escorted by craft which bore the nobles of the Realm, my barge rounded the final corner and came into view of the Tower. Instantly there sounded the deafening report of cannon marking my arrival. At the blasts my babe jumped, startled, in my womb, and I was amazed that he had been able to detect the reverberations. I sat and quietly rocked for a moment cradling my stomach, soothing him as best I could, not wanting him to be afraid.

I was assisted from the barge by the Lieutenant of the Tower, Sir Edward Walsingham, and its Constable, Sir William Kingston. Heralds surrounded me as we processed along the gravel path along which stood, at attention, officers at arms. Glancing along the row of gentlemen of Henry's court, I recognized Lords Carlisle, Richmond, Windsor, Lancaster, York, Chester, and Sandys. The elderly Dowager Duchess of Norfolk followed; her designated role to ceremonially bear my train. When we arrived at the King's Bridge, before entering the Tower I turned and called out to all within earshot, thanking them with great warmth – the Mayor, the officials, and the citizens – for the magnificent celebration they had staged for me that afternoon and assured them that never would I forget it as long as I should live. With that, I made my way to the Royal Apartments - those that had required so much of Henry's time and money to be carefully refurbished for this very event.

Once I stepped inside and my eyes adjusted to the dimming light, I was stunned by the sight. The previously drab and damp Great Hall had been transformed into an exquisitely ornate cavern – a gleaming riot of colour and decoration wherein long tables, laid with white cloths and shimmering candelabra, groaned under the weight of plates piled high with foodstuffs for a festive supper.

Henry greeted me just inside the doors, and grasped me by the shoulders, pulling me to him and kissing me most lovingly. Offering thanks to his courtiers, he dismissed them from his service for the evening and led me by the hand to my chambers. Once we were alone, I relaxed into a chair thick with padding and silk brocade and smiled broadly at Henry. His eyes glittered; it had been a long while since I had seen that gleam – the look of the young, excited boy about him.

"Did you enjoy your special afternoon, my love?" he asked with keen anticipation.

"Henry – it was indescribable. I have never, ever seen anything like that river tableau in all my life ... it was an absolute delight! Thank you so very much, my darling. Oh, I adored the dragon! However did they *do* that? The fire on the water was astonishing."

"I am sure I don't know, but one must engage the right people to accomplish such feats, and *that* I do know how to make happen," he said with an offhand wave. A satisfied chuckle underscored his pleasure as he came to me for a proper kiss, which I was more than happy to bestow upon him!

"Now, my Queen, take you to your inner chambers where your ladies will help you out of your finery and into something more comfortable. Indulge in some repose, and then I will join you for a private supper. We will sup early, for it is off to bed with you. You have important days ahead, and I want to be certain, above all, that you and my son are well rested and not subject to the strain of fatigue."

Stifling a yawn, I allowed Emma, who had arrived at the Tower earlier, to escort me to my changing suite and bedchamber. I had relished the first day of my coronation celebrations very much. Very much indeed.

The next day, Friday, was mine to luxuriate in at leisure. I made good use of the opulent renovations Henry had ordered in the King's and Queen's apartments in the Tower. After awakening at almost mid-morning, I breakfasted with several of my ladies. Then, because the weather was so lovely, we walked and sat in the privy gardens which were abundant with exquisitely hued roses while we listened to music, played cards and lolled in the sunshine, chatting and giggling as the day wore on languidly. Henry, himself, had a full diary of ceremony and official business. He was to create eighteen new Knights of the Bath in a rite which would commence at dinner that day and conclude on Saturday morning when he would dub almost fifty men Knights Bachelor. Many of my friends and supporters were amongst those numbers, and it served as a fitting backdrop for what was to come. I had no official place in these formalities, though, so could remain hidden from the crowds, rest, and gather my strength.

In the early evening, I was requested to grant a brief audience with a relatively new ambassador from the French court of François I, Monsieur Jean de Dinteville. The Monsieur came from a most illustrious family belonging to the *noblesse d'épée* – nobility reaching back many centuries. It was said that he was elegant, learned, and quite handsome. Most intriguing to me, however, was the fact that he was a close friend of Jacques Lefèvre d'Étaples, the renowned French humanist and theologian. I would certainly entertain a visit from Monsieur Dinteville this evening, and anticipated lively future discussions with him as a member of my court.

He swept into the chamber, a flourish of velvet, gold, and a feathered *chapeau* with which he dusted the floor in a dramatic bow. He was young, perhaps late in his twenties - thirty years of age at most - yet he had that charming *savoir-faire* so well adopted by Frenchmen. His features were regular, his dark beard full but neatly groomed, and his clothing rich yet tasteful.

"Your Royal Highness," he greeted me, "I bring the most respectful, forthright, and truly heartfelt wishes of joy and congratulations from *Mon Souverain*, François. If only he could be here to share your great and deserved honour tomorrow."

"Merci beaucoup, Monsieur." I studied him closely as I spoke, and felt that we would be friends. "I am grateful for the sentiments you bear from François. I, too, wish he could be with us, but I am greatly pleased that you are present to stand in his stead. And, once the pageantry has concluded, Monsieur Dinteville, I intend to spend time with you discussing that which you have learned from your wise friend, Monsieur Lefèvre d'Ėtaples. I am a devoted student of his writings, you know, and have been for some years."

"Indeed, so I have been told, Your Highness. It will be my great privilege to converse with a woman of such profound beauty and grace, who clearly possesses the intelligence to match. I do not wish to occupy you overmuch on this important evening, but I did want to say that I am deeply honoured to be a part of the procession tomorrow, leading you to Westminster.

I will count the hours until then," whereupon, with a warm and captivating smile, he bowed once more and backed from the room.

Once Dinteville had departed, I remained seated to enjoy my rare solitude, and soon became lost in thought. I was on the brink of the most momentous two days imaginable. I had married the King of England, and in doing so, became his Queen Consort. In Henry's mind, this designation was not sufficiently worthy of me. He continued to believe firmly, as did I, that we were part and parcel of one another, each the other's second self. Therefore, he believed nothing less would be acceptable but that I be a Queen anointed and crowned. The holy and ancient ritual of coronation would be sanctified by God, and no one could dare deny my royalty henceforth.

Events of the past year had nurtured my confidence. I had learned, often as the result of missteps - and at a not-inconsiderable cost to my pride - to hide any appearance of fluster by pointedly assuming a calm and patrician air. I was well aware that many courtiers and their ladies thought me haughty and arrogant, but that caused me no concern. They were mere acquaintances; sycophants and grovellers who simply wished to gain Henry's attention and favour. They could not possibly know my thoughts; they knew not the true me. I had, by careful design, become quite accomplished at maintaining a particular affectation to protect myself from frequent affronts delivered by those who clearly resented me for the position I had achieved. Oh, I freely concede I did lean heavily upon Henry's strength at times but now, on the cusp of my Queenship, I was fiercely determined to conduct myself in such a way that all and sundry would know me to be as laudable a Queen as had been Katherine.

As I remained in the Presence Chamber, unusually but delightfully alone for a few minutes, on that evening of 3 May 1533, my lips twitched in a wry smile. For all my headstrong determination and staunch resolve as I assumed the role of England's Queen I knew myself to be simply Anne …

Nan Bullen. A country girl from Kent.

•

I had made certain Henry would not be disappointed in me, for I knew just how to play my part. In preparation for this momentous day, Master Cromwell had worked ceaselessly to ensure every detail would be carried out to perfection. As for me, I had read and reread the *Articles Ordained by King Henry VII For the Regulation of His Household*, for it contained explicit instructions for '*the Receaving of a Queene, and the Coronation of Her*'. I intended to follow those ordinances precisely.

I retired that evening, readying for bed in the extravagant chamber Henry had constructed for me in the Tower, confident that the ceremony to come would not be soon forgotten by England's peers or its subjects.

On Saturday, I was slow to arise and lay abed surrounded by pillows which propped me up just enough so I could lazily nibble on cheeses and sweets brought to me by my ladies, striving to be as rested as possible for the procession later that day, and for the coronation on the morrow. I was relayed the good news that, again today the weather promised to be fair; something for which we all heaved sighs of relief. With Lucy and Emma fully occupied performing a thousand tasks, my sister Mary, Anne Zouche, Honor Lisle, and Bridget Wingfield assisted me in preparation for my appearance at the coronation procession.

I bathed and had my hair washed, dried and brushed out with lemon oil to make it as lustrous as a seal's hide. We giggled and chattered all the while, and let out peals of laughter recalling the deadly serious demeanor assumed by the dressmaker, Master John Skut, upon his departure for a trip to France: his official mission being to design and sew a gown of the very latest French fashion; the one I would wear during the coronation procession. When informed of his selection for this honour, his eyes nearly popped out of his head, his mouth soundlessly opened and closed, and he was struck speechless. The dear man had then prepared for the trip as if he had been instructed to retrieve the Holy Grail personally.

The result of his efforts, though, was fine. So very fine. A fitted gown of white satin accented with golden threads, and created so cleverly that at once I looked elegant and graceful, yet the fullness of my pregnancy was clearly visible. I was to be a vision in white. Pure white, too, would be the litter in which I would be carried, and even the horses and their caparisons which accompanied me. Glinting in the late afternoon sun would be ample touches of gold: the lacy, woven gold of my coif draped over my dark hair, and the golden circlet, studded with gems, which would rest upon my head.

My hair, in all its shining glory, would be loose, falling to my waist as is ordained for a Queen crowned.

It grew late before we were ready, my ladies and me. The days waxed long now, so the mellow afternoon sun slanted through the windows of the Tower, light catching the golden floss woven into my gown as its train slid across the floor. Our assembly took shape at the gate, and thus did the coronation procession commence.

In the lead was Monsieur de Dinteville, proudly heading a group of French nobles and ambassadors. In homage to my close affiliation with France, the Frenchmen set the tone for what was to come; brilliantly appareled in rich blue velvet trimmed with gold. Their horses, wearing magnificent trappings of blue silk patterned with white crosses, shook their heads impatiently; tack jangling. And then we were off!

Marching forward, hooves crunching the fresh gravel strewn over the streets, the French brigade was closely followed by the sombre city judges then by the newly appointed Knights of the Bath, each elegantly swathed in purple velvet and white miniver. Next came a showing of the powerful and wealthy of the land, so numerous that I had never seen such a sight … abbots, barons, bishops, earls and marquises, dukes and the Lord Chancellor; the Mayor of London along with ambassadors from Venice and Aquitaine and, accompanying them, the High Constable of England, Charles Brandon, Duke of Suffolk, bearing the ceremonial verder of silver.

Before me rode my chancellor, Lord Audley, his head deferentially bare. As he advanced, I resituated myself in the litter, pulled the mantle of ermine loosely about my shoulders, arranged my hair a final time then took a deep breath and lifted my chin, smiling, so the crowds might see me clearly. Directly behind me were Lord Borough, my chamberlain, and William Coffin, Master of the Horse, who led the ceremonial white horse, tacked with a lady's side saddle and trappings of fluttering white tissue.

Following the horse processed my ladies – the eminent ladies of the realm. First were my ladies-in-waiting all clothed in gold, and directly behind them came the *grande dames* of England: my lady mother along with the Dowager Duchess of Norfolk and the Marchioness of Dorset. Trailing them were the younger noblewomen, riding horseback in cloaks of red velvet, and then an extended company of peers and important merchants, black velvet coats marking their wellborn status.

I felt remarkably well. The late afternoon sun warmed me, and the measure of the litter rocked me gently as we progressed along Fanchurche Street. It demanded no effort to offer a warmly smiling countenance to all, turning my head from side to side the better for them to take in my full beauty. The further we rode, the more astonished I became at the gorgeousness of the decorated buildings: the houses and shops hung with colourful arras, textiles, and richly hued carpets. Across the narrowest parts of the street gold and silver tissue billowed in the light breeze while everywhere, spilling from each window and doorway and crammed body to body along the processional route, throngs of people gawked at the spectacle, waving and cheering.

When we arrived at the juncture of Fanchurche and Gracious Church streets, my litter halted in front of a stage erected for the occasion. There, a lovely pageant was performed by the merchants. The Mount Parnassus had been constructed, and above it was the fountain of Halcyon. On the Mount sat Apollo and Calliope, offering me unending praise, whilst all around sat Muses playing stringed instruments and singing sweetly. I sat attentively smiling and nodding, noticing that the fountain was designed such that the townspeople could approach it and partake of the Rhenish wine which flowed continuously. 'Twas little wonder then that, in that particular area, every face I saw bore a broad smile!

Eventually, we resumed progress, stopping at Leaden Hall for the next pageant. A small mountain decorated with red and white roses served as the setting for a snow-white falcon which emerged to settle on its very pinnacle. With a fanfare of music, an angel materialized and set a crown of gold on the falcon's head, talons sunk deep into its sweet-smelling bed. The white falcon had been chosen as my special symbol - it figured large in my badge, representing me and the majesty and grandeur I would bring to my Tudor marriage. Next to the falcon was a theatrical portrayal of Saint Anne, with her children all about her. Then, just below the stage a further group of children, whose recitation referred to the fruitfulness of Saint Anne, where one sweet child had been chosen to deliver a verse composed for me. In a tremulous voice, he cried out:

> *"Honour and grace be to our Queen Anne,*
> *For whose cause an Angel Celestial*
> *Descendeth, the falcon as white as a swan,*
> *To crown with a diadem imperial!*
> *In her honour rejoice we all,*
> *For it cometh from God, and not of man.*
> *Honour and grace be to our Queen Anne!"*

Watching this tableau, I rested my hands on my swelling belly, acknowledging the message and feeling privately relieved that I was already fulfilling the great expectations placed on me.

We passed conduits in Cornhill bubbling with wine and were given gifts by the local ladies before proceeding on to Chepe, which proved a wonder of gold and silver with swathes of crimson velvet hanging from every building. A festive atmosphere was at hand, yet the crowds were well behaved and controlled by the Constables. At every window pressed a multitude of faces, all clamoring for a better view. Once again the fountains ran with both white wine and claret in an abundance no one had ever seen before.

We continued on our route, and came to the Cross of Eleanor at which place the Aldermen waited, whereupon Master Baker, the Recorder, approached me, bowed low and handed me a gilt purse which contained one thousand marks in gold. I nodded in grateful acceptance before addressing the standing Aldermen, assuring them I was honoured and would do my utmost to serve them well as their Queen. We then turned toward the gate of St Paul's where I was greeted by yet another pageant consisting of beautifully draped ladies sporting banners on their heads bearing Latin inscriptions, who encouraged me by advising that, when I bore my son, there would indeed arise the dawning of a new and golden world.

As we entered the churchyard a most joyous sight greeted me: a staging which bore well nigh two hundred children of all sizes and ages. Their shy, smiling faces melted my heart. Several of the older ones recited verses, nervously shifting from one foot to the other but nevertheless projecting their voices loudly enough to be clearly heard. Their appearance was welcome refreshment because I had begun to tire, my face beginning to feel frozen into a smile, though my heart was still indefatigably jubilant.

The procession continued, passing Saint Martin's church and Ludgate; choirs singing and bells pealing with undiminished enthusiasm as we entered Fletestreet, where yet more wine flowed from every aqueduct, until finally winding through Temple Bar toward Westminster Hall.

With barely a moment's hesitation, my litter was borne into its immense cavern. Even though I had been hailed by the splendour of vivid colour and an abundance of gold throughout the afternoon, I drew my breath at the sight of that magnificent Hall of Westminster, adorned for the occasion. I knew it to be the largest hall in England and Europe, and Henry had not missed the opportunity to feature its importance. With his consummate finesse, he had directed the purchase of the most costly tapestries, which were to be hung on every available expanse of stone wall; myriad gilt candelabra, each as tall as a man, lined its length, glowing with masses of the purest white candles; tables were set with exquisite white drapery while, to my left towered an immense cupboard stacked with gold plate and vessels each piled high with the most aromatic dishes. And, soaring above us was the hammerbeam roof, its ornate oaken timbers gilded and painted in bright hues with the carved heads of angels overseeing all that occurred below.

The litter halted once it reached the middle of the Hall where I was helped down, all the while praying my legs would hold me after having sat unmoving for so long. Leaning upon the steadying arm of the Lord Mayor, I was led to the south end of the room to ascend four stone steps to the dais. There I was seated at the King's High Table. On its smooth, dark marble surface was my place setting of gold. Immediately I was served a goblet of hippocras. I indicated to the servers that they should provide my ladies with the same. Gratefully we drank, and as the liquid warmed my throat and stomach, I became infused with the requisite vigour to address the assemblage in a strong and clear voice.

"My Lords and Ladies, respected Mayor and gentle subjects: I am honoured this day, beyond my imagining, by your generosity and gracious esteem. The events of the day have moved me greatly, and I am anxious to serve you, if God be willing, to the very best of my ability. I look forward with humility and deference 'til tomorrow when I will be anointed as your Queen. Therefore, may I express my most profound gratitude for all you have done for me today. I retire from you, then, with humble regard and the promise of my singular dedication on the morrow. Good evening."

Following which I nodded in grateful acknowledgement before, surrounded by my ladies, being led to a door at the south end of the Hall and out to the royal barge waiting quayside, ready to transport us to the welcome respite of my chambers at Whitehall.

Once on board, what a clamor of female voices was heard! Each lady, at last able to speak once released from the watchful eyes of the senior nobles and city officials, let loose with a torrent of excited chatter, gossip, and observations on this most special of days. It was a welcome relief to chortle at the exaggerated fervour of many of the merchants, guild leaders, and sheriffs as they made certain their representation was seen as the best of the day; to sweetly recall the children's faces as they sang; and to exclaim over the expectant crowd which had stretched and craned, some hanging most perilously from crumbling windows, to watch the spectacle unfold.

My beloved ladies made certain I was well wrapped against the breeze on the river and raised my feet so they rested on a cushion. So tenderly concerned were they with my welfare that they fluttered about, tucking blankets here, adjusting pillows there: all the while marvelling at my endurance, being, as I was, six months with child. I loved them for it, and could not hope for a better end to a long and tiring, but wondrous event.

The final pleasure of that memorable day yet awaited me. I was impatient to see Henry and to relish the evening with him in our privy chambers before the most solemn service on the morrow.

I had so anticipated talking with Henry late into the evening, describing for him every detail and each observance of the extraordinary day. But I found that once I had changed into a more comfortable gown and hungrily consumed roasted venison, stewed rabbit, viand ryall – a dish prepared with rice, spices, wine and honey - and a whole cherry pudding, all accompanied by wine, I could scarce keep my eyes open. I bid my husband the King good night with a sweet kiss and welcomed the assistance of Maggie along with Lucy and Emma, who readied me for bed. I fell immediately to sleep while they prepared my wardrobe for the following morning, for it was sure to come early.

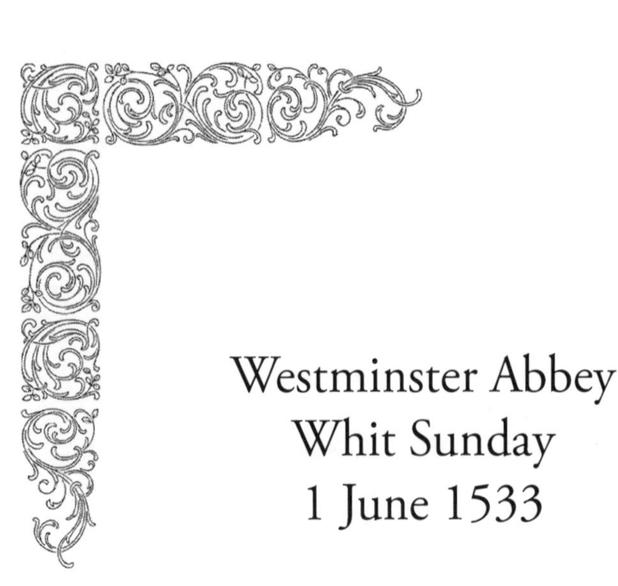

Westminster Abbey
Whit Sunday
1 June 1533

AWAKENED SHORTLY AFTER dawn by my maid Emma, I stirred and stretched in my bed. I felt refreshed and prepared to take on the day. An exceptional day, one altogether unimaginable and momentous. On this day I would, as had others before me for untold centuries, become a consecrated Queen of England.

For a moment, as I lay there idly watching the pale sunlight play on the darkly polished wood of my chamber walls, the prospect seemed preposterous. For the first of many times that day, I felt dreamlike. Memories flooded my head unbidden. I re-lived, as if it had been but yesterday, that narrow sliver in time when Henry and I had intently regarded each other on the hunting field; our intimate encounter concealed by that swirling pearl-grey mist … how it seemed so long ago! November of 1525, when I was twenty-four years of age and, under that compelling gaze, had fallen deeply in love for the very first time in my life. And now, a woman of thirty-two years, I was married to my love the King, carrying his precious son. By God's eyes, the time that had passed between our fateful rendezvous and this day had been an onerous journey; one not for the weak or tremulous, that much was certain.

I had been mightily drawn to Henry, and he to me. My consistent refusal to his request that I became his mistress had, at times, been almost impossible to uphold. But as we grew in closeness we were surprised by the depth of our rapport – and we read on the concept of the 'second self' as described by Aristotle in his *Ethics.* Soon we came to regard ourselves in exactly this way: each as the second self of the other; it was as if we had known each other all our lives, and perhaps even before – in some boundless and eternal way. We would achieve only good for the other, based as it were in the unity of deep friendship. And it was just such strength that somehow enabled us to endure years of frustration while Henry had sought to dissolve his marriage to Katherine of Aragon. It had bound us ever more tightly even as we survived the great plague of sweating sickness which had killed so many through that horrible period during which, due to our separation, we truly came to recognize the depth of our love. And from that time forward we were one, eventually living as if we were husband and wife, though not yet wed. We travelled to France - a couple betrothed - and presented a unified front to the French King, and to the questioning nobility of England and France. Once we had returned to London as *Henry and Anne* - with Katherine at last banished forever - blessedly, we conceived a child: the son for whom Henry and I both yearned. We married, though the Pope had never given his dispensation. With that act of defiance, Henry had staked his place as the Supreme Head of the Church in England. And as his wife and the mother of his expected son – his second self – my destiny was made manifest: I would be crowned Queen. Not merely a Queen Consort! No, I was to be an anointed Queen of England – royalty bestowed upon me and my issue by God, never to be withdrawn unto my death. I would be, in every way, a fitting match for my husband...

"*Madame*! Your Highness! You must arise right now lest we have scant time to ready you!"

Sensing the urgency in Emma's voice, my reverie was broken, whereupon I pushed the coverlets aside and scrambled from my bed. Not wanting her to be fearful we would delay the day's schedule, I handed myself over to her. Maggie, Mistress of the Wardrobe, entered the room briskly, and when my eyes met her blue ones which were filling with tears, I could see that she was overwhelmed with the enormity of what was to take place. I grabbed her hand. "Maggie, don't. Please – you, of everyone today - must be my rock. I need you! And good that you are here, for who else will help me, swaddled in these heavy robes and furs, to find a pot every time I need to pass my water? Which these days seems to be every few minutes!"

She laughed aloud, and with that, the moment grew light. I thanked the Lord that my longtime dearest friend would be with me on this day. We went to the adjacent closet where my bath had been drawn, to begin the long process of preparing for my coronation day.

For yesterday's procession, during which I was on view to the people of London, I had been a vision in shimmering white. Today, though, I was to wear the colours and *accoutrements* of royalty. The kirtle, so skillfully designed and sewn by Master Skut, was of a most vibrant, blood-red crimson velvet, its lustrous, silky gloss unlike any fabric I had ever seen. Draped over that elaborate kirtle was a rich purple velvet robe. The intensity of colour lying one against the other was brilliant – almost an assault to the eye – relieved only by a liberal application of fluffy powdered ermine, the white fur edging gown and robe alike. My hair, brushed to a high sheen, was swept under and pinned, and atop it was affixed a remarkable caul made of seed pearls set throughout with rubies and diamonds. The effect was a lacy, bejeweled web which held my dark hair in place. On the crown of my head was set a golden coronet. I wore a necklet of pearls, each one the size of a large pea. And as for my toilette: my face was lightly buffed with a tinted powder to afford it an even sheen. The very lightest touch of cochineal rouge enhanced my cheeks and lips. I added no adornment to my eyes. I wanted my face to represent my genuine, innermost self.

At exactly thirty minutes past the hour of eight in the morning, with my ladies-in-waiting about me, we again processed into Westminster Hall. Assembled there were the Mayor, aldermen, sheriffs, members of the clergy, and many of the nobility, uniformly clad in brilliant crimson and gold. Upon my arrival, they bowed in unison while I was led to stand under the golden cloth of estate. Before me, stretched a royal blue carpet, upon which I would walk, barefooted as was the ancient custom, through the Hall and on to the High Altar in the Abbey.

The assembly positioned themselves in order of rank. Oh, if only I could fairly describe the sight! The members of parliament in their ceremonial robes along with the city officials led the procession, with the bishops, archbishops and abbots closely following, outfitted in their pontifical vestments and mitred hats. Then walked the nobility: Knights of the Bath, barons, and viscounts, and finally, wearing crimson velvet furred with ermine, the earls, marquesses, and dukes. Preceding me went the Marquess of Dorset, bearing the sceptre of gold, and the Earl of Arundel, grasping the rod and the dove. A pace behind came the Earl of Oxford, High Chamberlain of England, conveying the crown of St Edward, and finally the Duke of Suffolk: Brandon, who for that day was High Steward of England holding in his hand the ceremonial ivory rod.

Only then did I begin to walk under the gold canopy of the Cinque Ports. Carrying my long train once again was the Dowager Duchess of Norfolk, fulfilling her responsibilities as the highest noblewoman in the land, second only to me. It must have been difficult for her as the path was long and the train heavy. But she withstood the stiffness of her aging limbs and handled her task admirably, closely followed by the highborn ladies, gowned in scarlet velvet with narrow sleeves trimmed in lace, crimson mantels furred with ermine, and gold circlets upon their heads. Slowly and ceremoniously we paced along the carpeted path. I held my head high and looked about covertly for Henry. I knew he was to be positioned some place where, hidden from view, he would watch the solemn rite. It was not his day - instead, it was mine - and he would not overshadow me by his presence.

We entered the great Abbey of St Peter. At once its mysterious beauty overwhelmed me: a veritable forest of dark stone, its ribbed vaulting soared heavenward. We glided silently past ancient tombs, their ominous presence reminding me of my mortality, even on this day. Smoke rose and swirled from a multitude of torches and candles, and the sharp, biting scent of incense burned my nostrils. Lightheaded, I drifted in a semi-hypnotic state while the glorious voices raised in melodic chant faded until all I could hear was a buzzing, as if my head was filled with a swarm of bees. I feared I might faint, but somehow my feet kept moving ever forward as I approached the High Altar where I was assisted up several steps, and seated in the gold-draped Coronation Chair – that venerable relic in which Monarchs of the realm had been crowned for hundreds of years.

Once settled I breathed deeply to try and dispel my dizziness. A slight movement behind a lattice screen placed high above the congregation finally allowed me to glimpse Henry, whose vantage point was out of sight of those in attendance. I wished he were next to me, his vigour a stronghold of support. But I took heart knowing he watched me, and even that merest sight of him had caused my haze to dissipate. The ages-old cosmati-paved floor of the altar had been laid with thick carpet, and I descended from the chair to this most revered place and slowly lowered myself to the ground to lay prostrate before the Archbishop of Canterbury, Dr Cranmer. As I lay there, he prayed over me. In truth, I heard nothing he said; instead, I tried my best to remain immobile despite lying uncomfortably on my swollen belly.

After what seemed an eternity, I gratefully accepted Cranmer's hand in helping me to my feet to resume my seat in the Chair of St Edward. Intoning the stately rites, the Archbishop - a friend who had singularly found the way for Henry and me to marry - placed upon my head St Edward's Crown, the sceptre of gold into my right hand, and the rod of ivory with the golden dove into my left. The choir erupted into a *Te Deum*, clear notes resonating throughout the massive space. Dr Cranmer approached me and removed the terribly heavy crown, which after all, had been made for men, and replaced it with a much lighter version which Henry had had smithed especially for me before the Holy Mass then commenced.

As Cranmer conducted the liturgy, I observed my surroundings. It was eerie to feel enclosed by the imposing carved burial vaults of the distinguished and holy: Edward the Confessor, Henry VII and his wife Elizabeth of York, Eleanor of Castile and Edward Longshanks … their ghostly presence was palpable and the hairs on the back of my neck prickled. The ethereal voices of the choir, men, and boys, were lifted in a psalm. Transfixed I watched as a young boy of about seven or eight years, positioned in the front row, fidgeted and shifted from foot to foot, singing angelically all the while. This child was robust - a picture of health - with a shock of vibrant ginger hair and bright blue eyes, face crimson-cheeked and adorable. I was overcome with a sense of longing for a boy just like that one – and pretended, for only a moment, that the impish, chubby, sweet red-headed child was Henry's and my son. I could not draw my eyes from him, and prayed earnestly – with the greatest devotion I was able to conjure – that God would bless us with such a gift.

Mass finally concluded, I went to the shrine of St Edward with an offering and a prayer that I serve England with God's good grace, after which I turned in preparation to recess from the Church. But before I took a step, every duchess and countess raised their arms in unison to acknowledge my new Queenship by placing upon their heads their coronets and circlets of gold, many interwoven with flowers. It was a lovely sight and one that gladdened my heart. Thence, supported on one side by my father, Earl of Wiltshire, and on the other by Lord Talbot, we began the recessional to depart the Abbey. I glanced upward and again caught Henry; his face pressed to an opening in the lattice … I swear I saw him wink at me as I passed by! And at that small but welcome gesture, I allowed my lips to relax into a smile – my first true smile as Anne, the Queen.

Westminster Hall had been made ready to host a magnificent coronation banquet, its massive space suffused with as much warmth and grandeur as could be installed into such a normally bleak old gallery. Arras, vibrant with reds, blues and gold threads winking, lined every wall. Four great tables extended the entire length of the hall, all draped in white linen. Torches burned and sent smoke heavenward. Hundreds of candles shimmered and cast a golden light on masses of silver and gilt plate stacked atop buffets throughout the room. On the raised dais was the King's High Table, above which had been raised a canopy of gold damask with golden fringe. Alone at this imposing table, reputedly carved hundreds of years ago from the dark Purbeck marble quarried in Dorset, I found myself acutely conscious of the spirits of the many kings and queens who had feasted, governed and asserted their divine royalty from this very place.

In the aisles between the tables, astride white horses which were caparisoned in crimson velvet with gold trappings, rode … yes - RODE! … Charles Brandon, the Duke of Suffolk, and Lord William Howard, who represented the Duke of Norfolk, absent due to a diplomatic mission in France. Both men were fairly studded with gleaming jewels and made an astonishing sight directing members of the retinue to their seats from those lofty positions on horseback.

As if by magic, my mother materialized at my elbow, with Maggie close behind. Anne Zouche led the way and the three of us quickly entered an antechamber which had been furnished as a withdrawing room for my rest and refreshment before the lengthy banquet. The instant the door closed behind us, all three fell to busily fussing about me, first leading me to a seat cushioned with pillows while expressing concern for the exhaustion I surely must feel, before solicitously arranging a thickly padded stool under my feet. And then the strangest thing happened. Maggie abruptly halted her ministrations and looked at me, stricken. So much so that I instantly became alarmed.

"What *is* it, Maggie? What's causing your distress?"

But she didn't answer. Instead, she lowered her gaze and slowly sank into a deep curtsey. I swallowed hard, reached for her hand, raising her to her feet. Only then did she meet me eye to eye.

"Your Grace," she whispered uneasily. "My most humble apology for forgetting my place, and for such common behavior about your royal person. May I offer you the deepest respect and loyalty any subject has ever held for a queen."

It was at that point I noted her lashes were wet with tears.

At this, my mother and Anne stopped what they were doing, and both dropped into curtsies with downcast eyes. "Your Grace," they murmured in unison.

Respectfully they stood before me, and we were suddenly uncertain of the new relationship which had been forged between us just an hour before. We looked at each other awkwardly, my lips trembling with emotion as I nodded and wholeheartedly said, "Thank you – thank *all* of you. You are the most important women in my life, not merely my subjects, and I do not know what I would do without you!"

An even longer moment passed. Then - and I could not help myself, I swear, although I tried to hold it aback – a snort escaped my nose and, however inappropriate it may have seemed, I could not contain the laughter which followed. Holding my sides I let loose a torrent of unrestrained guffaws, and they joined me. In a trice, we were as children in the sober surroundings of a chapel when all you wanted to do was scream with ill-timed hilarity! Desperately we tried to muffle our mirth lest the servants wondered what silliness had overcome us, whereupon that made the matter ever funnier for it had no stopping. We roared until tears ran down our cheeks and were mopped with the glorious velvet of our gowns.

Only finally did we begin to gain control. Maggie, still giggling, looked about, finding a basin of water and linen cloths so we could dab at our eyes and freshen our faces. Every few minutes another explosion of chortles would rise, unbidden, to the surface until at last we recovered our composure.

What a much-needed release that had been! For me, and for all of us. Thank the good Lord that my first few minutes as Queen had not been witnessed by any but my most loved and trusted companions. Revitalized, they tidied my gown and jewels while I hastily rearranged my expression in a manner more suitable for a newly crowned Queen of England.

The door opened, one last deep breath and then I swept forward to be seated at the High Table to dine with my subjects for the first time.

The King's Table was raised well above the many hundreds of guests below. To my right, at a table several steps down, was Archbishop Cranmer. Standing to each side of me, ready to do my bidding, were the Countesses of Oxford and Worcester. They stood during the entire dinner service, and when I went to wipe my lips, or remove a bone or piece of gristle from my mouth, they held a linen cloth before me so no subject would see his Queen engaged in such a crude act. Beneath the table at my feet sat two high-ranking servants of the household, who would assist me in any way needed.

At the long tables arrayed before me were, to my left, the Mayor and Aldermen of London. Next, stretched a table filled with duchesses and countesses, while on the opposite side of the middle aisle were seated the men: earls, barons, the Lord Chancellor and, at the far right, the barons of the five ports and masters of the chancery. The premier earls were designated for the occasion as chief servers, each of a specialty: a carver, a butler, cupbearer, larder – their status affording them the privilege of serving the Queen. All in attendance were hatless as a sign of obeisance.

A fanfare of trumpets blasted the arrival of the first course, and samplings of each of a score of dishes were placed before me. And so it began: course after course, each dish more marvelous than the preceding. Every course was followed by the presentation of spectacular *sotelties* – fantastical edible creations made to appear as if they were sculpted: ships moulded in wax carrying sweetmeat cargoes within; lions rampant; a jelly superbly crafted to look as if it was the façade of Whitehall Palace. Roast pork and venison, rabbit, veal, and lamb – stewed, baked, in pies, steamed with herbs … dish after dish after dish appeared until a positive *mountain* of food towered before me! Impressive indeed, but *oh*, how I wished my ladies were nigh so we could have a giggle at how excessive it seemed.

A lovely consort of minstrels played as we ate, and shortly another trumpet flourish announced the second course. This course was equally immense in scope with fish of every imaginable kind: sturgeon, salmon, lampreys, pike and bream. On and on it went as the afternoon hours waned. I very quickly appreciated the practicality of the cloths the countesses held in front of my face at my signal. In this way, I could be seen as tasting numerous dishes, but could then spit the unswallowed food into a basin. How else was I to remain polite and appreciative for such a feast without eating till I became sick? So I smiled throughout, and gamely tasted, chewed, spat, and nodded my approval of dish after dish, course upon course.

I imagined that Henry and the ambassadors who were his private guests, ensconced in a closet off to the side near the cloister of St Stephen, thoroughly enjoyed the magnificent array of food accompanied by the finest Burgundian wines.

At times, I needed to remove myself from the table and retire to the antechamber to stand, stretch my legs and relieve myself. The feast lasted all afternoon, and never was I so glad to see the hippocras being poured, indicating the meal's conclusion. I washed my hands in a scented basin of water held for me by my ladies, then rose to step forward into the middle of the hall. A solid gold cup was brought to me, along with a gilt tray of spices and delicate sweets. I detected a confection made with cinnamon and nutmeg, took a sip from the cup, and addressed the Mayor and his aldermen to thank them; my words accompanied by the warmest smile I could muster, for their painstaking efforts in presenting a celebratory feast which would never be forgotten.

Finally, under the golden canopy of estate, I was led to the great doors, at which point the canopy was presented to the Barons of the Cinque Ports. There a litter awaited me, and thankfully I climbed aboard to be transported to a barge which would row me back to Whitehall.

It was six o'clock in the evening on the fourth full day of coronation events.

The new Queen was mightily tired and ready to go home.

That evening, deliciously and comfortably attired in a black satin dressing gown edged in white ermine, I reclined against velvet cushions in my privy chamber. A sharp rap on the door was the only notice Henry had given before he strode into the room, eyes agleam and smile broad. He hurried to my side, bent down and kissed me, stroked my cheek and pulled a chair from the table so he could sit beside me without having me rise to my feet.

Resting his elbows on his knees, he gazed wordlessly at me for a moment, then said "Well, my Queen, it is done at last. You now are my consort and friend in every way. And well you should have that special honour, Anne. It is completed before you bear our son."

He raised himself up, drew a deep breath and nodded with the satisfaction he felt at having been victorious, all his desires and plans having come to a triumphant conclusion – with just this last, the arrival of his expected son and heir, imminent.

"How feel you, sweetheart? How did you enjoy your day? You are now revered, admired - and, above all, respected. That is significant, is it not, Anne?"

"Oh Henry, it was brilliant! Truly it was. Every minute of the last four days was near to overwhelming. I am so grateful and humbled by your generosity that I cannot begin to tell you what was most extraordinary - the procession through Westminster on Saturday, the exquisite ceremony in the Abbey, or the opulent banquet in the Hall … were there truly eight hundred mouths served? I cannot fathom the complexity of such a task!"

I took his strong hand in both of mine and squeezed. "While all the time, my darling, you have no idea how often I sought a glimpse of you and longed for you to be next to me!"

I held him a few moments more, then added wistfully, "How I wish my brother George had been there. He has worked so hard and long on our behalf, so that we would see this very day. I do wonder, was it necessary for him to be on the Continent just now, with Norfolk? Could not that business have waited?"

I frowned then, thinking of my dour and disagreeable uncle. Lately, I avoided him whenever possible. One would think he would be inordinately pleased – even grateful, by God's blood - that he and his Howard brethren were now closely related to the reigning Queen. But it was not so. He had made no effort to hide his growing disapproval of Henry's stance in separating from the Church of Rome. Norfolk remained loyal to the Pope, and his refusal to modify his beliefs bred a very visible dislike of me, seeing me as the instigator of Henry's defection. His relationship with his brother-in-law, my lord father, had also taken a downturn.

I guessed that Norfolk took a vindictive pleasure in the fact that my beloved George missed my coronation. Surely the man must have been pleased to have had a good excuse not to attend, himself. And though I pined for George, I was just as glad not to behold Norfolk's sour face.

Dwelling on Norfolk, I was reminded of another unpleasantry. Without thought, I demanded, "Oh, and Henry - where was Thomas More? I know he will never disavow the

Pope, and there has been considerable disagreement between you, but he has long professed himself as your friend. Yet the righteous Sir Thomas could not manage to appear at a ceremony which he well knew meant so much to you?"

My throat tightened, and I heard my voice grow sharp.

"Moreover, Cromwell has told me that More was sent twenty pounds for suitable clothing by the bishops, which I understand he was all too happy to accept. God's teeth, Henry! The wretched man could not even bring himself to *dine* with us at the feast?"

It was to prove a mistake, but I was sore offended, and indignation had taken hold. Glancing his way, I saw an ominous frown darken Henry's expression. Briefly, I regretted my comments, but too late: they had been uttered.

Jubilant mood deflated, he quietly replied "His convictions stand in the way of sensibility for Thomas. He could not be forced to attend. I did receive a note from him, in which he wished us good favour and said he would pray continually for our well-being, and that God might bestow His grace upon us."

I thought little of the crumbs More had offered Henry, and rolled my eyes in response.

At that, my love turned abruptly from me and made to leave the chamber, whereupon I was instantly contrite for spoiling our moment of celebration. Jumping from my chair I caught his arm, turning him to me and embracing him tightly, pulling his head to mine and kissing him long. When we parted, and I looked into his eyes, I saw his deep desire. But I could not fulfill it – we must not come together as husband and wife. Nothing could imperil my pregnancy, and we simply could not lie together: not even on this momentous, long-awaited day.

We had lain apart for some many months now, and briefly I wondered if he was tempted to seek release with other young ladies of the court. Though I knew the practice to be common amongst noblemen, the thought was abhorrent to me. Henry and I were so closely coupled that his loyalty felt absolute, as was mine for him. So I shrugged the concern aside, laid my hand gently on his manly cheek and murmured, "Soon, darling. It will be soon."

The day following, Monday the second day in June, was replete with festive events. Whitehall was bedecked and the newly constructed areas for recreation - the tiltyard, lawns and gardens, tennis plays, and banqueting house - all hosted tournaments, competitions, a myriad of gala feasts and masques in my honour. I attended as many games as I could, displaying my newly acquired royal jewels and elaborate wardrobe. In the evening, there was a *soirèe* in my chambers with music, dancing, laughter and flirting amongst my closest courtiers. A delightful time was had by all the guests, while I, too, enjoyed myself immensely.

Covertly, though, I had my sights set on bigger things than masques and balls, feasting and pastime. What I longed for was to be effectual in the governance of the realm: to be seriously regarded as someone whose decisions were justified and meaningful. I wanted – as I had determined some years ago – to be a woman with a voice. Now, as Queen, I intended my reign to be remembered. There was much I planned to do, God willing; changes I proposed to make which would benefit the poor, the illiterate, the afflicted. While at Hever - oh, how long ago it seemed, now - I had told my mother that I wished to use my learning – my education – and my passionate interests in much the same way as I had observed Marguerite, Queen of Navarre, do so fearlessly. At the time, my lady mother had told me she wished she had been able to use her resourcefulness in ways that women rarely, if ever, were permitted. But she did not scoff at my dream, instead, she endorsed it.

And now here I stood, with ample opportunity, and all the world, for that matter, at my feet.

Windsor
Summer 1533

I STRETCHED, GROANING AS discreetly as I could manage.

I had spent the entire morning sitting, then standing, in a partitioned area at the east end of the Queen's Presence Chamber. This room's angled windows caught the morning light in just such a way that Holbein, the court painter, chose to use it regularly as his temporary studio.

Master Holbein was still basking in the success of his brilliant designs which had been on display during the coronation. He had created the scenery for the tableaus, insisted upon specific table settings for banquets, and had taken charge of the extravagant decorations along the processional routes. His collaborative work with Master Cromwell on that undertaking had bonded them firmly. I was no less an admirer of his work than of the man himself; gruff and reclusive as he was. He had already painted an excellent portrait of me, which Henry adored. Now, though, he was diligently engaged in the completion of my full-length, official coronation portrait. He had finalized the preparatory cartoon for the painting, which he accomplished swiftly since I was to stand, positioned at an angle just so, with my hand on a stack of books gazing directly at the viewer. Once the cartoon was finished and its content transferred to the final canvas, I merely needed to visit him while he worked on the actual painting when I could sit, attired in my regalia, simply so he might observe and record it accurately.

This morning, after adding some detail to my portrait, I watched fascinated as he finished an impressive painting I had commissioned of him several months ago. The piece was complex, yet it drew the eye as well as the imagination. It featured the French ambassadors Jean de Dinteville and Bishop Georges de Selves. Dinteville, de Selves, Holbein and I were all proponents of the new theology. Bishop de Selves, in addition to making a visit to England to provide the younger ambassador with instruction from their King, had brought me a treasured message of encouragement and support from Marguerite, Queen of Navarre – François' sister and the beloved adviser who had most poignantly shaped my intellectual development while I was a young court *protégée* in France. It had been because I was so overwhelmed with gratitude at this gesture that I'd insisted de Selves play a prominent role in the composition.

The origin and evolution of the painting had been the joint contrivance of Holbein, Dinteville, and myself. It was replete with symbolism, and to my delight incorporated a puzzle challenging the viewer to decipher it. I had a special zeal for such cryptic devices, as did Henry. And Holbein had, indeed, done a consummate job in creating this one. The gentlemen were backed by a green brocade curtain - Dinteville especially, gorgeously attired. The floor upon which they stood was of *cosmati* paving – exactly the pavement of the High Alter at Westminster Abbey, the one upon which I had been crowned Queen. Placed strategically on the table between the two men were some symbolic items: a calendar device which indicated the date of the official announcement of my Queenship, a globe, a lute with a broken string, a book of mathematics demonstrating division, and a Lutheran hymnal. These mystical images, along with the merest suspicion of a crucifix hidden behind the green curtain, all spoke to our conviction of a religion free from the dogmatism of the Roman church. It confirmed my connection with the French humanists. It was an acknowledgement of my ascendancy to Queen. And, overall, Holbein's signature style of realism, accomplished through his brilliant touch and vivid use of colour, created a masterpiece in which one could become completely immersed.

•

Henry and I prepared to receive visitors in the King's Presence Chamber. June was drawing to a close, and I had been Queen for just a few weeks. There was much I wanted to accomplish, and to that end, I spent a good deal of time with my advisors discussing and learning about matters of state which pertained to me and, I readily admit, some which extended beyond the ordinary reach of a Queen Consort. Meanwhile, instead of following a standard progress for the summer, my cherished husband remained close by, hunting in the environs of Windsor Park or journeying no more than a few hours from the palace, so he could be certain to be near should I need him in the last weeks of my pregnancy.

The pages announced Ambassador Carlo Capello. I smiled as he entered for I very much liked this charming, quick, well-mannered gentleman from Venice. To my mind, he represented all that was attractive about the flourishing - nay, even intriguing - capitals of the Italian regions. I had read a great deal about Venice as well as Florence and had oft thought how wonderful it would be to go there, and to see those marvelous sights for myself.

With a deep bow and a very pleasant greeting to Henry and me, Capello began his audience by thanking both of us effusively, on behalf of the Venetian Signory, for the great love we bore their state. Henry nodded encouragingly. Indeed, there was little which aggrieved Henry these days, ecstatic as he was about impending fatherhood, and his elegant Queen beside him.

I seized the moment. "*Signore Ambasciatore!* We welcome you and thank you for your service. The King's Majesty and I are kindly disposed to the state of Venice, as I hope you know. I am personally humbled by your respect, *Signore*, for I well know that God inspired His Majesty to marry me: most certainly His Grace could have found a greater personage than I, but he would *never* have come across someone more anxious and ready to demonstrate a Queen's love towards your Signory. Will you most kindly do me the favour of reporting this message to them?"

"Ah, *si*, Madame, *si, si*! I will do so *immediatamente*. The illustrious gentlemen will be overjoyed at your compliment. *Molto grazie*, Your Highnesses."

I knew he longed to kiss my hand but, showing great restraint, he bowed as deeply as was humanly possible and backed from our presence smiling broadly.

Henry looked at me with unabashed admiration. "Well done, my love. And now, as that was our last audience of the morning, I shall take myself to the hunt field. Are you feeling good this day? Hearty?"

"Yes, Henry. I will assuredly be fine until you return." I grasped his hand as we shared that loving look known only to husbands and wives. "Off with you, then, and I shall see you this evening."

•

On 5 July, I remained inside, protected from the heat which shimmered on the stone pathways around and about Windsor. It was a remarkable day for two reasons. The first was the announcement of the death of Henry's sister Mary, the wife of Charles Brandon, Duke of Suffolk, who had herself been Queen of France as a young girl, and in whose entourage

I had served. She had been ailing for some time. In recent years she had borne no love for me, so I concede forthrightly that I grieved little at her passing. It seemed that Henry was scarcely moved, either.

The second, and by far most significant event of the day, was the release of an official proclamation issued by King Henry VIII which blazoned the following message:

> *Whereas the non-legitimate marriage between the King's Highness and the Lady Katherine Princess, relict-widow of Prince Arthur, has been legitimately dissolved by just ways and opinions, the divorce and separation having been made between his said Highness and the said Lady Katherine by the Right Reverend Father in God the Archbishop of Canterbury, Legate, Primate, and Metropolitan of all England; and therefore the King's Majesty has espoused and taken for his wife, according to the laws of the Church, the truly high and excellent Princess, the Lady Anne, now Queen of England, having had her solemnly crowned and anointed, as becoming the praise and glory and honour of the omnipotent God, the security of the succession and descent of the Crown and to the great pleasure, comfort, and satisfaction of all the subjects of this realm;*
>
> *It has been ordered, amongst other things, for the perfect and secure establishment of what is aforesaid, that no person or persons, whatever their state, grade, or condition, shall attempt ...to instigate any act or acts, or derogate from any of the said processes..., concerning the said divorce, as also the solemnity of the legitimate marriage contracted and concluded been the King's Highness and the said Queen Anne, under pain of incurring the penalties and provisions comprised in the Statute of Provision and Præmunire.*
>
> *By reason whereof, and because the said divorce and separation is now made and finished, and the King's Highness is legitimately married, as afore heard, it is a thing*

therefore evident and manifest that the said Lady Katherine may not for the future have or use the name, style, or title, or dignity of Queen of this realm…, but by the name, style, title, and dignity of Princess Dowager.

Considering which, the King our most excellent lord, whom we ought greatly to fear, although he in nowise suspects his loving-subjects of having attempted any act or acts, or any other thing that can be done, moved or said, contrary to the true intent of the said Act, nevertheless, in order that his said humble and loving subjects may have clear, open, and manifest notice of the great perils, damages, and penalties which are specified in the said Act has ordered a proclamation to be made for the open clearness and publication of the aforesaid things, so that all his loving subjects, as likewise others, if they choose, may escape and avoid the said great pains, perils, and punishments above specified.

God save the King.

And God save anyone – *anyone!* – who would dare to cross him.

Palace of Placentia
Greenwich
Late August
and September 1533

THE BIRTH DREW nigh. I remained appreciative of my condition, surely, but rued that my pregnancy had come to its term in late August, as it was hot as Hades that year, and I grew terribly uncomfortable. My ladies did all they could to assist in keeping me cool, applying damp cloths to my head and neck, and constantly providing a stool or bench to prop my swollen feet. At night I rolled from side to side, futilely seeking a suitable position for sleep. I wondered just how women willingly chose to give birth time after time. I had always wished for more than one child, but, dabbing the sweat from my forehead and neck and turning on the mattress for the hundredth time I readily dismissed the notion, determining that I would think on it once this baby was safely delivered. And so day followed discomforting day, inexorably proceeding to the moment when I would take my chamber.

Workmen were, even at this late date, placing the finishing touches on the luxurious suite of rooms in which I would be confined, along with my close ladies-in-waiting and a bevy of midwives, until I gave birth. Once I retired to these rooms as was customary, in great likelihood two weeks or more before my expected delivery, no male would henceforth be admitted. I would not see Henry's, or any man's, face until I had been delivered of a child. The mysteries of childbed were the domain of women alone.

Instead, Henry and his closest companions would hear Mass every day, praying for my safe delivery and that of our baby son.

Henry and I left Windsor and were rowed to Whitehall, where I gathered items I wished to have with me in the chambers during my lying-in. I wanted to be certain I had specific books and other reading material, a particular lute that I enjoyed playing, and a favourite book of hours for my devotions, amongst other things. Also at Whitehall, I would be reunited with my two dogs, the white greyhound Jolie and my adorable little spaniel, Purkoy. I missed them so very much since they had spent the summer being cared for in Westminster. But I had insisted they be allowed in the privy chambers with me during my confinement since they would afford me great joy and keep me well entertained.

Henry had put Cromwell to the mission of gathering certain jewels and plate previously belonging to the Lady Mary when she had been a young princess. Katherine caught wind of this and informed Cromwell's agent that the collection had somehow disappeared, even though she made noise that she would act the dutiful wife and provide Henry with anything he desired. All this while her servants paraded to and fro bearing new livery embroidered with 'H' and 'K'! Being present when Thomas reported this to Henry, I snorted loudly with contempt and did nothing to hide my derision. The woman had become utterly simple-minded during her exile. Either she had lost her senses, or she was possessed of a lionheart - I knew not which but cared even less! She had ceased to worry me and, despite her, *my* infant prince would have clothing, jewels and plate of a magnificence which would astound the world. We certainly did not need Katherine's and Mary's cast-offs.

Once I had collected the belongings I wished to have with me, we set off for Greenwich. All that remained before I took to my chamber was to confirm the lists of ladies who would be permitted to come and go within the apartment. I had included several ladies known at court as highly captivating in the art of gossip, several who excelled at storytelling, and a few most accomplished musicians. We were amply equipped with cards and games. Accompanying us would be Jane, a fool to whom I had taken an affectionate liking. She would have an official position in my household, and as she delighted me and my close companions with her giggles and innocent witticisms, it seemed perfect to include her. And I had arranged for official reports to be delivered to me, should something of significance occur within the realm while I was in confinement. I wished to be entertained as a form of distraction, but I very much wanted to remain aware of the state of the kingdom.

On Tuesday morning, 26 August, I attended the service with Henry and other courtiers in the Royal Chapel. Afterward, we were served spiced wine in my Watching Chamber. I was restless and apprehensive, and hated saying my final goodbye to Henry while others surrounded us, but that is what I was required to do.

I looked deep into his eyes while clinging to his arm a moment too long, but at last, I gathered myself and, along with my closest friends, entered the Queen's Chambers; the great door creaking to behind us.

Once the portal had been closed, it took some minutes to adjust to the dim light within. The suite of chambers, positioned along the easternmost side of the palace, overlooked the expansive gardens, but there was no view of the late summer blooms to be had, for every wall, every inch of floor, the entire ceiling - even the windows themselves - were draped in rugs and arras of incomparable richness. Certainly, once our eyes had become accustomed to the candlelight, we delighted in the dazzling colours of the tapestries that provided some compensation.

The ladies who attended me, and who would regularly stay with me in the apartment until after my delivery were Nan Cobham, who, along with Eleanor Paston would act as the chief midwives. Eleanor - Lady Rutland - had six children of her own, and was very knowledgeable about the medical assistances women required to aid labour and childbirth.

Nan Cobham, also a mother of six, had been trained by other vastly experienced midwives and had been called into service at the deliveries of many noblewomen. I had confidence in them both. Also, Lady Bridget Wingfield had been my friend for some time, and I found her demeanor to be serene and calming. She, too, had borne multiple children, and the combination of her temperament and her familiarity with birth gave me a sense of assurance.

Also amongst the select few was my sister-in-law Jane Rochford. I had warmed to Jane in recent years: although we had not started our friendship on good grounds, I now saw her as caring for my brother George, which was important to me. I'd decided, therefore, to include her even though she and George had no children of their own. And of course, there were my dearest Maggie, Lady Lee, and Anne Zouche. Jane the Fool would also remain in attendance to keep our spirits high with witty observations, and my lady mother would visit me though she was too apprehensive to be present for the birth itself. I would be happy to see her when she chose to call upon us.

As Eleanor, Bridget, my maids Lucy and Emma, and Jane busied themselves unpacking and arranging my personal items which had been delivered earlier in the day, Maggie, Anne and I, followed closely by Purkoy and Jolie sniffing into every nook, examined the surroundings which would be home to me for the coming weeks. The rooms were richly arrayed, to be sure. The scheme followed closely the Ordinances published by Henry's grandmother, the indomitable Margaret Beaufort, Countess of Richmond and Derby, in 1486 when her daughter-in-law Elizabeth of York was pregnant with her firstborn son Arthur, Henry's deceased brother. This dictum was entitled *'Preparation against the Deliveraunce of a Quene, as also for the Christening of the Child of which she shall be delivered'.*

In the style and manner characteristic of the doughty Countess, the lists were exacting and particular, and in my case, they had been followed precisely. The centrepiece of the largest chamber was the Queen's bed: new, and utterly enormous. Henry had spared nothing to ensure that I would be comfortable and have plenty of room in which to stretch out. It was arrayed with luxurious crisp white sheets which could be seen peeking from under a crimson velvet counterpane embroidered in gold and edged with ermine.

Atop the bed were four large down pillows, both long ones, and square, covered in fustian. The mattress itself was of a thickness and fluffiness rarely seen. Somewhat wryly, I reflected that the contrivance sat so high I would need a stool to climb in. Its sparver, the gorgeous circular curtain which hung from the ceiling and surrounded it, was of crimson satin embroidered throughout with the arms of the King and my emblems, beautifully edged with a fringe of blue and gold silk. It presented an imposing sight – almost too magnificent to sleep upon!

Nearby stood an ornately carved sideboard upon which sat bowls of gold, and one of silver gilt. In the adjoining wardrobe hung mantles of velvet and satin, all edged in ermine, for me to snuggle into as I rested. At the foot of the immense royal bed was a pallet, also generous in size and appointed with the same extravagance - sheets, down bolster supporting crisp-laundered pillows and a delightfully soft counterpane, but in blue rather than crimson. One of the ladies would be with me, sleeping in that pallet at all times. The rest of my ladies' beds had been dressed in nearly the same level of finery but placed in an adjoining chamber.

It was customary to keep the windows draped, mostly to avoid draughts which were thought to be harmful during the labour and delivery of a baby. In January, this may have been sensible, but this was August, and such a counter-intuitive practice made no sense to me, in fact, I thoroughly disliked it. Longing to gaze out of the open window to the lawns and gardens below I made my disapproval known but, Queen or no, was soundly overruled. The windows remained hung with heavy tapestries with the grudging concession of one, where I might go and draw a quick breath and peek at the sun when necessary.

We kept ourselves well occupied. It was too dark to sew or embroider, but we listened to music, played cards, gossiped, and read. As my term drew near, mostly I read from books of hours, praying diligently for the healthy delivery of my child, and that I might bear him with grace and courage. I also regularly read the Bible and treasured having my favourite with me: that which had been translated into French by the scholar Jacques Lefévre d'Etaples. Henry and I shared the two beautiful volumes, both bound extravagantly in rich, soft brown leather. On the cover of the first book was embossed the scripture '*For the law was given by Moses*', and on the reverse cover of the second, '*Grace and Truth were realized through Jesus Christ*'. Each book bore our initials, H and A, imprinted with the Scripture, in gold.

There was ample time, also, to reflect. Often, my mind would strive to imagine how the birthing would be. But I had no physical experience of such magnitude with which to compare, so I remained perplexed, even though I had asked every mother present to describe her labours, over and over.

To distract myself from the ordeal to come, I spent time each day contemplating exactly how my court should conduct itself, and what I would like to accomplish. Before my confinement, I had given each and every member of my household a beautiful girdle-book of psalms which they wore attached to chains about their waists. Furthermore, I encouraged my ladies to study them meticulously so that we could discuss passages together. Resolute that mine would be a court which would do much good for the impoverished in the realm, I believed strongly in giving to the needy. So my ladies would sew to provide clothing and other necessities – especially, I thought as I sat in the opulence of my surroundings with women there to serve my every need – for those poor mothers who had little to ease their childbirth, and even less to provide for their infants. It was a cause which inspired me greatly, and I determined to make a difference using the power God had bestowed upon me.

I had already set expectations that the behaviour of my all female retinue would be genteel and refined at all times, although this in no way meant we would exist in a sombre, sanctimonious setting as did Katherine and *her* lacklustre attendants. I loved laughter, visual beauty, witty and brilliant conversation, courtly romance, music, and dancing! All would play a significant part in my surroundings and in my households as I built the dazzling court I envisioned, alongside Henry.

On Sunday, the third day of September, we had just finished dinner when my mother, Nan Cobham and I were informed that we had a visit from Elizabeth Brereton, the wife of Sir William Brereton of Henry's Privy Chamber. Immediately I requested that she be admitted since I wanted to observe her and share conversation one last time before my baby's arrival. Out of several candidates, I had chosen Elizabeth to be wet-nurse for the infant. The selection of a wet-nurse was an important decision made by noblewomen who were about to give birth. Most aristocratic mothers did not feed their children unless absolutely necessary. Queens certainly would not do so since it was known that, during the period of nursing, conception was suppressed and bearing royal heirs was a primary function for a queen. Thus the choice of who would nourish the new prince was a crucial one. Her temperament must be altogether pleasing and calm. She must be healthy above all, and possess no vices which could plague the quality of her milk. In my opinion, she should, additionally, be literate and well spoken. And she must be available, and have a proven history of producing ample milk, as my baby must never go hungry.

It had not been easy to find such a candidate but, happily, Elizabeth fulfilled all of these qualities. Furthermore, she had just weaned her second son, little Henry Brereton and, despite the fact that Elizabeth was some three years older than I, I felt this maturity could only count to her advantage. A second cousin to the King, her son was a comely child, which I knew because I had made it my point to have him in my company. He was robust, with stout little legs and already toddling despite having only just passed the first anniversary of his birth. All these qualities were in order, yet I was an anxious mother-to-be, and I needed reassurance.

As the four of us sat and pleasantly conversed, sipping lightly spiced wine, both my mother and then Nan cast me a look indicating their approval. I sighed with relief. Now, truly, all was in place. It was only a matter of waiting.

In the pre-dawn hours of Thursday 7 September, I awoke with a low ache in my back. I had felt well until now, though I had occasionally experienced what I thought were the beginnings of labour, only to be mistaken. This ache was persistent, so I signalled Eleanor, who slept in a bed alongside mine. She placed warm cloths against my lower back to ease the discomfort, but I could tell by her expression that she believed my time had finally arrived. After a while, she had me arise and walk about the chambers.

By now all the ladies were fully awake, cups of warm posset being passed about, the hearth well stoked and the rooms readied. A birthing chair was moved into the main chamber while the pallet bed was prepared with new sheets and a covering of white linen. I went to my *prie-dieu* and, though I could not kneel, selected a book of hours then clutched the devotional to me as I walked and walked the chamber floors. At the hearth, Eleanor Paston was stirring a concoction which she had me drink to ease my cramps, and I was glad to do so for the contractions of the birth process had undoubtedly started. I desperately wanted to lie down, but Nan and Eleanor urged me yet to walk, saying it would help the baby move into place and shorten the labour. Anne Zouche trod the floor with me, and Jane the Fool, though plainly apprehensive, held my hand and tried, albeit somewhat unsuccessfully, to make me laugh.

I walked, then rested, and all the while my contractions grew stronger. The ladies comforted and encouraged me, but nonetheless, I trembled. Every moment in my life which heretofore had required me to be bold and fearless paled in light of what I now faced. I loathed that I was losing my grip on any sense of control until, eventually, I was helped to the pallet and laid upon it, legs apart and acutely conscious that I presented a most undignified posture for a Queen of England. Meanwhile, my women were on all sides uttering soft reassurance, aiding as my engorged belly assumed complete dominion over my being. It did as it was going to - royal frame or no: muscles pulling upward in waves that felt as if they would lift me to the ceiling. After each contraction I lay panting and dry-mouthed, trying not to cry out – for it was not pain, exactly, but the immense force of my body performing this ancient ritual all on its own which rendered me helpless and frightened.

I heard my ladies calling to me, encouraging me, smoothing the hair on my head, and then, as my body began to quake uncontrollably, I heard Nan tell me to bear down. Eleanor's strong arms were kneading my belly now, helping the baby to move, and there were ladies at my shoulders and back, supporting me into a sitting position while I gritted my teeth and pushed with all the strength I could muster.

Through a haze, I heard my voice cry "God's blood, I will tear end to END …!" but Eleanor retorted severely, "No you will *not*, my lady! Keep *PUSHING!*" whereupon I made an effort more mighty than any I ever remembered in my life.

… and suddenly it was done.

With immense relief, the child slipped from my body, and the pressure ceased. I took a great gasp of air and collapsed against the sweat-soaked pillows.

No one said anything.

Jesu! Did the baby live?

I heard the cry then, and instantly I knew.

I had been delivered, not of a boy-child as that wispy-bearded old fraud, astrologer Robyns had, oh so confidently, predicted … but of a *daughter*.

She was washed and smoothed with rose oil, as was I by my beloved ladies. They wrapped her snugly in her swaddling cloths then Nan Cobham carefully handed her to me murmuring, "Your Grace, you have a beautiful daughter. She is perfect in every way. Never have I seen a lovelier baby. I bear great happiness for you and His Majesty the King."

"Thank you, Nan," I whispered and reached to take my infant – my baby girl – into my arms. I was numb from the experience of birth although it had been uncomplicated, as they go, and I felt blessed for that.

Holding my daughter, I coddled her, and simply gazed into her face, rosy pink and seemingly, God be willing, full of health. Her fluff of hair was bright ginger, just like Henry's. Her eyes were wide open, peering up at me with an uncanny curiosity and awareness. I instantly melted with love.

As her tiny body snuggled ever closer to mine we contemplated each other – mother and child; I could not imagine her to be any other than who she was. Strangely and after all, she was precisely the baby for whom I had longed during my pregnancy.

I realized then, with a start, that I had somehow known, even from her first stirrings, that our child would be a princess.

•

Henry had been immediately informed of the birth but decided I was to have the evening to recover before he visited. That night, I slept soundly even though my body was aching. Lady Elizabeth Brereton sat up with the other women and suckled my child, comforting her when she fussed, allowing me much needed rest. Very early on the following morning, she was brought to me, and I spent a goodly while holding her, cosseting her, and becoming acquainted.

I was taken aback, really, to find how pleasurable it was to rock her in the crook of my arm. Her warmth, her gaze of awareness, her tiny, perfect humanity caused me to throb with maternal love for her. As our eyes met, I was infused with a determination to protect her, to be responsible for her wellbeing, and shield from her all evil. It seemed that she understood and that she gained from my touch the reassurance she needed, for she was content and quiet. At any moment, I would hear the sharp rap on the door of the chamber, mere seconds before my husband would sweep into the room to greet me and meet his daughter for the first time.

Contrary to the way I had always envisioned this meeting to go, now I was filled with misgiving. The palms of my hands were damp with sweat, my mouth dry. What bearing would he assume? Would his face be red, as it was wont when he strove to hide his anger? Or would he be ominously quiet – scowling even - which was a portent of retribution when he was displeased? I considered the possibilities, knowing all too well his dark moods, and though when we last parted it had been with an abundance of love and good will, I could not pretend he would be pleased with the birth of a daughter. After all, I had nigh to *promised* him a son.

But then I grew resolute. The more I speculated, the less apprehensive I felt: instead I became heated and indignant that he – or *anyone!* – might dare diminish the magnificence of my daughter's entry into the world or disregard the fact that she was a royal princess, mighty in her own right.

Quickly I assembled a mental array of sharp retorts I would launch when Henry challenged me. King or not, he would rue any word he uttered about my child which was less than commendatory. My breath came quicker, and I felt my ire rise as I imagined our encounter. In agitation, I arranged the soft blankets swaddling her, fluffed her shock of hair, and then smoothed mine, which was loose and arranged about my shoulders.

The expected quick knock preceded Henry's entry, and his immense presence – I had almost forgotten how his countenance filled a chamber. His eyes sought mine as he came to my bedside, and I was ready – jaw clenched – to defend my child.

We regarded each other silently for what seemed a long while. Finally, he reached out and stroked my cheek, then gestured for the baby to be handed to him. His expression was calm, and as I placed the sweet bundle in his large but slightly awkward grasp, I softened just a bit.

"She is beautiful, is she not, sweetheart?" I hazarded rather more tentatively than I had intended.

He drew her closer and peered into her perfect face. His eyes rested long on her pronounced tuft of bright ginger hair: I held my breath … and then a broad smile spread across his features. She was his issue, even though a girl-child, and her wide-open eyes observed him with a keenness exceptional for a tiny infant.

"She is indeed," he said. "She is gifted with extraordinary beauty indeed."

"Your Grace, I am pleased that you think so. I surely am. Look how serenely she studies you. She knows you are her father, and already feels secure in the protection of your strong arms. As I know she will always be."

His gaze left the baby's and met mine. "She will be safe with me, my Anne. You have done well, darling. Shall we bestow our tiny beauty with the name of Elizabeth? Let us honour the memory of my lady mother and your beloved mother who share that name. There can't be anything more fitting for our princess."

I exhaled quietly. "I thank you, Henry. It's perfect. I had hoped that would be your wish."

He smiled then. "My other wish, wife and Queen, is for your swift recovery. I have missed you greatly. And now that we have produced a gorgeous daughter we must become reacquainted with each other. Our next child will surely be a son."

He squeezed my hand tightly, and I smiled in return while relief flooded me as he bent low to brush upon my brow a tender kiss. "I shall visit you and Elizabeth again very soon, my lady."

But as Henry straightened, and before he turned to take his leave, plainly I saw the look on his face. His lips smiled.

But his *eyes*?

They were bleak.

Thomas Cromwell arrived later that day bearing the official pronouncement of Elizabeth's birth, which by tradition came directly from the Queen and would be ceremonially presented to my Lord Chamberlain, Lord Cobham. It was Cobham's duty to proclaim the new arrival, and forthwith commence celebrations. The churches would sing a *Te Deum* in Elizabeth's honour; bonfires would blaze in the town squares accompanied by wine which would again flow from the fountains for the people to drink and rejoice. Little wonder that they would love me, their queen, on this day.

The document had been drawn up for some weeks, written out by the scribes. It was only that, now, a small correction was required.

The letter *S* would be added to the word *Prince* telling everyone that the King and Queen had produced a daughter. It would now read '*Princes*'.

I scanned the parchment page, reading the words: *"By the Quene*

Right trustie and welbiloved, we grete you well. And where as it hath pleased the goodnes of Almightie God, of his infynite marcie and grace, to sende unto us, at this tyme, good spede, in the delyveraunce and bringing furthe of a Princes, to the great joye, rejoyce, and inward comforte of my Lorde, us, and all his good and loving subjectes of this his realme…"

My heart swelled with pride, knowing that this was the first important decree in Elizabeth's life. It mattered not to me that the document needed correction. The final phrases admonished the people to give, *"with us, unto Almightie God, high thankes, glorie, laude, and praising; and to praye for the good helth, prosperitie, and contynuall preservation of the said Princes accordingly."*

I mouthed the words silently and felt tears of gratitude and joy burn behind my lids, then swallowed past the lump in my throat and instead focused on a matter of practicality. "Thomas, are preparations for the christening well in hand?"

"Yes, Milady. It will be a beautiful event, with all suitable solemnity; as grand a christening as has been seen in many, many years. I will provide you with every detail before the day so you may imagine what it will look and sound like as if you were to be there."

"Thank you, Thomas, although I surely wish I could attend in person," I grumbled. "Does it not seem to you heartless that a woman must stay entombed in these dark rooms for so long, both before and after the birth? And miss her very own child's christening? It certainly does feel so to me. Sometimes I wonder who created such dictums that we must all blindly follow. I presume, at least in this case, that it must have been a man?"

A wry smile briefly creased Cromwell's face. It spoke more of his true opinion than had he made overt comment, but Thomas was a prudent man and well understood his place, so he merely rose, bowed low, and offered, "I will return within a few days, Your Grace, with a complete schedule of the proceedings for your review. Until then, please remain well, and I offer my sincerest felicitations to you, and to the Princess Elizabeth."

And with that, he backed out of the door.

In between visits from my beautiful baby girl, I received guests. One of my new and highly favoured silkwomen, Mistress Joan Clerk, was to call in the early afternoon to show me the progress she had made creating my Elizabeth's christening robes, a break in my closeted monotony that I looked forward to with delight.

Meanwhile, a ridiculous counter-suggestion had been made by some of the elder stateswomen. They proposed that Elizabeth should establish a custom by wearing the christening garment which had attired Mary, the previous English princess to have been baptized. Upon inquiry, I learned that the robe was of Spanish lace, made by Katherine's Spanish needlewomen. It was implied that any and all of Henry's children should be christened in that same gown.

I had attended to them quite politely as the idea was presented by the Dowager Duchess, Lady Norfolk. Not halfway through her speech, though, I ceased listening, albeit doing my very best to maintain a pleasant expression. The instant her mouth stopped moving I shot her, along with the other ladies who accompanied her, a look intended to convey that my imminent decision was final and that no further discussion on the topic would be tolerated.

"Thank you most kindly, ladies. I see that you have given this notion a great deal of thought. How generous of each of you. However, there will be no consideration whatsoever of Elizabeth donning the robes worn by Mary. On the contrary, *Elizabeth's* gown may well begin a tradition to be followed by other, yet to be born, children of Henry's and mine. But *my* child, our true Princess, will certainly *not* wear a Spanish gown unrepresentative of the beautiful craftsmanship of our skilled English seamstresses! Furthermore, I feel certain that, if asked, Mary's mother would balk at providing me with the garment anyway, and instead will keep it well hidden – as, for that matter, would I if I were in her circumstance. And lastly, ladies, an old Spanish gown of pale, washed-out lace would do absolutely nothing to show off my child's exceptional beauty. So, no, I have seen to it that her first significant garment will flatter her- will complement Elizabeth's Tudor hair and colouring - so that all who observe her will plainly see her conspicuous likeness to her handsome father, the King. But again, I thank you for your visit."

With a brief nod to each, they were dismissed and out, with downcast eyes, they filed one by one.

Spanish, indeed! Cobbled together by Katherine's ungainly outfitters! I think not.

Mistress Clerk was a rare talent, and I felt fortunate to have made her acquaintance. She had previously sewn gowns for several noblewomen from north of London, in Essex. Living in Braintree, she had apprenticed with some of the best and most notable seamstresses and silkwomen in an area widely known for its expertise in fine craftsmanship. Once I had commissioned a gown from her, on a trial basis, and examined the result quickly produced, I had been left awestruck by her fine workmanship and even finer sense of colour and fabric. Indeed, I'd immediately requested that she move to London for a position as a regular provider of clothing for me, and for Henry, and now she would sew for my child as well.

She entered my chamber with a graceful curtsey, and efficiently lifted from her large sack various materials and pieces of partially completed garments. A lovely lady, witty and vivacious yet respectful, I enjoyed spending time with her looking over and selecting beautiful swatches of luxurious silks and velvets and discussing items which would comprise a new wardrobe for me and gowns for the infant Elizabeth. It afforded a welcome respite from my continued lying-in, which had begun to feel extremely wearisome.

I held my breath in anticipation while from a linen wrapping, Mistress Clerk carefully lifted a magnificent creation of deep, rich purple silk velvet - Elizabeth's royal christening robe. Although only partially complete, one could already see that this gown would prove extraordinary. Lined with incomparable crimson satin, when I reached out to touch it, I was amazed by its supple softness. I sighed with satisfaction as my fingers stroked the splendid texture of cloth falling in folds like violet liquid. Its neckline had the beginnings of silver and gold embroidery, delicately placed: the entire gown to be edged in a fluff of white ermine. There even came with it a tiny matching cap, also satin lined, which pleased me because it was as smooth and soft as my baby's skin, and would cause no chafing or discomfort for her.

How elegant she would look in this, her first important frock! Needless to say, she had to be beautifully garbed at all times, and thus would come to know the importance of conveying the right personal impression through her attire. I could be certain of that because I would instruct her, just as I had been taught when I was a mere girl in France.

On the morning of 10 September, my chambers were astir with activity: everyone preparing for the christening. I, on the other hand, sat propped in bed as I had been for the past four days … and God's eyes but I was in a foul humour! So much so that most of the women who were serving me, and the nurses who were to prepare Elizabeth, gave me a wide berth. And who could blame them? My head pounded with a relentless ache; my breasts were sore and swollen with unused milk even though I had been tightly bound with linen to suppress the milk flow, and my temper verged on the uncontrollable – just as it always had at certain times of the month, but far worse.

The cause of my dissatisfaction was evident to all. I could not stop lamenting that such a wonderful, miraculous event - the baptism of my long-awaited child – was to take place without me. How did other queens, other noblewomen, bear up under such trying conditions? I had no idea, and so I continued to ruminate, scowling, while wondering if Henry would even bother to come to my rooms to see me before he joined the guests for the mass and the ceremony.

True, he had visited a few times in the last few days and had held Elizabeth briefly on each occasion. With me he was exceedingly polite, smiling and seemingly pleased with our daughter, expressing his anticipation for having me back at his side, but nevertheless, I sensed a gulf had opened between us. It did not surprise me. After all, I had wondered at length how we would conduct ourselves once we were truly alone and tried to persuade myself that the easy cadence of our former affection would resume quickly. But, at that miserable moment?

Well, frankly - I simply didn't care!

I glanced up from the book I held, merely as a form of distraction, to find Maggie sweeping across the room to my bedside. She pulled up a chair, sat down, took one look at me, and said, "Oh my. No wonder you are sitting here all alone, in the midst of a whole crowd of people. No one has the courage to come near you, I see."

I could not help myself. A single, self-pitying tear traced its way down my cheek.

She reached over and took my hand in her cool one. Even her touch was soothing.

"Anne, I know how you are feeling. I remember the days following the birth of baby Henry, even though it was almost three years ago. While I rejoiced in the fact that I had survived the birth, and my baby boy was hearty and robust, I had never felt so low in my entire life. I longed to coddle and feed him, but, just like you, I could not. Instead, I had to watch his wetnurse suckle him, and it about broke my heart. My breasts caused me agony, and my mood was always dark. It seemed there was nothing I could do to shake it, even while acutely conscious that I should be happy and grateful. The midwife assured me, however, that the despondency would pass. She encouraged me to hang on, just as I do now with you, and soon I would feel like myself once again. I hardly believed her, but the days passed quickly, and I did come round, as will you. Once finally able to step outside into the sunshine, after my churching had taken place, I improved vastly."

I clung to her hand, still sniffling pathetically.

"I feel I will never again escape this room – these accursed walls! I hope I never see those wretched tapestries again: I care not a whit how costly they were!"

"And you won't have to. As soon as you are able, Anne, we will walk in the gardens every day. Better still, I will stay at Greenwich and not return home for as long as you need me. And think! You will be well recovered in time to enjoy the beautiful autumn – your favourite season, yes? Have faith, my Lady! All will be well."

It was then that she leaned in and spoke quietly. "Anne, is your sadness because you birthed a girl? Do you cry because you feel you have failed the King?"

Using both hands, I roughly brushed my tears away. Maggie handed me a linen square, and I blew my nose. I hesitated just a moment longer, then with an emphatic sniff, "No. No, I do *not* feel that way, and it is certainly not the cause of my malaise, Maggie! I only need to look at Elizabeth and am filled to the brim with pride. She flourishes by the day and seems uncannily alert, full of life. And always she reminds me of Henry – her hair, of course, but also, her lips, and the shape of her little face are his. He sees it, too, and is pleased. He immediately assured me of his happiness and his certainty that we would beget a son."

… and here I lowered my voice to a rumbling growl, mimicking him, "Anne, we will yet have sons. We are young: both young enough to have a boy child – in fact *many* boy children!"

At that, Maggie and I shared an incredulous look at my temerity, then spluttered with laughter. My imitation of Henry, as well as the fact that he had called us 'young' - which seemed rather preposterous - sparked our mirth. Together Maggie and I had always been able to laugh so easily; her objective was achieved.

My gloom lifted while Maggie called for one of the assistant midwives to bring me a herbal tisane to ease my bodily discomfort. As I sipped the warm infusion of lemon balm, mugwort, and rosemary, sweetened with a bit of honey, I did indeed begin to feel better.

We spent a while longer discussing the christening and the celebration banquet, and I told her all I knew about what was to take place. I asked her to make certain, in my absence, that the baptismal water was warm enough, and that there were no draughts in the centre of the Church where Elizabeth was to be held. She promised that not only would she ensure these things on my behalf, but that she would remember every single detail to recount them to me tomorrow.

I thanked her, kissed her, and let her take her leave so she would not be late.

The ceremony was to take place in the Church of the Friars, adjacent to the palace. Henry had been christened there since the Franciscan Friars were much beloved by his father, and by his mother as well. The resident friars had always served the court well, being advisors and confessors to the Catholic nobility when the court lodged at Greenwich although now, of course, there existed discord based upon Henry's distancing himself from the Church of Rome. Still, there were those Franciscan brothers with whom Henry, and his courtiers, remained close: indeed some would still serve at the religious ceremony.

Otherwise, the church would be filled with nobility and clergy. I hoped Elizabeth would comport herself as befitting a royal princess, and not cry or fuss. Once the ceremony was concluded, the guests would present their gifts to the baby, then after having partaken of refreshment would come to my chambers to show Henry and me what they had given to the mighty Princess of England, Elizabeth.

I had at last perked up and called my maids to come and help me prepare for my visitors. I might be bed-bound, but it would never do to look anything but my best.

The days passed excruciatingly slowly while herbal remedies, brewed by one of the skilled midwives who had also apprenticed as an apothecary, fortified me. As my body regained its vigour, I also became strengthened in spirit by a renewed zeal to serve as an enlightened, reformist queen. Now that my pregnancy and the birth were behind me, my thoughts were consumed by the possibilities for change which beckoned me as the crowned and anointed Queen of England.

I requested books and writings that instructed me on the lives of some of the women I most admired, beginning, of course, with the beloved mentor and heroine of my youth, Marguerite d'Alençon.

Marguerite had been the first woman to make me aware that a lady need not merely sit placidly and prettily, convention-bound to never enter into any conversation of substance. Instead, Marguerite deliberately provoked debate, prodding those involved in such a way that she created an opening with which to propose her ideas, however radical. I had loved watching her interact with learned groups of men.

Next, I read about Catherine of Valois, who, after a desperately neglectful childhood in France rose nevertheless to a position of power as the wife and queen of Henry V then ruled after his untimely death to, ultimately, enter into a relationship with Owen Tudor, a Welsh soldier. Their union produced Jasper Tudor, a figurehead of the future Tudor dynasty.

The boldly enterprising Eleanor of Aquitaine and the tenacious Margaret Beaufort also stood forth as relevant females for thought-provoking study. And finally, enthralled, I turned to *Le Livre de la Cite des Dames - The Book of the City of Ladies -* by Christine de Pisan.

Born in 1364, Christine had been an ingenious thinker and writer in a time when most women had little or no knowledge of how to even read or write, much less the wherewithal to challenge standard rules of belief. The daughter of a Frenchwoman, she was born in Venice to an Italian father who had taken her to France at an early age and provided for her the then-unthinkable - a thorough and broad education. She was an avid reader, being well versed in multiple languages, and thus fortunate to become wed to a man greatly supportive of her intellectual pursuits. He died, however, at a young age, leaving her to care for herself and her children. But Christine was no woman of faint heart. Employing her talent for language, she began to write. At first, she composed poetry and prose, but soon initiated a written analysis of women and their place in society. I marvelled at the way she condemned the depiction of women in literature, and instead argued for their education and ability to have a voice in the world.

With keen enjoyment, I devoured, again and again, *The Book of the City of Ladies*, delighting in Christine's creation of three mythical figures: Lady Reason, Lady Rectitude, and Lady Justice. They carry on conversations with each other, and with other notable women in history who have come to live in the fictional 'city'. They discuss why women are or are not suited for certain jobs, why they have been denied the education they deserve, and recount the inventions and the many advantages that women have provided to humanity throughout the ages. Above all, I delighted in her work's melodious French, and her ideas, so artfully presented, inspired me.

Increasingly I grew restless for my churching: that small traditional ceremony which declares a new mother fit to re-enter the world after having given birth. I felt ready and impatient to assume the role of Queen. I wanted to rule alongside my husband. I wanted to implement change in the realm; not merely in religious practice, but for the good of all England's subjects.

Whitehall
October 1533

AS SOON AS I was able, I was rowed downriver to my suites at Whitehall. Long had I waited for that day of my return, as I felt it to be *my* palace. The rooms were beautiful and very comfortable – after all, Henry and I, together, had designed the Queen's apartments in preparation for the major renovation of Wolsey's York Place into a luxurious palace for the King and Queen. And after my long confinement, I needed to escape Greenwich for a while.

It was there in mid-October when the air had turned crisp, and the blazing hearth fires warmed the handsome palace chambers at night, that I arranged a tryst with my husband. It would be the evening in which we would reunite as husband and wife – in total privacy.

To my surprise, I found myself to be anxious. Henry had regularly come to my apartments at Greenwich where, while our interaction had been coolly courteous, he'd never failed to demonstrate great pride in baby Elizabeth. He'd held her and cosseted her, and discussed at some length who would make up her royal household, for she would, by the end of the year, have an established residence of her own, where she would be cared for by a meticulously selected staff.

Picture it so: Henry and I cooing over our beautiful baby, smiling at each other when she smiled, or blew a tiny bubble, or pushed her fist into her mouth – did it not create a lovely family tableau? But the harsh truth remained: Henry needed a son, and I – his 'second self', his parallel, his beloved consort who had been preordained to provide him with that which was only good – I had, quite simply, failed to deliver him of one! Oh, I loved Elizabeth with my whole heart and believed that she was all I had ever hoped for. But I was rational, too, and fully aware that Henry would not be satisfied with merely another daughter, no matter how bright and beautiful. So, truly, it was left to me to renew our closeness, and, God be willing, to bear more children with the great hope that the next one would be a boy.

As I had done little more than a year ago, I carefully planned Henry's seduction. It was of the utmost importance that we not only share a marriage bed but that he fall once again deeply and irretrievably in love with me.

With the help of my steward and several of my ladies, I planned an elegant light supper which would be served in my chambers for just the two of us. I arranged, too, for a single lutist to play for us as we dined, for Henry loved the lute and its sweet harmonies rarely failed to make him feel sentimental. Lastly, I set the stage with a table laid with gold and silver plate, an abundance of candles placed low on the furnishings to create an intimate, ambient light, and with just a hint of incense burning to scent the air.

Once those details had been attended to, I paid mind to my appearance. When Henry was to join me for supper, I would be clothed in a soft grey gown of velvet. I would wear a circlet of pearls to add lustre to my face, and my skin would be enhanced by a soft flush of pink powder.

... and thus came the night upon which so much depended.

Once our supper had drawn to a close and the servants clearing the remains had been dismissed, I retreated to my bedchamber where two of my ladies helped me out of the grey gown, and into an unstructured, but close-fitting robe. Mistress Clerk had created this special garment that I was to wear strictly for Henry's pleasure. It was made of light, very beautiful white satin, fine and fluid. My hair was loosened and brushed about my shoulders, my jewelry removed … and then I waited.

Henry opened the door quietly and stepped into the warm, fire-lit chamber. His eyes met mine, then travelled the length of me as I stood before him in only a gossamer layer of white – nothing more – with every curve accentuated by the flickering light. I knew I looked virginal… glowing … white silk slipping over my body with my ever luxuriant hair lying on my bare shoulders. I wanted him to remember why he fought for me – why he married me – why he loved me still.

Without words, we came together. As soon as I was close to him, his scent – that personal redolence which was distinctly his – immediately aroused me as it had always done. He buried his face in my hair and ran his hands over my body, feeling the slip of the satin. Gently he pulled my head back, so I looked him in the eyes and I could immediately see that his ardour had been renewed. He gazed at me as he had always done, with a mixture of lust and pure adoration. His voice was husky: whispering close to my ear.

"Anne, how I have missed you; holding you; pressing my lips to yours …"

Then his mouth was on mine and our kisses somehow sweeter than I remembered them to be. As we lay together on the soft bed, strewn with furs, I sighed in sheer pleasure. Once again I was with the only man I had ever really loved.

And as that sensual night progressed, I was left with no doubt that my King truly did love me.

The next morning we sat together at a small table in my bedchamber, breaking our fast; eating silently, having exhausted our conversation for the time being. As he relished his cheese, grapes, and fine white manchet, I studied him. He had passed the forty-second anniversary of his birth some four months previously. Lines had become etched at the corner of his eyes, and under his neat beard, there was distinct evidence of some heaviness in his cheeks, settling into jowls. His ginger hair betrayed threads of grey, and his broad, powerful body had thickened somewhat, to be certain, but his eyes were lively as ever, his smile quick and infectious, and his potent allure had not waned at all. He was still the most vibrant, finest-looking man I had ever encountered and, without question, my attraction to him remained as compelling as it ever had been.

But my thoughts could not be swayed from a particular topic which tormented me. I had told myself over and over to let it go: never to bring it up. But the seemingly opportune silence, and my feeling so close to him after our night together loosened my resolve.

"Henry, I have never felt such contentment and joy with you, my darling, as I do this morning," I smiled, offering him all my charm. "I feel complete, having been back in your arms once again."

He raised a querying eyebrow over the rim of his cup, and I saw his pleased look in return.

I hesitated for just a moment. "But … I can't help but wonder, my love. It is only because I am so devoted to you that I need to ask …"

He waited.

I could have stopped there. Or I might have substituted another, more agreeable question. But I forged ahead.

"Did you feel the need to take a mistress while I was restricted by my pregnancy?" My heart was pounding. "Henry, did you have another who loved you?"

Instantly his eyes narrowed while his expression grew hard. In a mere second, his warmth tempered, the set of his jaw and shoulders clearly indicating displeasure.

"And if I had? What would you think to say to me, Anne? What would be your response?"

"Only that my heart would be broken! You are mine, Henry, and I yours. I want you to be touched by no other woman's hands or lips. Is that too much to ask of my husband?"

For what seemed an eternity he sat without responding, regarding me impassively. When he did eventually reply, his voice was cool.

"Indeed, I love you, Anne. I have loved you like no other woman in my life. And I have sacrificed much for you, that you well know … but do *not* deign to feel as if you can tell me how to conduct myself! I am a man, and I am King. Should I choose to take a mistress, I can, and I WILL do so!"

The knot in my stomach, which had made its presence known as soon as the question had left my lips, tightened even more cruelly at his response. I was dismayed. I had fully expected him to commit to me and only me, and to promise eternal fidelity … oh, how foolish I had been! Now I must bear his response with grace, or further anger him and jeopardize the delicate bond which had been built the evening before.

He looked me directly in the eye then. "Having said that, though, I will, in this case, provide you with the answer you seek … I had no other woman in my bed. I waited for you."

There fell a silence between us. Then followed, "… I hope you grasp the significance of what I declare?"

"Indeed, it is a salve to my soul, Henry. Please indulge me. I asked only because I simply could not bear to share you with another. You mean that much to me."

"And you to me, Anne."

The words reassured … but his tone? I wanted it to envelop me with warm certitude.

It did not.

As he rose to depart, he took my hand and pressed it to his lips. Quietly he said, "So be it, then. We can only hope that our love last evening has conceived us a son."

He let go of my hand, turned and went from the room, leaving me to wonder.

Greenwich
Autumn 1533

MY PHYSICAL STRENGTH returned as the colourful days of the harvest ebbed. I delighted in again riding out with the hunt, and though my once bold recklessness on the field - a powerful attraction to Henry – had been tempered by a concession to safety now that I was a mother, still, we enjoyed many afternoons on horseback. Henry and I did also spend some goodly time hawking in the fields adjacent to the palace. Never again would I take for granted the ability to breathe deeply of fresh, cool air and look heavenward to gaze on eternal, celestial blue skies!

I rambled through the gardens and woods, sometimes with Jolie and a few other hounds trailing, oft-times with Maggie, who, true to her word, had stayed to walk with me once I had recovered.

As for Henry and me? Our love affair regained its passion, and mostly we were merry together during the day while at night he came almost always to my bed where we would share the intimacies of husband and wife. That is not to say, however, that we never quarrelled. Oh, truly we did so! And when embattled in disagreement, neither of us retreated. We were so like each other - stubborn, and proud! At times, we bickered over the simplest of things while, at others, our rows had as their source more weighty matters.

I had begun to sit with Henry in his Presence Chamber when he heard reports about matters of state, having taken advantage of one of his more indulgent moments to ask if I might learn by listening to the dispatches and requests made by ambassadors and other statesmen: a request to which he agreed. Thus, it was that, together, we read official letters and documents delivered by Cromwell and composed replies. All in all, Henry was gracious and lenient in allowing me to participate in a more active way than had many previous queens, including Katherine, although at times my views and my outspokenness seemed to strike a raw nerve in the King, and I would feel him bristle next to me. This was fair warning for me to contain my eagerness. Often, though, I took no heed. It would be my folly as I continued speaking, expressing my opinion, and suddenly he would turn on me and snap a sharp command for me to hold my tongue and sit silently.

I did not take well to those incidents. Oh, I never forgot that he was King - had he not made *that* eminently clear? But my nature and our familiarity provoked me to assert what I intended: what I hoped to develop as my right as Queen. I fiercely wanted to have a voice, and by God's blood, believed that I would make it happen.

As the year waned, life took on a deliciously turbulent pace. I describe it as such because I found, ever more so, that I enjoyed being fully absorbed in the day's many and varied activities. I became immersed in the requests of the realm's subjects; the decisions to be taken; plans being devised. I confess to relishing the effect of the power I had achieved. I recalled the meeting to which I had been invited at Hampton Court some years past, when – as the only woman in a room full of learned men – we convened to discuss the political and theological implications of Henry's demand for a divorce. At that time, I had had to struggle to create an opening in the debate in which I might insert my personal views. And at that time, I had quietly determined, should I marry the King and become his Queen consort - not knowing, then, that I would be crowned and anointed as a Queen in my own right - I would work toward advancing a setting within the English domain which would encourage women to speak their minds.

And so my daily routine became ever more meaningful and varied. I oversaw the goings on in Elizabeth's nursery: indeed, would visit her frequently, conferring with Lady Margaret Bryan, who had been appointed my daughter's nurse and head of her growing household.

I sat in while we were advised about the deepening discord between Henry and his nephew, James V of Scotland, over Henry's position with Rome. I also listened, but judiciously did not offer comment, while the portly and somewhat pompous Bishop of London, Edmund Bonner, briefed Henry on his meeting with Pope Clement VII.

In that context, Henry had sent Bonner to Marseilles to discourse with the Pope while simultaneously visiting King François. The intended purpose of the meeting had been to encourage Clement to convene a general council which might review the divisive situation existing between the Pope and the King of England as a result of Henry's decision to dissolve his first marriage and marry me, thus asserting his supreme authority. Henry, despite everything which had transpired, still saw the wisdom of improving relations between himself and the Pope.

In addition, he had tasked Bonner, while in Marseilles, to assess the current attitude of the ever fickle François. Henry and I had, on many occasions, discussed his mistrust of François, and were both agreed upon the criticality of maintaining a good rapport with the man even if only to glean intelligence enough to guard our backs. I daresay, though, that there were many times when Henry would have wished damnation upon such diplomacy and, instead, provide the haughty François with a solid thrashing.

In his droning voice, Bonner described at length how the Pope, instead of listening statesmanlike, had persisted in interjecting during the reading of the official document, loudly proclaiming his belief that Henry held no respect for him. The bishop then described how François, ever the splendid one, had made an entrance during the meeting, bowing and scraping before His Holiness to ensure his continuing good favour. The Pope and François then caused Bonner to wait aside, humiliated, while they chatted and laughed together for three-quarters of an hour, nigh unto six o'clock, when they finally parted with great cordiality.

Only afterwards had Clement permitted the conversation with Bishop Bonner to resume, again continuing to pepper the topic with disapproval and patronizing comments. Worse, and most insulting: after all was said and done, when Bonner returned at the Pope's request the following morning, he was informed that the effort was to be denied anyway.

How I seethed at this account! While I did not warm to Bonner in the first place – he had been a loyal aide to the late Cardinal Wolsey and, in truth, reminded me of him; overly large and self-important - neither could I stand for anyone contriving to make Henry out a fool. My loyalty, even though I had a strong affinity for France while François affected a great fondness for Henry and me, was to Henry and Henry alone. However, I continued to do my best to learn from my esteemed sovereign, who, somehow, maintained his comportment during this, and other frustrating reports. I had to admit that my response to such resentment, were I to be the sole source of governance, would be much fraught with irascibility.

•

It was an unusual day – and a delightful one. Grey, heavy December skies did nothing to dampen our spirits as my brother George, and I rode far out into the woodland beyond the palace. It was an exceptional opportunity because George, as one of Henry's most devoted and trusted diplomats - he having apparently learnt well from our father - was rarely on English soil these days, much less at the same location as I. My daily schedule had also become increasingly committed, affording me little chance to escape the confines of the palace for an entire afternoon. Thus did we both grasp that special moment of freedom to distance ourselves from inquisitive ears, anxious to talk privately and apprise each other of the goings on in our lives.

No one, except perhaps my lady mother, knew and understood me better than George. I loved him so much, even though he had always been my vexatious little brother. Although a few years younger than I - he on the cusp of reaching thirty years of age and I being thirty-two – now we were adults the difference mattered little. Mind you, there had been times during our youth when that unruly child's relentless teasing and jokes made me want to box his ears. Nevertheless, throughout the years we had spent together: growing up and running free at Hever - from being tutored by our schoolmasters and bickering amongst ourselves and Mary when we played cards and games at the manor during long winter's nights, to thrilling over our attendance at the first glittering court events when I returned from France - through all that, I had always been aware of George's devotion to me. It was plain on his face and had been so even when he pulled my hair as a child. I was his older sister, and he saw me as wonderful, smart, strong and capable.

I, for that matter, observed him with equal admiration as we rode from the stableyard and out into the fields. It was as if a slip in time had occurred. I could hardly believe I was looking at my little brother, now a man's man, tall and splendidly attired in a way that showed no effort: strictly with a casual charm, an affectation probably perfected by interacting with stylish European courtiers while abroad. Handsome; square-jawed, with a thick crop of dark brown hair and bright blue eyes he was, above all, engagingly witty. George had always had a quick tongue and a capacity for creating innuendo which was uproarious. He drew people to him and was thoughtful and courteous to all - or, that is, all of those we considered friends and allies: a quality which made him a sought-after companion in the most fashionable circles.

But what probably roused the most envy amongst certain courtiers was the fact that he had become a boon companion to Henry. They kept company whenever George was at court, talking, laughing, and invariably competing. Often when they were together, playing tennis or primero at the card table, their familiarity and jocular ribbing would seem as if they were merely conventional brothers-in-law – not King and subject. Henry appreciated George's friendship greatly, awarding him choice assignments, and paying him generously for his diplomatic work as well as those regular winnings George wrested from his sovereign while betting on their respective prowess at sport.

It afforded me great contentment, knowing we had both achieved remarkable places, representing England to the world in the year 1533.

I glanced at him as our horses negotiated a stream, picking their way between the rocks in the flowing water.

"George, did you hear of the latest demand Katherine has made of Henry?"

"You mean the one with which she has continued to perfect her already excellent skill of groaning and grumbling?" he grinned. "Demanding of the King that she be moved to more suitable quarters? Yes, I did hear about it. In fact, I've also heard tell that Brandon is laying low, keeping well out of Henry's line of vision because he fears that he will be sent to Buckden to haggle with Katherine about where she will go, and what and whom she might take with her. I'm only thankful that task won't be assigned to me."

I smirked. "Yes indeed, you'd best be enormously grateful for that, brother. She is not someone you'd want to argue with."

"*Obstinada*, no?" he laughed as our horses scrambled up the bank.

"*Obstinada*, most assuredly! And worse, she has taught her half-Spanish daughter well. So well that I know not which one drives Henry into a greater frenzy. Mary is at that horribly fractious age anyway - seventeen and totally convinced she knows all. It doesn't help that her father can also be one of the most intractable men I have ever met when he sets his mind. Their letters and messages to each other have been dreadful. She has been planted there, at Beaulieu up in Essex, mostly alone with her small household, for months. She has not seen her mother in a very long time and, as far as I know, Henry has rarely stopped by either - yet she still refuses to relinquish her stance that she is the true royal Princess, and my Elizabeth the bastard."

He afforded me a sideways glance. "Don't you feel at all sorry for her, Anne?"

I thought about that for a moment. "Strangely enough, I do in a certain way. Now I'm a mother I have a different view of the forced separation under which they live. It must be impossibly hard to be forbidden to see your child. But they are so unreasonable, George! Especially as their situation could so easily be rectified."

"Yes, one would think at this point, that Katherine would give in. It is painfully obvious to all that she will not ever re-establish her position as Queen, and most assuredly, Henry will never, ever return to her as her husband. All she need do is recognize you and Elizabeth, instruct her daughter to do the same, and I am certain the King would willingly allow them both to dwell together in a much more comfortable house, with plenty of servants to see to their needs."

I turned in the saddle to face him. "I have thought of soliciting Mary's friendship if only she will acknowledge me. Do you think I should? Will it make me look weak?"

"On the contrary, Anne, such a generous act would only demonstrate your kind nature. I hope you do so. Somehow I feel that the overture will not be received well, but you should try, anyway."

"I will think on it. Thank you, brother … and now, to change the subject, just try to guess what I am giving Henry at Christmastide."

"A bevy of scantily-clad dancing girls, perhaps?" he chortled.

"You are just as incorrigible as you always have been, Lord Rochford! But as much of a jester as you fancy yourself, you are not far from the truth."

He looked at me blankly while I explained, "I have had Master Holbein design a gorgeous table fountain. It is being smithed right now by Heyes and his apprentices. It will be very large with several tiers, made of gilt but with rails of gold, and strewn with diamonds and rubies."

"It sounds stupendous – just like our King."

"Oh, it is. But the best part? Into the bottom basin will spray scented water – from the nipples of naked nymphs!"

I giggled with glee, and George joined me with a boisterous laugh. "Henry will love that gift, with certainty! You are such a minx, my Queen. And you know how to keep your King intrigued. Bright girl."

I gave him a wink. He spied the open field spread out before us. "Anne, let's have these splendid steeds stretch their legs. We have rambled all afternoon: now let us have a real gallop."

He looked over to check if I was ready to spur my mare for a race but instead saw me shake my head definitively.

"Sorry, George, I cannot do that."

"Yes, you can."

"No, I can't."

We were immediately children again: urchin siblings squabbling, but with great love.

"YES, you can!"

"No, I can *NOT*, George!"

"Well, of course, you can. Have you become a milksop, Your Royal Highness?"

"It's impossible." I cut him short emphatically. "Because, dearest George, I am again with child!"

•

And so December unfolded as both the best of months, and also the most difficult. I truly rejoiced in my pregnancy. I had conceived so quickly after having given birth to Elizabeth, that both Henry and I felt fruitful, and young – just as he had predicted. He was elated at the news and resumed his loving behavior. He cared for me and fussed over me, ensuring my wellbeing. Our relationship had resumed its firm footing, and for this, I was very happy.

My contrasting sorrow arose from the inevitable: my baby daughter would be taken, with her governess Lady Bryan, her devoted nursemaid and cradle-rocker Mistress Parry, and the other household we had so carefully selected, miles away to Hatfield House in Hertfordshire. There she would live and grow, being cared for by a large retinue, to be quarantined far from the potential disease-causing air of London and its environs.

Certainly Hatfield was a lovely, solid and comfortable house surrounded by rolling hills and beautiful, fresh countryside. Its security was undeniable, and would be paramount. Those individuals who would be admitted to the property would first be thoroughly scrutinized. No hint of sweat or plague would be allowed to penetrate the estate. The disadvantage was that, while I intended to visit her as much as I was able, she would no longer be under *my* roof, in her cheery nursery just a short walk through the hallways. I would not be able to rush to her cradle and sweep her up in my arms, kissing her sweet little face whenever I chose. I was proud of her, and knew the establishment of her important household was right, but oh, how my heart ached!

I was only too glad I had the expected baby to think and dream about.

Christmastide was merry at Greenwich. We had much to celebrate and to give great thanks for. Henry was mightily pleased with his audacious table fountain, and in exchange, he bedecked me with jewels.

So, 1534 gave promise to a marvelous year. We were in good health, the state of the realm was stable, religious reform had taken a firm foothold, Henry was at last ruling independently of the Pope, and my proponents were at least as numerous and as powerful as my detractors. Most importantly, Henry and I were closely united as we awaited the birth of what would surely be our son.

Whitehall Palace
Early 1534

I WAS SURPRISED TO find this pregnancy entirely different from my first, even though I had been well advised by my midwives that it was often such. Whereas not much more than a year ago I had scarcely suffered from queasiness, and thought it only to be poor digestion, now in the harsh deep winter I tired easily and was constantly nauseous: so much so that the nasty puke basin accompanied me everywhere as I moved about my chambers, especially in the morning hours. In fact, I had to change my morning routine quite drastically, finding that I often vomited without much warning. So, I stayed in my rooms until at least noon, nibbling on dry bread and sipping very weak ale, the combination of which sometimes helped to settle my unruly stomach.

It was cold – very cold – this winter, and I was told that there was a thick sheet of ice covering the Thames some miles below Gravesend. Domestic goods and all communications had to be sent by land across Kent and Essex as the frozen Thames was impassable. Thankfully, my chambers were warm, the hearths and braziers being continually fed by house stewards, but I constantly worried about Elizabeth, and demanded regular updates on her wellbeing. I harped on Henry to ensure that there was firewood aplenty at Hatfield. He humoured me and offered reassurance that his tiny Princess would not be cold.

And as day followed bitter day, a further concern preyed upon my conscience. I could not stop thinking, when the ferocious wind howled about the eves at night and I was snugly tucked into my warm bed with ample soft and thick coverlets, of the poor – especially the children and the pregnant women – who had so little, and whose houses were thinly constructed of wattle and daub, with nary a hearth to provide heat. So, to alleviate my guilt over the care and comfort I received, I ordered a massive quantity of canvas and flannel then commanded all of my ladies, and also drafted women from the surrounding noble homesteads, to sew shirts, smocks, and sheets for the poor and indigent. With the flannel, we made petticoats. As items were completed, I had Henry's guards distribute them amongst the many parishes surrounding London, offering each poor family some warm clothing and two shillings apiece. It was not much, but it gave me peace to know that their suffering had been lessened, if only a little.

As the weeks wore on, I felt slightly better. Still, though, my sense of health was not nearly as robust as it had been in my third month of pregnancy with Elizabeth. So I rested as much as I could, took great care with the food I consumed, and hoped matters would improve.

Taking advantage of a short break from the cold, Henry had gone to Hatfield to visit Elizabeth. I knew he had an additional mission, however. His daughter Mary had also been moved to Hatfield House not long ago, with the intention that she would serve in her sister - my Elizabeth's - household. As expected, this news had been unwelcome, and Mary reacted rudely, initially refusing to go. Only after an ugly altercation did she sullenly pack her belongings, and allow herself to be transported to her new home. Henry hoped he would be able to smooth her discordant feelings and convince her to accept her new position, paying deference to Elizabeth, and to me.

I had wished him well on his departure suspecting, meanwhile, that I would be greatly surprised if he returned with good news.

One sunny afternoon, I sat in the short gallery which led from the King's Presence Chamber toward the privy chambers. A weak beam of light spilled through the windows, and I sat on a bench reading one of a packet of letters I had received from my good friend Honor Lisle. Honor and her husband Arthur had moved to Calais shortly after my coronation where Lord Lisle now served as Lord Deputy of that city. I missed Honor; we had been close, and I loved her because she was extremely lively, full of high spirits and humor, and could always make me laugh. She was fashionable, and we had enjoyed talking together about the new and ever changing styles coming from the capitals of Europe.

Happily, Honor was a great letter writer – I do not think she was able to *write*, herself, but she had a command of the language and was witty, so she dictated her many missives to a handful of scribes whom she trusted and used frequently. The letters were always amusing and full of interesting gossip in which she would tell me all about the wives of the prosperous French merchants who came to Calais to trade and conduct business: what they wore, what they liked to eat and drink, and who was having illicit affairs with whom.

We also shared a love of animals and birds – at least, of some of them. Indeed, I had a great affection for my horses and dogs – especially for Jolie, my hound, and Purkoy, my little spaniel. I did not mind cats, and I held a particular liking for kittens … but *monkeys*? Some people I knew actually kept them as house pets. Oh, I had such a distaste for the strange little creatures. In fact, seeing them look about with their beady eyes and grin and grimace like tiny people sent chills down my back. So I kept my great distance and left explicit instructions never, ever to gift me with a monkey. Honor, on the other hand, always had a myriad of pets in her household; all of them wandering in and out – dogs, cats, birds in cages, peacocks parading across the lawns. She even gave names to certain fish in her carp ponds! So she had sent me a gift along with this group of letters, all delivered by the Lisle's devoted gentleman steward John Husee - a little bird in a delicate cage called a linnet. It had a red breast and a greyish-blue head, and it trilled and sang constantly. How I loved it! He was such a little fellow of great cheer, and I kept him in my sitting rooms where his lively voice could be heard greeting me every morning with the sunrise.

I sat contentedly, enjoying reading the letters. From the entrance to the gallery, I heard voices but continued my reading. Only when a peculiar tone – clandestine; somehow conspiratorial – caught my attention, did I glance up. Standing just outside the doorway of the Presence Chamber, and unaware of my presence, were my Uncle Norfolk, and the repugnant Spanish ambassador, Chapuys. Their heads were bent toward each other, and their voices low but emphatic. It was clear from their posture and facial expressions that they were collaborating on something because shortly they both nodded in agreement and shook hands. Only then did they look up and see me watching them. It was uncomfortable for them both, as I gave each in turn a pointed look of contempt.

Even the mere sight of the snide Chapuys made my skin crawl. How I disliked him: particularly since I had learned that he referred to my daughter as 'The Bastard'. He might call me whatever he chose – I knew that it was often 'Concubine' – and I cared not, but since he'd dared to disparage my child, he was now, even more so, my sworn enemy. I fixed my eyes on them, unblinking, until they both averted their gaze. Norfolk bowed; Chapuys barely inclined his arrogant head then they quickly retreated into the Chamber from whence they had come, undoubtedly seeking another exit so as not to have to pass directly by me.

My growing irritation ruined the pleasantry of the hour. But I will admit, I also worried. My uncle was becoming ever more conspicuous in his antipathy towards my family and me. What were he and Chapuys planning? And when and why, for that matter, had they become co-conspirators? The bond did not bode well.

Suffolk, too, now took opportunities to make his differences with my family and me well known, but he was careful. He had long been one of Henry's closest companions, and his dislike of me threatened that friendship, and hence his standing at court. However, it was well known to me, and to Henry too, that Charles Brandon had resented me and my position from the early days of my courtship with Henry.

It seemed as if that afternoon was a sinister harbinger of turbulence to come.

Shortly after the incident in the Whitehall gallery, I was having supper with Henry and decided to tell him about it. I knew it to be a risky decision, for Henry's humour had not been good of late. He had returned from his trip to Hatfield greatly displeased by Mary's behaviour, and I knew he had no idea what his recourse with her might be. But we were enjoying good conversation, and he was eating a savoury roasted lamb, one of his favorite dishes, so I carefully described to him the scene I had encountered. When I told him that Norfolk and Chapuys had shaken hands in obvious collusion over something they wished to keep private, he stopped eating and put his knife down.

"I will tell you what I suspect was the topic of their agreement, Anne. Yesterday, Norfolk told me Chapuys wished to speak with me. When the ambassador was received in my chamber, he said that six months ago he'd heard of the new title assigned to Katherine. Of course, he insists upon continuing to call her 'the Queen'. He had also been told about the change in title for Mary, from Princess to Lady."

As usual, when we discussed a subject of great distaste, I aimed to arrange my expression so I did not appear as a hysterical woman ready to give vent at any moment. But it was not easy.

Henry continued. "Chapuys had asked Norfolk and Cromwell to tell me that such conduct was not lawful, thinking that the message would be better received from them, instead of himself."

He snorted and looked as if he smelled a bad odour. "He then asked for leave to make such a representation to Parliament. I made him squirm by staring at him long and hard, but saying nothing. Then I told him, in the tone of exaggerated patience I typically use with Master Chapuys, that he was in truth well aware I am married to my lawful wife, so perhaps I misunderstood his intent? Perhaps there was some strange confusion, because since I am lawfully married, and my first marriage has been pronounced unlawful, then by rights my first wife can in no way be called 'Queen' nor hold property given to her in consequence of the marriage. Furthermore, nor could the person he called 'Princess' be legitimate, nor able to succeed. And …"

He was beginning to turn red by then, recalling the disgraceful scene caused by the ignorant ambassador. "… and that even if Mary *were* legitimate, her disobedience alone is sufficient to merit disinheritance while, as for his request to go before Parliament, Anne …? It is not the custom: the damn fellow has no such power, and I was appalled by his demand."

"Henry! The man's impertinence! How dare he cross you thus! Can you not have him deported? How long must we bear his snake-like character and his poisonous treachery?" I was ready to summon Chapuys myself and threaten him with the worst form of torture I could conjure.

My hands shook as Henry continued. It *was* Chapuys, after all – persistent to the point of obnoxious ignorance – so, of course, the encounter had not ended there.

"He stood before me, not budging – not cowed in any way, and even quoted from our own English history saying that, concerning the sentence of divorce given by the Archbishop of Canterbury, it should be as little regarded as the sentence which King Richard caused the Bishop of Bath to give the sons of

King Edward, declaring *them* bastards! He added that there was no doubt Parliament would do as I wished, as I had married again and had forbidden Katherine to be called Queen, and she was not summoned to Parliament, nor had any person to speak for her. And then, Anne, although he did hesitate for a few moments, he doggedly went on: persevering in his overbearing way that all the Parliaments could not make his Princess a bastard, and even if my marriage with Katherine were annulled, still the Princess Mary would remain legitimate, owing to the lawful ignorance of her parents."

By this time, Henry saw that I was deeply upset. I had paled, and my hand laid upon the table was clenched.

"Mine own sweetheart! Are you ill? I am sorry, and never intended to dismay you so!" He covered my hand with his big, warm one, and his touch brought me reassurance. I drew a deep breath. How I hated Chapuys!

"Anne, let me tell you how I ended the meeting. I informed him that, according to the laws of the kingdom, his so-called Princess was unable to succeed, and there was no other Princess except my daughter Elizabeth until I have a son which I firmly believe will happen soon. I looked him in the eye and told him that his arguments I found trite and meaningless, and that, day by day, my respect for him diminished more, while if he believed he intimidated me with his connection to the Emperor, he was surely mistaken. And with that cutting remark, I brusquely dismissed him."

He leaned across and brushed my cheek with his lips, to convince me that all was well and that he had matters to hand. I did feel better, for a short while.

But as winter gave way to March, disorder became the rule.

Greenwich
Whitehall
Spring 1534

DESPITE THE AMPLE presence of stewards milling about ready to do my bidding, I reached across the table to pour more wine for Archbishop Cranmer, with whom I was dining after Mass.

"Please, Madame. There is no need for such effort on your part." He made a motion for me to cease and summoned a servant.

"Thomas, it is nothing. And why should I not provide for the needs of my dear friends when they are my guests? Anyway, there is much that I require from you today, regarding news and advice. Tell me what you know of the Pope's ruling on Henry's nullity suit."

I leaned forward, anticipating his account. I knew that Henry had been informed of the most recent developments, but had provided me no detail. I imagine he wished not to grieve me, in my condition. But I had to know!

"Milady, I am told that the Vatican consistory, a council of twenty-two cardinals, was convened in late February, continued to meet into this month of March, and last week, on the twenty-third, its finding was pronounced that the marriage between His Grace King Henry and Katherine was valid and their issue thereof legitimate. The King has also been enjoined to take back Katherine as his wife."

Cranmer did not miss the dark look his news produced. His voice assumed the tone he used when conveying trouble: soft but firm – factual. "The council still requires the signature of the Pope, but that is only a formality. The matter is done, as far as the Curia is concerned."

I drew a deep breath. "And what did Monsieur du Bellay do when he heard this report? Did he press on in representing our case, as he knew his duty required him?"

Jean du Bellay, the former French ambassador to Henry's court, and an ally as far as I was concerned was now Bishop of Paris and had been designated to be an advocate in Rome for François, and for Henry as well.

Cranmer was quick to rejoin. "With certainty, Your Highness. Bishop du Bellay relayed that he planned to discuss the matter yet again with his Holiness before his departure, which I believe he did, although I have since been informed that His Grace has now left Rome for Paris: his royal master, François, not wishing him to stay longer. It was felt that the finality of the matter must be accepted, and the news delivered to our king in total. The report is that the Bishop was well aware of how terribly discontented His Majesty would be with him, especially because of the assurances contained in his last letters. He told François to inform His Majesty at once, before he might hear of it from Charles and the Imperialist diplomats who, naturally, are triumphant that at last, the Emperor Charles's aunt Katherine has been vindicated."

He lowered his voice then, to ensure confidence.

"I am told by very reliable sources that the French are much grieved they cannot send better news. They feel – as of course they would – that events will show how François endeavored mightily to prevent one of the greatest troubles desecrating the Church and perhaps all of Christendom. They feel they have omitted nothing in attempting to attain Henry's desired outcome."

I sat back in my chair and let out a heavy sigh. I cannot say I would have readily agreed with the French envoy's perspective. "And Katherine knows of the determination, I assume?"

"I have no doubt, Madame. She has her messengers."

"Oh, how *marvellous* for her," I snapped sarcastically. "I can picture the scene now … her tawdry, dismal gowns already packed; trunks ready and waiting by the gate; worn-to-the-bone Spanish prayer books assembled - all to be transported in triumph from gloomy Buckden back to her rightful place here in Henry's beautiful court."

I uttered a loud and resentful laugh at that point, whereupon the waiting stewards looked up suddenly, taking notice of the sharp change of tone in our previously discreet dialogue. "Such an immediate move will, *of course*, be in response to the King's command when he denounces me, and recalls her as his wife and Queen, obediently following the instructions of the Pope and the Curia!"

Cranmer's wiry eyebrows lifted, startled by my venom. "You do not fear that as a consequence, do you, Madame?"

"No, of course not! But, although the ruling comes as no surprise, it seems an ignominious end to seven long years of battle. And how I despise that Katharine and Mary will feel exonerated in any way. This will do plenty to inflame the already shameful behavior Mary exhibits for her father, *and* to me, for that matter! I have extended the hand of friendship to her twice now. Both times it has been rebuffed with absolute contempt." I shook my head in disgust. "I tell you, my next tactic is just to go head-to-head with her in a full-blown rivalry. We will then see who wins: her death or mine."

My esteemed and wise friend paused. Then, gently, he placed his hand on my arm. "I advise you, my dear Queen, to avoid such statements of renunciation. They are not representative of your fine character. And, truly - you do not know what the future holds for you and Mary. She is, after all, a young and impassioned girl. In time, she will mature and become softer as we all do."

One grey brow arched quizzically nevertheless. I suspected he was wondering just how much softer *my* attitude had become as I aged.

"Thank you, Thomas. How fortunate Henry and I are to have you as a friend, advisor, and our Archbishop. You are right, as you always have been. I will follow your good counsel and strive to be more prudent in my thoughts, words, and actions."

He offered me a benevolent smile, which I returned, most graciously.

While, privately, I still clung to my lingering resentment.

•

My ladies and I sat courtside, cheering on Henry, William Brereton, Henry Courtenay, Brandon, my brother George, of course, and a few others who were involved in a rousing tournament of tennis at the new, very beautiful courts which Henry had constructed in the yard at Whitehall just a year prior.

We were enjoying ourselves, being served food and wine by ushers who ran to and fro from special kitchens which serviced that sporting facility. Nan Zouche, Bessie Holland, Maggie Wyatt Lee, Mary Scrope and I spent the afternoon watching, cheering, and gossiping while I blithely showed off the new gown designed for me by Mistress Clerk, which showed my pregnancy to its greatest advantage.

The lightheartedness of the day was a welcome respite from the burdensome thoughts I had been carrying with me: the disappointing ruling from Rome, followed closely by my anxiety while Parliament was in session to evaluate Henry's prospective *Succession to the Crown Act*. That proposed Act would declare Elizabeth as being the true successor to the Crown of England unless Henry and I had sons, who would, only then, supersede her right to the throne. Its text designated Katherine as Princess Dowager, and by the complete absence of any mention, it bypassed Mary as a successor under any circumstance.

Although I had been guaranteed by both Henry and Cromwell that the Act would be passed, I was not at all certain and prepared myself for confrontation. The Act embodied, within its content, a requirement that all subjects take an oath of loyalty. And should any amongst them refuse? Well, they would then be guilty of treason. It would place a formidable burden on my adversaries.

As I had been promised, on the last day of March the closing assembly of Parliament pronounced its endorsement of the Act. Allegiance to me, and to my daughter or any other issue I may bear with my husband, the King, was now law – with a dreadful punishment awaiting those who objected. At this news, I felt a great relief. But not without a certain tinge of misgiving.

As we nibbled on gingerbread and spiced wine and selected almonds from a large bowl, we giggled and gossiped in low whispers, leaning in to be heard. Mary Scrope, whose husband was William Kingston, Constable of the Tower, told us, with eyes widened, that her husband had reported exceedingly grotesque behavior by the imprisoned Elizabeth Barton, the so-called Nun of Kent. I was particularly interested in this news because Barton – a demented religious zealot – had been a tribulation to Henry and me for many months. Born to an impoverished family in Kent she, as had been reported, began having fits and spasms as a young girl. It was after one of these episodes that she started uttering prophecies. It was not surprising that the poor and gullible townsfolk followed her, listening to accounts of her visions with a swelling number believing she had been imbued with some mystical power. More and more frequently her look took on a deranged aura while her outrageous prognostications became increasingly focused on fanatical Catholicism. Soon Barton took up the subject of Henry's divorce from Katherine, and to the crowds who surrounded her, ranted and raved about it.

It had been on Henry's and my return to London from our trip to Calais two years prior that she had waylaid us and confronted Henry directly. As I'd looked on, she had made her declarations: eyes wild and rolling in her head, crinkled hair escaping her cap and whipping about her face, spittle flying from her mouth as she spoke in varying inflections – some loud and growling, others high and melodic, and still others with her mouth seemingly closed – a sight which made my skin crawl. She had craned her neck then stretched as far as she could towards Henry, spitting that, should he proceed to marry me, he would surely die a painful villain's death within the month.

Horrified at her effrontery, I had wanted to look away from the spectacle of her, but could not … but then the situation became farcical when she told Henry that she knew he had been prevented from receiving communion while in Calais due to his great sin, whereupon *she* - who had been present, but of course invisible - had received his host instead, directly from the Virgin Mary!

At this revelation, I exploded in unbridled laughter, the result being that the crazy crone whirled her head to glare at *me* next, while directing a look so terrifying that I could not help but reimagine it for days. Not for a moment, though, did I believe she was anything but a brazen charlatan and, indeed, seemed to have been proved correct for in that autumn she had been arrested, along with a whole group of deceitful men who had the gall to call themselves monks, on suspicion that they had jointly and severally colluded to bring about the downfall of His Majesty the King. Archbishop Cranmer had been called in to question her. Consistent with my expectation, he'd found that she, in collusion with the monk Edward Bockyng, had constructed lies and materials to feign her holy powers while, coincidentally, making a great deal of money by doing so.

Mary Scrope told us that in the two weeks since Barton, Bockyng, and several other accomplices had been attainted of high treason, they had behaved in a manner barely short of barbaric during their imprisonment: all the while Barton still attempting to assume the appearance and demeanor of an ascetic visionary.

In response she, along with her cohorts, had been thrown into the deepest dungeons of the Tower, where they wailed and howled all the night and day. Mary said her husband had told her that none of the guards would agree to go near them, so frightful were their screams and writhings. Indeed, Constable Kingston was forced to induce guards with extra payments just to approach the miscreants' cells to throw in scraps of food and push pails of water through the hatch doors. Now, all that was left for the Holy Maid of Kent was to await her execution, which was imminent.

While I listened, I shivered and pulled my silken wrap more closely around my shoulders. The suppression of those who would defame Henry and me, my daughter, and my marriage was both necessary and warranted, but hearing such bald description of its reality somehow turned my stomach. My heart pounded strangely, leaving me feeling weak and light-headed.

My ladies saw that I gripped the bench while my complexion must have turned pale because Maggie and Nan quickly gave me a sip of ale, then got me to my feet and helped me back to my chambers, where I took to my bed until the next day.

•

By the end of March, and just before Parliament was prorogued until the following autumn, all of its members were sworn to the succession as described in the Act. Commissioners were dispatched far and wide across the realm to take the oath of the men and women of England. Mostly, their efforts produced great consent.

But there were detractors. Notable amongst them? Katharine, of course – who fought belligerently against any urging to sign such a document.

The others were John Fisher, Bishop of Rochester and, most distressingly, Henry's former advisor, councillor, Lord High Chancellor and dear friend, Thomas More.

But there could be no tolerance of weakness. As the only recourse to their persistent defiance, both were arrested and locked in the Tower.

Fisher was not a man well known to me. He had never been an ally, having always championed Katherine and her cause, so his imprisonment caused me little concern.

But More? His arrest hit me hard. Sir Thomas had always seemed an enigma to me – exceedingly soft-spoken and gentle, with a dignified bearing and warm manner who had invariably conducted himself with cordial deference in my company. And to Henry he had long been a confidante and true friend, advising and caring for him with a genuine affection that was indisputable. But having said that, for such a learned man his viewpoints often seemed unwisely resolute, and in certain matters he was as indomitable as were many of the antiquated monks who shuffled about the monasteries buried deep in the countryside. As the Great Matter had progressed on its turbulent path to the final outcome, More had taken pains to be certain Henry knew he held no actual opposition to our marriage but, as Henry drew further and further apart from the Roman Church and the Pope's jurisdiction, Sir Thomas had nevertheless become increasingly distressed. Finally, at the critical moment – when Henry looked to Thomas to sign the Oath of Supremacy - that great religious lawyer and statesman could not, and would not, do so. Henry tried ardently to convince his friend, knowing what consequences would be required if he continued to refuse. I saw plainly how the disagreement weighed on him; not only was it a singular indictment of Henry's position of supreme authority, but a betrayal by a mentor he had well and truly loved. While he told me of their fruitless discussions, eyes downcast, he appeared heavy and forlorn, and when he departed the chamber, the slope of his shoulders caused me great sorrow.

There was something indefinable about More's imprisonment which seemed symbolic, as nothing else had to date. It caused me to reflect, quite unpleasantly, on the conditional nature of that which I had so naively believed to be certain.

To cheer myself, just before Easter I planned a visit to Hatfield, longing to see and play with, and kiss my little lambkin, Elizabeth. I had several trunks packed because I planned to stay for several days, at least. Sheets of rain battered us as we lumbered across the winter-rutted roads, but nothing could contain my excitement at seeing my baby girl. Since Elizabeth and her retinue had assumed residence in December, I had received regular reports from Lady Bryan, and always promptly replied, usually sending packages with velvets for Elizabeth's gowns, along with soft flannels and fustian for her bedclothes and blankets. Lady Bryan assured me, in the interim, that Elizabeth was as bright and intelligent a baby as ever she had known. I could not wait to see her.

Once settled into my chambers, bathed and dressed in dry clothing, I hurried to the nursery. At its threshold, I stopped to admire the snug, comfortable setting in which Elizabeth spent most of her time. The tapestries lining the walls were brilliant with colourful forest animals and birds: the great bay window allowing a flood of bright sunlight through its leaded panes. At both ends of the large and spacious room hearths burned cheerily, keeping the room delightfully warm. I gazed about me for just a moment before, suddenly, a little head, clad in a linen bonnet revealing a shock of vivid ginger hair, popped up above the edge of the deep wooden cradle, brilliant blue eyes, wide open, staring at me.

I rushed to sweep her into my arms and cover her with kisses. She tilted her head back to study me carefully, then buried her face in my neck. And, as happened every time I was with her, my heart swelled near to bursting with love. She *knew* me! Even though I had not seen her for what seemed too many weeks, she knew I was her mother, and nuzzled me as I hugged her.

Lady Bryan joined me, and we spent the rest of the afternoon playing with my little Princess. I delighted in watching her bounce on sturdy little legs when we held her upright, vigorously rock to and fro on her hands and knees, and even attempt some crawling steps. I exclaimed in satisfaction when we peeped into her mouth to see several teeth emerging from healthy pink gums. While Elizabeth sat happily on a rug waving a wooden rattle and mostly pushing it into her mouth to gnaw on it, Margaret told me of the happenings in the household. I inquired after Mary, who had been living at Hatfield now for several months.

Margaret looked uncomfortable. "Your Highness, I rarely see her."

I stretched to wipe a bit of drool from Elizabeth's chin. "What mean you, Margaret? How is it you never encounter her – in the halls, at meals, walking in the courtyard?"

"Well, Madame, I am told by her serving staff that she remains in her chambers. She is served her morning meal, and then reads and prays in her apartment. When it comes time for dinner, she usually claims she has a headache and takes to her bed for most of the afternoon. I have no idea if she sups with anyone for I am busy caring for Elizabeth at that time, preparing her for bed."

I was confused. "But does she not come to the nursery to visit her sister? Has she ever taken her for a walk in the gardens on dry days?"

"Never, Madame. She has been in this room but once, and that for a mere blink of an eye." Lady Bryan appeared flustered at bearing such unseemly news."Even then she did not look upon the baby – not at all."

I pursed my lips as I put Elizabeth's toys in order on her play rug.

"Well, *that* will surely change. With immediacy!"

Late the following morning I sat in my small receiving chamber, awaiting the arrival of Mary. I had issued an order for her to see me. The page returned to report that the Lady Mary was not feeling well, and thus could not keep the appointment. I sent the young man immediately back to her, with an irrefutable command that, unless she appeared in my chamber at the appointed time, her father the King would be informed, and he would be highly displeased.

So I sat, drumming my fingers on the arm of my chair, and waited. A full quarter hour after the designated time, a crier arrived at the doorway and announced, "The Lady Mary, Your Highness."

Dragging her slippered feet, eyes to the ground, Mary entered the chamber. She cast me a surly glance, and her hands moved to the sides of her skirts. At the same time, her head gave the smallest bob while her knees barely eased. Her curtsy was as disrespectful as one could manage without neglecting it altogether. I ignored it.

"Good morning Mary," I called in a voice studied in its civility. "How fare you this day?"

"Not well, Madame." Her reply so muted I could barely hear her, even though she stood just a few paces away.

"Speak up, Mary, I can scarce hear you! How has your time been here at Hatfield? Do you find it an improvement over the large and drafty Beaulieu? Are you happy here?"

She remained obstinately silent. It grew awkward, yet I waited, determined that she answer me with some propriety.

Finally …

"Now that you ask, Madame, I will tell you. I am *most* unhappy. I feel unwell almost all the time. And …"

"And …?" I encouraged.

"… and I never stop thinking about my lady mother: the true Queen of England, a Princess of Spain; a woman with the noblest lineage, who is forced to languish – ill and without the comfort of me, her daughter, nor any of her beloved friends and servants - in a dank and inadequate dwelling, as if she had committed a most heinous crime. My *mother*! The woman all of England adores and demands to see resume her rightful place upon the throne! So NO, Madame - I am not at *all* well!"

By the time she had finished her speech, she had drawn herself erect, squared her shoulders, and was glaring at me with blazing eyes. Eyes filled with hatred.

Coolly I met her stare. Just as I had once, years ago, with her mother when I was first the object of Henry's love, and at a royal banquet Katherine had surveyed me accusingly – then, lifting my chin, I looked directly into Mary's eyes. Not for a second would I have this truculent young woman feel entitled to speak to me in such a disrespectful way.

Deliberately I kept my voice quiet and composed.

"Mary, if I were you I would hold my tongue and never again utter such treacherous words about your mother being the true Queen. We both know very well that the most learned men in the world - foremost among them your noble father the King - have found that statement to be false."

I drew a deep breath, then.

"However, I still wish to offer you a sign of peace. If you will acknowledge me as your Queen, and if you will honour your sister Elizabeth as the true Princess – and *especially* if you will visit her, cherish her, and treat her as a sister is meant to ... well, then I am prepared to love you as a daughter in return, and to entreat your father to bring you to court with all of the comforts and deference you would be owed as the King's child, even though your status is, as we know, illegitimate. You must surely see how generously he has benefitted his son Richmond, and I feel confident that your endowments will be of no less value."

I paused, giving her a chance to consider that which I had proposed, assuming in the meantime, an air of benevolence.

She did not rush to respond. No, she made me wait. While doing so, I could not stop thinking of how the child needed a sharp slap to address her insolent disobedience. It mattered not whether she favoured me: noble and well-brought-up children were taught never to display rudeness to their elders. It confirmed for me that her mother had done a poor job of raising the girl. Still, I kept smiling, albeit somewhat fixedly, until she finally did deign to speak.

"Madame, it is most unfortunate, but I cannot even bring myself to thank you for your proposition. In truth, I find it insulting! I will never – and I repeat, *never*! - acquiesce to your ridiculous assumption that you are Queen and that your child Elizabeth is the true Princess."

By now, her voice, created by the most ill of feelings, had reached a high pitch while tears made her eyes unnaturally bright. Lip trembling, she then added, "And threaten all you wish, Madame - I care *not* where my father puts me … he can throw me in the Tower if he so chooses. I will NOT change my position!"

She spun about without a backward look and fled from the room.

I did not see Mary – nor did I attempt to– during the remainder of my stay at Hatfield, spending as much time as I could with Elizabeth instead, reading to her, singing lullabies, and watching her inquisitive mind take in all that surrounded her. I knew without any doubt that she was an exceptional child, and my pride knew no bounds.

As I left to return to Whitehall, my heart heavy at leaving Elizabeth behind, I determined to put Mary from my mind. And that I did.

I was not to see her again for many, many months.

Whitehall
Hampton Court
Summer 1534

AFTER THE MELANCHOLY I had experienced in early spring, the blossoming of a beautiful summer came as a welcome distraction. The weather grew temperate while ample rain had prompted the roses, lilacs, and heather to flourish and release their perfume in the soft, warm air.

Henry and I enjoyed each other's company, entertained by talented musicians from across England and Europe who made a destination of the King's court as they travelled from location to location. We held suppers for our friends and made merry playing cards, gambling for gold sovereigns. On evenings when Henry was otherwise occupied, I held *soirées* in my chambers and my ladies, and the gentlemen serving Henry danced, flirted, and carried on in great high spirits while I observed from the comfort of a well-padded chair, hands cradling my swelled stomach. It was not unpleasing to note that every male courtier present strove for the opportunity to sit near me and pay me beautiful compliments, flattering my comeliness and engaging in the witticisms of courtly chivalry.

Eventually, the court moved from Westminster to Hampton Court for the duration of the summer. I was pleased to leave the city behind and to travel upriver with my retinue and become settled at Hampton Court, where I intended to stay for the duration of my confinement. My baby would be born in the pleasant and healthy surroundings there.

By early June, my household was fully established. I did love the palace, as everyone who visited seemed to, for, in addition to its very comfortable lodgings, the gardens were such a wondrous sight: harmonious bands of colour waving in the breeze while flowers of every kind bloomed continuously from early spring through to autumn. The walk from the house down to the river had been pleasingly designed to dazzle the eye and soothe the soul. Henry had commissioned the most talented gardeners in England to create new parterres extending both left and right of the central walkway which featured splashing fountains, neat and angular arrangements of flowers and plants, and, best of all to me, some areas – my favourites - offering a wild, natural look. Along those shaded terraces grew billowing grasses; deep green, cooling ferns; carpets of orange balsam with their cup-like flowers and lovely fragrance; beds of evening primrose, and iris of every variety. Tucked into hidden corners were carved stone benches, cleverly placed next to deep formal pools in which multi-hued carp lazed, graceful fan-tails swirling behind them like the trains of ladies' gowns.

If Paradise existed, then Hampton Court was surely it.

One afternoon my mother and I sat on a bench shaded by an ornamental tree, enjoying the garden's beauty. She had left her summer residence at Hever to pay a final visit before I went into confinement. As always, I treasured her company. In the morning, we had been presented the new celebratory medal which had been struck in honour of the upcoming birth of what Henry and I hoped – and fervently believed – would be our son.

"Anne, I can't help but find it so amusing to see that medal – such an official looking thing! – with your portrait on it, and your motto. I look at it, and all I can think of is the day – oh, how long ago it seems – when you were a maiden walking with your mother in the autumn garden at Hever, and we talked about how a marriage for love would make you happy. Truly, at that moment never could I have envisioned the life you now have. You are a mother, yourself; soon with two babies. And you've come to know how very much you wish for your children to be happy and their lives healthy and tranquil."

"I do, Mother. I think about Elizabeth every day and ponder on the life she will lead. I know that there is no conquest or accomplishment I wish for her more than her simple happiness and contentment." I wrinkled my nose somewhat wryly. "Mind you, I'm equally certain that Henry would not concur with that sentiment - instead, he will want her to make her mark upon the world in a resplendent, significant way … whereas I wish only for her, and for my unborn babe, to live halcyon lives filled with love and joy."

I smiled then. "The peacefulness I feel, sitting here with you in this wonderful glade, surely does not reflect my life's daily measure. Nor will it distinguish Elizabeth's, I fear. But after all, she is her father's child – and her mother's. Undoubtedly she will revel in any challenge which confronts her. And *my* son …?" I caressed my extended belly as if it were the baby himself. "… well, he will be just like his father: courageous, exuberant, a lover of life and all that it brings. He will be well able to adapt, and he will thrive, this I know."

My lady mother gave me a loving look while reaching to tuck a tendril of my hair, which had escaped, back under its hood, then we rose together to stroll back to the palace for dinner.

Henry arrived at Hampton Court with his attendants by the middle of the month. Never one to remain in place for long, especially during the summer, he'd travelled with a reduced household which included his closest Privy Council members:

Sir Edward Rogers - one of Henry's chief Esquires of the Body, and Sir William Paulet, his Comptroller. This small group finalized the route to be followed on summer progress, due to commence in July. In the latter part of the previous year, there had been talk of Henry and I visiting Calais this July, instead of our usual summer progress. It was thought that we should stay in Calais as we had done in 1532 just before we were married, and then travel on to Paris to see King François and Queen Eleanor. Not only would a visit strengthen the sometimes volatile bond shared by the two kings, but Henry and I would have an opportunity to discuss the possible marital union of our daughter, the Princess Elizabeth, with the son of François and his former wife, Queen Claude: Charles, Duke of Orléans. When Henry had first informed me of this possibility, I was thrilled with the anticipation of a new adventure. Not only did I have a taste for travel to locations outside of England's borders, but I would again visit the site of my youth and people whom I had once loved but had not seen in many years: chief amongst them being Marguerite.

But Fate intervened. A most benign and joyous Fate on this occasion. Shortly after the idea had taken form, I discovered I was pregnant. Of course, Henry was elated, and only too happy to postpone the trip until after I safely delivered so, in our place, George was tasked to go. He was to travel to the French king with all speed, first stopping at Paris to offer our hearty recommendations to the Queen of Navarre, if she was there. He was to say that Queen Anne, his mistress, rejoices greatly in the deeply-rooted amity of the two kings, and he was to offer gifts as tokens of our goodwill.

Most importantly, though, he would express our wish to have the much-desired meeting deferred. George would explain, in his perfect French, that though the King is very anxious to see his good brother François, it is impossible at present because his beloved Queen is so far gone with child that she cannot cross the sea, and the King would be loath to deprive her of his Highness's presence when it was most necessary, at the birth. George would, instead, seek deferment of the meeting until the following April, and press the matter most earnestly in all hope that the meeting of diplomacy between the two kings and queens, and François' eminent sister the Queen of Navarre might take place then, in France.

I had every confidence that George would succeed in his mission, his charm, and diplomatic skills being, at this stage, unsurpassed. I waited assuredly for his return and a full report of the goings on at the French court. In the meantime, I continued to hear and resolve petitions put before me, provide approvals for my financial affairs with Master George Taylor, my Receiver-General, and pursue my patronage of selected individuals who advanced the cause of religious reform, or who excelled in the arts.

On a balmy evening in early July, I had walked the privy gardens with Henry after supper. We'd talked about his intention to stay near to hand, but visit some of the local villages in the coming weeks before my confinement. In any case, he would be easily reachable, and I had no cause to worry. He was very protective of me: even as we walked, he kept his arm about my shoulders, a gesture which felt safe and gave me great comfort. At the staircase which led to the King's and Queen's apartments, he kissed me and wished me a good night. Contented, I climbed to meet Lucy, my chambermaid, at the entrance to my privy chamber. With the familiar ease that came from our years together, she led me to the closet to prepare me for bed.

Tucked in, I read for a short while until Lucy came to snuff the candles then settled back among the pillows and drifted easily to sleep.

… And then … in the pitch-black of the night I awoke with a start, my forehead covered with a clammy sweat, heart pounding in terror …*why*?

I scrambled to sort my thoughts; to understand what had awakened me. As realization dawned, I felt sick, as if I were to vomit from fear.

It was the babe! It was not moving in my womb. How long had it been since I last knew it to be active? Desperately I tried to recall the last time - the last moment – I had felt a kick, a turn, *anything*. I strove to remember. Nothing throughout the entire day before … meeting with my councillors … dining with Henry…walking in the garden - nor even during the night, for that matter, when it had become commonplace to feel the baby shifting its position. No movement at all. Oh, how could I *not* have been concerned …?

I could scarcely breathe in my rising panic. I had naively assumed the baby was simply at rest, but now I could not escape the dreadful truth.

I called shrilly, panic-stricken, for Lucy to fetch the midwife, Nan Cobham, who was staying in a chamber close by until the birth. While Lucy, in her robe and carrying a lantern aloft, flew to summon Nan, Emma quickly lit candles and the hearth then came to my bedside to hold my hand, dabbing gently at my brow with a cooling cloth. She looked so frightened, but I could not even speak to tell her what was wrong. For her part, she just patted me a little too helplessly while repeating over and over, "It will be alright, Madame, just breathe. All will be well."

By the time Nan arrived, hastily dressed and bearing a look of alarm, the pains had started. They spread upward from my lower back, agonizing enough to make me gasp with their severity. I began to cry. There was no possible way my baby, coming now – too soon – could survive. I prayed, and both Lucy and Emma prayed aloud with me as they hurriedly collected more cloths, heated water, and placed pillows at my back.

I was frantic for God to hear me and my entreaty! If only He might still work a miracle. Between gasps, as my body heaved I implored Him to allow this one, oh so special infant, to live. Nan bent over me and valiantly did her best – it was much too late to summon other women to help. Through what seemed like a thick fog I heard her call to me to push, and she pressed on my belly, aiding the child to emerge quickly in the hope it might be saved.

I pushed.

And prayed.

At the end, though, I heard a quiet sob. It may have been Lucy's, or Emma's.

Nan remained at my feet holding the tiny baby who had just been born.

No sound came from the child. No cry. No intake of breath.

She had died.

•

Maggie sat next to me on that same stone bench I had shared with my mother several weeks prior. Sunlight dappled the grass which carpeted the small corner garden, and I could hear the soft splashing of the fountain which fed the pool, while vaguely aware of the heavy scent of lavender emanating from a nearby, sun-kissed bed. Idly I wondered if I would ever again enjoy the smell of lavender – it had once been my favourite, but now it just seemed cloying: a further intrusion into my grief.

Maggie, one of the few people in the world whose presence I could tolerate during that ghastly time, sought my hand and laid hers atop it. Briefly, I glanced up at her with what I knew must be red-rimmed eyes, full of sorrow. I had never imagined – not in any way –that a human being could endure such personal anguish. At times, my thoughts were so painful that I wished for eternal sleep to relieve me of them.

"Anne, I hesitate to speak," Maggie ventured "I have many things to say, but I know – how well I know – that you will not wish to hear them. Your reaction mirrors precisely how I, myself, felt when my first baby died just a single day after his birth … no one could comfort me; like you I was inconsolable. But my love for you, dearest Anne, compels me to be candid."

She put her hand under my chin and lifted my face, so I met her gaze. "And you must listen. Anne - you *must*! Because you are not like other women – simple country women, who, when they birth a dead child, can be left to grieve until they feel ready to re-enter life. You are Queen. And cruel as it may seem, you have no choice but to resume your duty."

I looked at Maggie silently, biting on my trembling lower lip to steady it as she pressed on.

"Anne, you still have a daughter who needs you. She is a wonderful, glorious child, and you cannot leave her entire upbringing to others. She must have her mother. And … there is Henry. I know – I have been told by some closest to him – that he, too, is grieving painfully. You cannot turn your back on him, Anne, although you may not feel he can soothe your heartache in the way you would wish. You *must* cling together! And you know this to be true: you must have him return to your bed as soon as you are able. You are his wife. You can still conceive and give birth to a healthy child."

I felt my tears well yet again.

"You cannot have him turn to another woman, Anne," Maggie pressed gently. "you must be there for him. You must give comfort to each other."

She waited while I composed myself. Bless my Maggie. Who else would be able - would *dare* - to say these things to me, at this, the lowest point I had ever experienced? I don't believe even my lady mother could have risked guiding me so frankly. And anyway, she was enduring her great despair at the loss of her grandchild; especially one who had held such promise.

I nodded slowly. "Thank you, sweet friend. My ears have heard your words, and I pray that my soul will respond." My doleful eyes sought hers while I clung to her hand. "Maggie, truly – what would I do without you? You are with me in the good times, and the bad. There is no way in which I can ever express to you the depth of my gratitude."

She smiled a kindly smile. "Ours is a unique friendship, Anne. From running wild as children in the open fields of Kent to dancing in the gleaming palaces of London. It's uncanny, is it not? But we have forged a partnership, and if it is up to me, it will remain as such until the day we die."

I hugged her long and tight and kissed her cheek. And in doing that, I felt a glimmer of hope – the first since that awful night of my baby's death.

Hampton Court
Greenwich
Autumn 1534

I REMEMBER ALMOST NOTHING about that autumn. As the trees turned from green to red, then to tawny and umber, I observed them with eyes which may as well have been those of a blind woman. I wandered the palace and its grounds not seeing, not hearing, often unaware of the courtiers who passed me and bowed or curtseyed a greeting. Maggie's advice swirled round and round in my mind, but I seemed stuck – unable to act – even though I wished to. I had never experienced such deep grief, and I was surprised by its all-encompassing nature and its vicious ability to siphon every bit of vitality from a person.

I now know that grief shows itself variously in different individuals. Henry, upon being quietly informed of the tragedy, shut himself in his most private chambers. He emerged to visit me once, and his face had so aged I was appalled. He did not look me in the eye but sat silently at my bedside for many long minutes. Only finally did he speak, whereupon he told me nothing would be said about the incident. No one, not even those closest to him, was to refer to it. We agreed that the child would be named Margaret, and we would have Cranmer arrange her interment with the utmost discretion. Following the conclusion of that sad necessity, Henry would carry on with his progress as planned, thus he would be away for some time. I did not reply. Before he stood to leave, he clutched my hand, squeezing it so hard that it pained me. But still he did not face me, could not bring himself to look into my soul … and then he was gone.

Perhaps it was better, after all.

I found that my fragility caused me to be filled with rancor. In that period, I feel certain that most everyone dreaded my company, even those closest to me.

In late September, I received my sister, Mary. She arrived at court, smiling and obviously happy, with a man whom she announced as being her new husband. One could feel her delight and pride as she stood next to her tall companion, William Stafford, a soldier in Henry's army, and a farmer of his family's modest property in Essex. Without the slightest trace of diffidence Mary glibly told me they had met while both were in Calais some two years prior, accompanying Henry and me on our trip. They had fallen in love, and Mary had taken upon herself - without even *consulting* me! - to marry the fellow: a match well beneath her station.

I was furious. I found that my pain quickly converted to ire – and the demonstration of that anger felt good; it gave me relief. So I let loose a torrent on Mary and the hapless Stafford. I told her, in a voice so cold that it even startled me, to leave court and not to return.

"*Ever*?" she said, her dismay reflecting surprise and hurt.

"Not *ever*, Mary! I will summon you if I require you. But I see no possibility of that anytime soon. So - GO!"

She turned from me with a woebegone look and slowly left the presence chamber. Once she glanced back, but receiving no encouragement, continued, her husband holding her arm to steady her.

As I watched her go, I felt as if I would choke with resentment.

She was pregnant.

•

In that same month, Pope Clement VII died. For him, I felt nothing. He had been our adversary for so long, and an incendiary in the heated arguments between conventional advocates of Catholicism and the new thinkers who fought for change and enlightenment. Oh, he had exuded authority - as Pope he was entitled to do so - but it was well known that the despotism of popes throughout the ages was a carefully preserved patina: it does not take much to cleave that polished surface and discover that what lies beneath is often a much less inspiring sight. With that knowledge, I had little confidence that the next Pope would provide any improvement at all. It was a matter of days before Alessandro Farnese was elected by the conclave and assumed his regnal name of Paul III. Only time would tell if he would be able, in any way, to mend the broken relationship between Henry VIII and the Roman Church.

I had my doubts...

By early October, I was only too happy to leave Hampton Court, desperate to escape the memories which met me around every corner. I wanted to return to Greenwich, where I hoped I could restore my spirit, and repair my marriage.

In addition to all that I endured over those sombre months, rumours churned that Henry had taken a mistress. Whereas during another time or place, I might have gone mad with jealousy, my reaction to the whispered news was deadened. Henry and I had met with each other only infrequently over these many weeks. In fact, I realized much later that I must have purposely avoided him, without an overt admission of such. I was just not ready to resume relations as husband and wife. I was still too raw.

So with great relief, I moved back to Greenwich, and quickly organized a trip to Richmond to see Elizabeth, whom, I admit, I had not visited for some time. I knew just the sight of her would do me a large measure of good, and felt lighthearted for the first time in a long while. I arranged a dinner and invited some my ladies. Some of the gentlemen of Henry's council attended as well. I was told, then, that the Lady Mary was also at Richmond, having been compelled to accompany Elizabeth as a part of her retinue. So I decided I would seek another meeting with that recalcitrant young woman in the chance she might capitulate and acknowledge me as Queen. In which case I would certainly treat her with the utmost largesse and hope to repair our fractured connection.

My mood was bright and for the first time since the summer's dreadful occurrence, I felt warmth and delight as I played with my child who had passed the first anniversary of her birth. She was so engagingly imaginative, constantly babbling while intently watching my mouth as I spoke to her. It was plain that she had a great desire to talk and be understood. Her uninhibited childish antics made me laugh – and how good that felt! Hugging and cuddling her provided a balm to my suffering like no other, and at last, I began to feel my outlook improve.

Mary, on the other hand, maintained her brazen effrontery. Defying my command to meet, she again feigned illness and remained in her room until I had left to return to Greenwich. However, I was changed since I had last encountered her, and instead of indignantly forcing her to an audience with me, this time, I left her behind, not caring one whit if I ever saw the young wretch again.

Nevertheless, although I placed Mary Tudor far from my thoughts, I had discovered that in the weeks since the tragic loss of Henry's and my child, Katherine still came frequently to mind. She lingered alone and in exile, a situation she alone had the power to reverse, but it was not that which caused my melancholy. Instead, we were now linked by a terrible bond: the catastrophe of a child lost – one so longed for, so joyfully anticipated - who had noiselessly slipped from one's grasp into eternity, like a wraith into the night. I began to understand the depth of her despair, and knowing that she had endured not one, but many such losses induced me to wonder how she had marshalled the strength to carry on.

By God's tears, I found that I now pitied her; the woman who had caused me so very much aggravation.

I wondered if somehow she had heard of our plight, and if so, was she at all moved by *my* misfortune?

Somehow I rather thought not. Justified, more than likely: gratified by my inadequacy.

As Christmastide drew nigh, I asked Henry if we might have Elizabeth stay with us at Greenwich, and he agreed. In the weeks of late October and November, Henry and I had spent several nights together, but they had been awkward. We'd been distant from each other, and our love-making had not been successful. My pain had now subsided sufficiently that I knew it was well past time for me to put my mind toward repairing the damage that my miscarriage had caused between my husband and me. I needed to get on with living and to find once again happiness and delight in my surroundings. So, even though we intended to have a quiet Christmas, I looked forward to holding intimate suppers with Henry, just the two of us, in the hope that I could reignite the flame that had once burned so brightly.

Greenwich Palace of Placentia
Christmastide 1534

I TOOK CHARGE OF the stewards at Greenwich, and with the help of the Lord Chamberlain, readied the palace for the festive season. I gave instructions that the Great Hall was to be laden with winter greenery, filled with holly – only branches which held the reddest berries - and fresh candles and tapers were to be added to every corner of every room. The Yule log would be massive, and I conferred with the Master Cook to be certain he and his staff were prepared to serve only the very choicest selections of beef and venison, the freshest possible breads and the most desirable sweets and spiced puddings. I took pains to ensure that, although we were not going to host a mighty banquet in this year, each and every small gathering would be pleasurable.

As a surprise for Henry, I had arranged a very special musical performance for him and our closest friends, on an evening just before Christmas. One of my keen interests was the financial support of artists who displayed rare progressive talent in their fields of endeavor. Dear Marguerite d'Alençon had been a true artists' patron in France and, as a young, impressionable girl, I had been fortunate enough to have been in the company of the illustrious musicians, painters and writers she had encouraged.

Thus, it was that, through a referral by the brilliant Bishop Richard Cox, a friend and true reformer, and a dean at Oxford, I came to know a man with prodigious musical skill by the name of Christopher Tye. Tye was then studying at Cambridge, and I had been told that he was a new master at composing and directing splendid choral music. The Bishop was most enthusiastic about his friend's abilities, and since I trusted and admired Cox so greatly, we organized a performance with Tye and a small choral group, so that he might perform several of his compositions for the King. I then met with Master Tye himself to discuss his program, found him to be exceedingly pleasant, and was amused at his excitement, which he tried very hard to control by striving somewhat unsuccessfully to appear dignified. It felt wonderful to become once again immersed in planning a special celebration – something joyous that I would look forward to.

That elegant evening supper was a great success. I'd wanted to take Henry's breath away like I had once been so adept at doing, so I took great care in selecting my gown and jewels. To help in that scheme, I utilized the skilled assistance of a new French maid, Simonette, whom I had recently employed, and who excelled at working miracles with hair and cosmetics.

Between the elegant vision of Mistress Clerk, who not only fitted my new satin gown - the colour of rich cream - so that it made the most of my figure, but also helped to select my jewels: a parure of deep blood red rubies - and Simonette, whose artistry with powders, creams, and colour for the face was simply unmatched– I once again glowed with youth and health. When all of the ministrations were complete, and we each studied the overall effect, Simonette and Mistress Clerk nodded with satisfaction – happy with their accomplishments. I, for that matter, found that my confidence had been restored.

I could not wait for Henry to see me, and I fully intended to demonstrate just how much I had missed our intimacy.

Just before joining Henry to greet our guests, I snatched a few minutes to peer into the room to ensure all was in readiness. The spacious Presence Chamber was bedecked with Christmas finery: the warm glow of candlelight reflecting on highly polished, rich wood paneling; the mantels over the hearths laden with greenery and red berries; the fireplaces crackling merrily and the tables set with pure white napery.

I looked about in approval. The buffets were stacked with sparkling gilt plate and serving pieces, ready to serve up their delicious contents once the guests were seated. Crystal decanters of claret added striking touches of colour, placed as they were on the white cloths of the sideboards. I noticed that, in accordance with my wishes, the censers placed in the corners of the room burned, releasing just the slightest winter fragrance of rosemary and myrrh to perfume the air.

Content, I smoothed my silken gown, arranged my ruby necklet, and went to meet Henry.

It proved a marvellous evening. The food was exquisite, the company engaging and, above all, that music …! Master Tye surely excelled. His choral singers had heavenly voices, and his compositions were uplifting and magical.

More pleasurable than anything else, though, was the way Henry looked at me when he greeted me. As we walked together through the halls of the privy chambers to the Presence Room, he kept his eyes on me. They glistened with appreciation. I knew him well, and I knew his expressions better than my own. My heart swelled with love in return – and relief. He took my hand as we walked, and we entered the room to meet our guests, hand in hand. We paused just past the threshold, and as we smiled at the assembled group, Henry raised my fingers to his lips and kissed them, signalling to all that I was his Queen, and his love.

Although that evening gladly marked the renewal in Henry's and my ardour and desire for one another, and while

I had determined to maintain an uplifted spirit, nevertheless the ponderous weight of the previous six months stubbornly refused to yield.

Just nigh to Christmas Eve, we received a plaintive message from the wife and children of Sir Thomas More, who had now remained incarcerated in the Tower for more than eight months. They sent a petition for his pardon and release, the letter adding that he was 'in great and continual sickness of body and heaviness of heart.'

Carefully I watched Henry's expression grow sad while the letter was read aloud. His mouth twitched almost imperceptibly, but I knew just what it signified. At the letter's conclusion, he sighed, and sat without responding for several long minutes while distractedly examining his hands clenched tightly in his lap. Finally, he looked up and, in the presence of several of his Privy Councillors, responded that unless More was prepared to sign the Oath – as he *should* do, out of respect for his sovereign – there was no likelihood of a release. At any time, he added, if Sir Thomas became more sentient, which would be wise, his King was prepared to reconsider immediately the punishment enacted upon him.

There was no mistaking it. Thomas More's imprisonment – no, in actuality, his refusal to honour the friendship Henry thought they had shared – grieved the King. He felt betrayed and, worse, bereft of the support of a man he'd trusted implicitly since his youth. Even if More now recanted his position, signed the Oath, and was subsequently released from prison, their bond was broken: it would never be the same for Henry.

Once betrayed, Henry never forgot.

•

The closeness and comfort we shared with each other were reinstated, and it felt wondrous to me. Not only did I still love Henry with an irresistible attraction, but he had always provided me with a powerful sense of protection through his great physical presence as well as the authority he wielded over his domain. It was reassuring, to say the very least, to be in his good graces.

We had resumed the practice of supping together, quite privily, on a regular basis. I loved those evenings because we were able to share chat – light, ambling conversation and laughter – which was so difficult to achieve when surrounded by courtiers and staff. We discussed ideas for building and design at the many royal palaces, we talked about art and music, our horses and of hunting and, of course, about our bright and beautiful daughter.

But then, one evening after Christmas but before the New Year, we had just finished our supper. As I rose, preparing to adjourn to another chamber, Henry grasped my arm. There was something about his touch which caused me unease.

"Anne, remain seated. I have something yet to say."

I was immediately filled with anxiety and realized how quickly I responded this way to any possible sense of disaster – whereas before I had suffered my great loss I had been much more resilient. I looked at Henry in dismay.

He reached out to touch my cheek. "Darling, don't worry so. Our daughter is fine and healthy. You and I are well …"

"Then what *is* it, Henry? I see plainly you have news – and it promises not to be good."

He held my hand, and his expression was compassionate. "Anne - your little dog Purkoy … he has died."

My hand went to my mouth. "What *happened*, Henry? He was young - and well! I had not received a message that he was ailing. Oh alas, my poor, poor Purkoy!"

Henry looked reluctant to reply. After a minute, he muttered awkwardly, "I am so sorry, Anne. Your little companion fell. He fell out of an open casement window from an upper floor of the palace. No one wanted to tell you, as they felt terrible, and everyone knows how much you loved him."

My heartache knew no bounds. Amplified as it was from the occurrences of the recent past, I broke down. I cried and sobbed while Henry held me in his arms, waving away the servants who stood by, and letting me weep on his strong shoulder, releasing all of the pent up anguish I held inside until there were no more tears to be shed.

At last, I pulled myself together.

It was very unusual. All at the same time, while I felt happy - grateful for Henry's love and his strength – I also felt unhappy: overshadowed by the spectre of loss. It seemed that this new dichotomy might become an inevitable pattern in my life.

In any case, I was more than ready to bid the year 1534 *adieu.*

Westminster
Spring 1535

WITH THE TURN of the new year, my perspective improved immeasurably. I felt well and fit, and looked forward to fair weather so I might ride and hunt with Henry, the court, and invited visitors once again.

The winter had been mild, and England revelled in an early spring. I took advantage of good travel conditions to visit Elizabeth whenever I could arrange it. Each time I saw her, I was astounded by her growth and development and felt proud to be her mother. I knew her to be a remarkable child; only on occasion did I allow myself to think what life would be like if my Elizabeth had a brother – a baby boy as dazzling as she.

The matters which proved dominant in those months involved a widening gap between ever more strident religious reformers in England and abroad, and the staunch conservative Catholics who were committed to maintaining their obdurate stance at all cost.

And that cost was proving to be very dear indeed. In May, four monks who had been spreading counsel against the King and his position as Head of the Church of England were arrested. Even under duress, none of them volunteered to change their position. So they were drawn from the Tower of London to be executed. Of course, I was not present, but I was with Henry when he was given a full account. They were hanged with ropes and, while still alive, the hangman cut out their hearts and bowels, and burned them. Then they were beheaded and quartered, and their bloodied parts skewered on spears in full view for the public. It was said that each, until the last, was made to observe his predecessor's execution fully carried out before he died, yet even while such horrors were being inflicted they each continued to preach: exhorting the bystanders with the greatest boldness to do well and obey the King in everything that was not against the honor of God and the Church.

My stomach churned as the report was given in all its gory detail, yet I kept my composure and willed my face to remain impassive; taking my cue from Henry, who sat listening as if he were being informed of the ledger expenses at one of his palaces. No emotion – no expression at all – crossed his features.

More and more often, now, affairs of state were being handled by Thomas Cromwell. His level of activity was relentless. The man seemed to be everywhere: involved in everything. To Henry, he was invaluable. And because Cromwell and I seemed to share the same dogma I, too, was tentatively satisfied with his conduct albeit there always remained a hint of mistrust on my part. I took note of how differently Henry and I responded to what I felt was the man's ingratiating behavior. Henry welcomed it, and in return allowed Cromwell even greater control. His confidence in his secretary was conspicuous. I, on the other hand, could not help but hold myself in check. Sceptical by nature, I had reservations about all but my closest of family or companions. Perhaps that is why the more trusting Henry could become so utterly devastated when he learned of even the slightest degree of disloyalty from those whom he deemed close to him.

Master Cromwell's handprint was all-pervasive. He oversaw the bills and invoices that came to the King for payment from the royal coffers. He heard arguments for and against clerics who opposed reformist beliefs. He directed the disposition of lands owned by Catholic monasteries which were now being dissolved due to a lack of funding and support from Rome and of course, above all, he kept tight control over the royal inventory of jewels, property, and assets.

Likely because of that dogged pace, Cromwell took ill just before Easter. His ailment increased in severity until we were informed that he might not survive.

At that same time, the Lady Mary also took dangerously ill – and this time, it was not feigned. Henry was visibly distressed at the news. I wondered how drastic a turn events might take if either, or both of them, died. But as the weeks went by, it became apparent that they were both to survive, though it took some considerable time for each to recover.

Once he was able to reappear at court and in Henry's presence, Cromwell assured the King that neither his abilities nor his vigour for matters important to His Grace were in any way diminished. Probably to curry his King's favour, Cromwell related that Mr John Smith, Dean of St Paul's, had sent a message about a jewel that Henry had once seen while at the church. It was a precious little cross with a crucifix of pure gold and a rich ruby in the side, garnished with four great diamonds, four huge emeralds, four large balasses, and twelve magnificent orient pearls. Apparently, Henry had much admired it, and now Mr Smith, with the agreement of his brethren residentiaries, offered it to the King, trusting accordingly in his charitable goodness toward the Church of St. Paul.

Personally, I had to conceal my cynicism. To me it was quite apparent that Cromwell had brokered this 'gift', not only to please the King but to ensure that Smith and the clergy of St Paul's were beholden to him, Master Secretary Cromwell.

All this he did, unfailingly, with his usual quiet, modest demeanor.

The man was shrewd as a moneylender and as cunning as a fox.

With me - the Queen and the King's beloved wife - whispering in one ear, and Cromwell the esteemed secretary in the other, Henry confidently oversaw the planning of the progress, which he and a select retinue would undertake commencing in July. After a lengthy discussion, in which I had been thoroughly involved, it was decided that the progress of the summer of 1535 should be significant. That of the previous year had, of course, been dampened by the terrible event just before Henry's departure, so this time, there was much to be accomplished. The travel would take place west of London, predominantly to villages and great houses rarely visited by Henry and his court. I had never been that far west, and was eager for adventure; certainly I was more than ready to escape the familiar surroundings we frequented, to ride and hunt, and to enjoy the summer months with abandon by Henry's side. Oh, and of course I wished to advance the cause of religious Reform – the locations we considered were ripe for such an influential visit: one which would convince the local landowners to adopt the tenets of Reform wholeheartedly.

It was decided that the party who had been selected to go on progress with the King would depart from Windsor, that palace being well positioned to commence our journey towards Bristol on England's west coast. Preparations were already underway. Endless supplies were gathered, horses and carts selected and readied, dozens of trunks and wooden crates were packed.

In the meantime, it was a certainty that the various landowners chosen to host the royal party along their way were also madly making ready. The expense incurred by receiving the King, and the preparedness required to accommodate much of his royal traveling company, was by no means insignificant. In fact, it might just strain the resources for a particular estate well nigh to insolvency if its master was not careful.

But the most meticulously laid plans ...

My unmitigated pleasure and clearly Henry's as well, in overseeing the packing and anticipating our summer tour was brought to an abrupt halt by the trials and subsequent indictments of Bishop John Fisher, and Sir Thomas More. Of necessity, our journey was delayed therewith, as the drama played out in a chamber at Westminster.

First, word by word transcriptions were delivered to Henry and me. The charges stated that Sir Thomas More did traitorously attempt to deprive the King of his title of Supreme Head of the Church. Led by Chancellor Audley, those who heard the proceedings included Thomas Cromwell; the clerk Sir Thomas Bedyll, and Sir John Tregonwell, a lawyer, as well as a number of the King's councillors.

More was first asked directly whether he would accept the King as Supreme Head on Earth of the Church of England, pursuant to the statute which was in place. He refused to give a direct answer, saying 'I will not meddle with any such matters, for I am fully determined to serve God, and to think upon His Passion and my passage out of this world.' His responses, as the charges were levelled, were articulate and heartfelt. But he remained unwavering, at one point admitting that 'the Act of Parliament is like a sword with two edges, for if a man answer one way it will confound his soul, and if he answer the other way it will confound his body.'

As the trial continued, More stated that he 'knew well the reason why he was condemned: because he had never been willing to consent to the King's second marriage; but he hoped in divine goodness and mercy, that just as St. Paul and St. Stephen who were persecuted are now friends in Paradise, so we, though differing in this world, shall be united in perfect charity in the other. He prayed God to protect the King and give him good counsel.'

It did not take long for the trial to conclude. As expected, More and Fisher were condemned to death for their traitorous beliefs.

We were told by numerous witnesses that on his way back to the Tower after his trial, one of More's daughters - Margaret - pushed through the archers and guards, and held him in her embrace some time without being able to speak. More, asking leave of the archers, bade her have patience, saying that it was God's will, and she had long known the secret of his heart. After he'd turned heavily away and gone just ten or twelve more steps, she returned and embraced him again, to which he said nothing, except to bid her pray to God for his soul.

When I heard this part of the account, I swallowed hard and sat with my eyes cast downward into my lap fearing that, if I raised them, they would fill with tears and spill over in an unseemly display of emotion.

And as for Fisher? To make matters worse, the new Pope had created him a cardinal of the Roman Church in late May. Henry had done what he could to block the appointment without success, and thus continued with his prosecution, arraigning Fisher on 17 June. Fisher's downfall proceeded swiftly from that date.

On 22 June, he was marched out onto Tower Hill and beheaded.

More remained in the Tower for several additional days, but on Tuesday 6 July was taken by guards from his prison to the open space in front of the Tower. Just before his death he asked those present to pray to God for him, and he would surely do the same for them in the other world. He then besought them earnestly to pray to God to give the King good counsel, protesting that he would die the King's faithful servant, but God's first.

His head was then smitten from his body by an axe.

Both Fisher's and More's heads were displayed on spikes near the Thames so that all might bear witness to their likely fate should they refuse to swear the Oath their sovereign required of them.

It soon became evident that he people of London and its environs were sore outraged by these acts. Both More and Fisher had been beloved by many: in fact, the double execution was to mark what surely must have been the lowest point in Henry's, and my, public favour as King and Queen in the two years since my coronation.

It seemed, therefore, a most opportune - and frankly, prudent - time for Henry, myself, and his closest councillors to depart the city.

Windsor
Severn Valley
New Forest
Summer 1535

BY THE END of the first week in July we were ready. The courtiers accompanying us included Thomas Heneage, Sir Francis Bryan, William Brereton, Henry Norreys, Francis Weston and my brother, George. I had also selected those of my ladies I wished to have as travelling companions; the remainder were to return to their families during the hiatus in formal court duties over the summer months. Margaret Dymoke would join with us, too, along with her husband Sir William Coffin, my Master of the Horse. Margery Horsman, my cousin Madge Shelton, who was new to my household, and my sister-in-law Jane Rochford were all eager to ride with Henry and me, seizing the opportunity to visit estates, monasteries, and locations new to them.

Our merry band of riders assembled early on a bright summer morning in the large courtyard at Windsor. The yard was clamorous with animated chatter, accompanied by the clatter of hooves on cobblestones. I was mounted on my favourite mare, Plume, a fine palfrey with a shining bay coat and silken black mane and tail, and was in high form wearing a new riding habit fashioned from tawny-green damask, new leather boots and a travelling bonnet which had peacock feathers waving from its brim. I like to think that, altogether, I made quite a statement. Additionally, my travelling trunks were packed to overflowing with newly designed clothing - the most current fashions in daywear, riding attire, elegant evening kirtles and gowns made from brilliant colors and fabrics plus, of course, a large suite of jewelry. I had kept Master Skut and Mistress Clerk very busy indeed during the past weeks.

Also at the ready, I carried my beloved English translation of the New Testament, along with the Bible translated into French, one which Henry and I shared and had read many times over. I wanted to be certain that any member of the families who would serve as our hosts would have an opportunity to see such treasures and read for themselves, if they had the ability, thereby reinforcing one of the central intentions of the Reformed church.

I sidled Plume next to Henry's large gelding, reached out and grabbed his horse's bridle, and once right alongside my handsome husband, leaned in to give him a kiss. In return, I received a broad smile and a wink. We had been looking forward to this journey together. We needed it.

The noisy confusion of mingling horses, riders, carts and dogs coalesced as the party set off along the long graveled entrance road to the Palace. Windsor's tower grew smaller and smaller as we fell into an easy order and rode deep into the wooded parkland in the direction of Reading.

We enjoyed fair skies and temperate warmth, ideal for riding, and I was thankful it had not yet grown too hot. The Abbey was a short enough distance from Windsor that our party arrived in the mid-afternoon: the spires of Reading Abbey visible from quite a distance as we approached. It was an impressive monastery, with expansive buildings, their fittings clearly demonstrating the trappings of wealth. I knew it to be a comfortable place to stay, and that Abbot Faringdon would prove a fine host, being accustomed to royal visits. We were to reside in the Abbot's house where the chambers were spacious and accommodating. The gardens, also, were very inviting and well tended by the resident monks and provided a lovely place to walk and talk, or merely for quiet contemplation. Our voyage was off to a successful start.

After a few pleasant days at Reading, we travelled on to Ewelme Manor. That visit was interesting because the estate had recently been owned by Charles Brandon, Duke of Suffolk, but although it provided a good location as a base for hunting in the surrounding area, it offered little more, in my view, the main house being crumbling, ill-appointed and damp. I had no liking for it whatsoever and was happy to move on to our next destination, the abbey of Abingdon.

This monastery was large and imposing, with an interconnected network of many buildings, the whole accessed by a substantial gatehouse where Henry and I were warmly greeted by Abbot Rowland, after which he and his attendants set about making us feel welcome by feeding us well and ensuring our every comfort. On Sunday 11 July we heard mass in Abingdon's large church and then made ready to travel early on the morrow to the Palace of Langley.

On the way to Langley, we instructed the drivers of the caravan of supplies and baggage to continue along the road ahead, while those members of the travelling party who wished to hunt joined the horses and hounds in the forests near Woodstock. Henry and William Coffin knew the red deer to be plentiful in that locale, and after a breakneck chase, we brought down a big buck. It would provide the kitchens at Langley with at least a small contribution toward the food we would consume over the days of our visit. I had been to Langley on a couple of occasions before and liked it well, as did Henry and his father before him: so much so, in fact, that the house had been in strong consideration as an alternative residence for Elizabeth. The Oxfordshire countryside surrounding the manor was lovely, marked by rolling hills, meandering streams, thick copses of trees, all giving visitors a feeling of peacefulness which was always pleasing. Once arrived, we settled in for an agreeable stay.

While we spent a goodly part of each day in the pastimes of the hunt, other sport, and general enjoyment, the King set aside time to attend to matters of state. Likewise, I was regularly apprised of business which pertained to me and acted upon it when necessary. Cromwell had remained behind for a short time to handle affairs in Westminster, but it was planned that he would catch up with the company once we reached Sudeley. So from Langley I wrote and dispatched several letters to him, requesting that he resolve the open position of abbot for the Abbey of Wallryall in Lincolnshire by appointing an individual who had been recommended to me. In a subsequent document, I assigned him the responsibility of handling certain issues with the wardship of a child whom the King had placed in my charge. Much like Henry, I found Master Cromwell's assistance to be ever more vital.

And thus, we moved on to stay at Sudeley Castle in Gloucestershire, only to find the accommodations a little less than satisfactory, the buildings being infrequently used. Nonetheless, the swarm of servants who had been dispatched to each site in advance of the royal party had done an admirable job of cleaning, arranging, and stocking the kitchens so our visits would be as enjoyable as possible. In the afternoons we hunted and rode out into the countryside, returning to the castle though its neighboring villages so we could greet the people who spilled out from their cottages, waving and cheering – often proudly offering us presents of cheeses or jam which they had specially prepared. In the evenings we ate and drank, played cards and games, laughed, and made merry.

One evening after supper, Henry and a few of his gentlemen were playing a game of Pope July at the card table: Henry Norreys, George, Henry, Madge Shelton, Margery Horsman and I sitting around the circular table bathed in candlelight. As it was Norreys' turn to deal, he passed cards to each of us. When he reached Madge, however, I noticed that, as he laid her card before her, his hand casually caressed her fingers resting on the table. I raised a quizzical eyebrow at her, whereupon she blushed and lowered her gaze. I was surprised, but not displeased. Madge was new to my household; she was my cousin, and she was young and very pretty. She was so grateful to have received a place as a maid of honour, and had made a great effort to be as helpful to me as she could. A charming young girl, she was quick to laugh and flirt and had a pleasant manner with which to keep company. It was apparent that several of our gentlemen thought so as well. Madge knew well how to smile to show off her dimpled cheeks, and flutter her eyelashes in the way which made any red-blooded male want to come close. I watched their little interaction with wry amusement.

Cromwell and some of the household were staying apart from Sudeley in a nearby abbey called Winchcombe. Assiduous as ever, Thomas seized the opportunity to conduct a thorough audit of the abbey and its connection to the people of the surrounding communities, including its finances, holdings, and practices. I took great interest in his review. Integral to true religious reform, I firmly believed that the deceptions concealed by many monasteries must be corrected. As was emblematic of the Roman Church and its clergy, a holy facade was carefully presented to the world. In truth, though, they were all too often fronts for hypocrisy, allowing the monks to live duplicitous lives, displaying a pretense of austerity when they were more pleasure-seeking than most of the hard-working country folk they were intended to serve.

Cromwell, amongst his many other titles and responsibilities, had been appointed by Henry to serve as Vice-Regent of Spiritual Affairs, with the purpose of supporting the King's role as Supreme Head of the Church. This post pleased Cromwell, and me as well. It meant that we could join forces to eliminate systematically the deceitful practices of the Catholic

Church still embedded throughout the kingdom, and with the emphasis of the law, strengthen Henry's autonomy and new principles of enlightened Reform.

At last, I felt as if I was beginning to fulfill my desire to voice my opinion, have it taken seriously, and to use my influence to create action and change in England.

The chaplains who had accompanied us on the journey – William Latymer, Matthew Parker, and others – did a fine job of speaking to the crowds who followed us. They preached and evangelized the new word; wherefore people listened, inspired. Many showed up day after day, nodding and shouting affirmation when the clerics made their points loudly and clearly. I was so gratified to watch the throngs grow every day. Undoubtedly we were making a difference! While the trip progressed, I became ever more content with myself, and my sense of authority. I was beginning to feel like the Queen I had aspired to be.

As our pilgrimage unfurled, so did my daily state of happiness and fulfilment. And I greeted it like a new and welcome friend.

Word quickly spread through the surrounding countryside that the King and Queen, with their colourful retinue, were about and could often be seen spending long days, well into the dusk of the summer evenings, traversing their local fields while hunting. As a result, the assemblages of curious and cheering onlookers increased in size each time we moved from location to location. Meanwhile, my endurance on horseback grew steadily, and due to those days spent in the open air and sunshine, the evenings laughing and enjoying good food and the company of friends, and the night-times most often cradled in Henry's arms, I felt better – younger and more vital – than I had for many years. I must have looked as well as I felt because Henry most often was by my side, and his admiring gaze, just as during our early years together, rarely left me.

Our blissful tour carried on. We stayed at Tewkesbury Abbey, then arrived amidst much grand ceremony at the town of Gloucester where the mayor, all the local gentry and most of the townsfolk paid us homage while Henry and I were gracious in return.

By mid-August, we had arrived at Thornbury Castle, the former home of Edward Stafford, third Duke of Buckingham – a hateful man whom Henry had executed in 1521 after Stafford brazenly and openly challenged the King's right to the throne. Construction to vastly improve the palace had begun before Stafford's death but, afterwards, Henry took control of the property, and when he and I spent almost two weeks within its thick walls, we became enchanted with its lovely grounds and elegant design. Our suite of rooms, located at the very top of the tower, was cool and delightful, offering a magnificent view of the privy gardens and bright green lawns sloping toward the River Severn below.

When our stay at Thornbury was regretfully over, we rode a short distance to Acton Manor. Acton was owned by the young and ardent reformer, Sir Nicholas Poyntz. Master Poyntz had been so overjoyed when he had been notified of our plans to visit that he had hurriedly undertaken a flurry of renovations on his lovely house in preparation. He proudly informed us that he had commissioned Master Holbein himself to assist in the stylistic design, and the results were magnificent. From Acton, we pressed on to Little Sodbury Manor, an estate owned by Poyntz's aunt and uncle, Sir John and Lady Anne Walshe.

The Walshes were dear friends and advocates of William Tyndale. I was fascinated by their close association with a man I had held in great awe for some time. To me, Tyndale was the embodiment of a radical thinker. I believed that his brilliance, combined with his fearlessness in expressing his ideas marked him as one of the most important men of our time. For that reason alone I was thrilled to be able to hear directly about him from people who had known him so well.

Tyndale was a native of Gloucestershire and a son of the local Hychyns family. Even as a child his keen intellect was already evident. As a young man he had developed a passionate interest in language and, early in his studies, had mastered fluency in seven languages. At an early age, he was admitted to Oxford, and then Cambridge, but, while earning his degrees, had become frustrated by the fact that a study in theology did not allow direct readings of scripture. Once he had left Cambridge, the Walshes hired him as their personal chaplain, and, because they respected his views, had him tutor their children.

I asked Lady Anne what it was like having him live under their roof.

"Oh, Madame, it was a curious experience, that is certain. He was kind to our two boys, but he was, ah ... different, do you know what I mean? After lessons were completed for the day he gathered piles of books and went out into the orchards. He would sit under a tree and read and read for hours on end. Once dinner was finished, he would go to the antechamber near the hall where he kept further stacks of books, parchment, and quills, and write furiously well into the night, having searched the house to seek out and use every nub of candle he could scrounge. "

My eyes grew wide, imagining the workings of such a mind. "Was he easy to speak with, Milady? Did he, for instance, relate to matters of everyday life?"

She chuckled softly. "Umm, that is a good question, Your Highness. At times he seemed to – but at others, one could see that he was elsewhere. Often he ate very little. He seemed to forget to eat! He was a tall young man - almost gaunt. And all too often ..." she wrinkled her nose at the memory, "he would neglect entirely to wash or to comb his hair. I needed to remind him, or the boys would not go near him!"

I chuckled and shook my head, thinking about how it must have been to have lived with a true genius under one's roof.

"After a short period, he became obsessed with a desire to go to London to pursue his interest. He was bound to obtain permission to translate scripture, and I would say he was single-minded about securing that; *insisting* that all men – women too

– should be able to read God's word in their own language … Oh, I did so admire him for his perseverance! And could not help but agree. So, eventually, we gave him some money, wished him well, and off he went to pursue his life's work. And, as I believe you know, Madame, he has not had an easy time of it."

How I enjoyed talking with this enlightened, educated woman! There were so few of us who valued reading, scholarship, or the acquisition of knowledge. There were even fewer who were willing to stand and express their beliefs to the world.

"So did you remain in touch with William, Lady Anne?"

"We did, but just for a while. He had poor luck in London. There were those who shared his beliefs, but few who were agreeable to risking their standing or prosperity by endorsing such a seemingly eccentric young man; even fewer prepared to underwrite his cause …" She frowned uneasily. "John and I were taken aback when we heard of an argument William had had with the scholar John Foxe. Foxe argued the necessity of following the edicts laid out by the Pope. By then, William had come to disavow the Pope and the statutes of the Vatican. In his very careless way, we were told that he replied, 'I defy the Pope, and all his laws; and if God spares my life, ere many years, I will cause the boy that driveth the plow to know more of the Scriptures than thou dost, *Doctor* Foxe!'"

She shrugged uncertainly then. "Well, Madame, as I am sure you can understand, shortly after that outburst it behooved William to leave England to see if he could gain a foothold elsewhere. We knew he had gone to Europe, but John and I knew not where."

Captivated, I said, "I knew that he travelled around Germany and the Netherlands, seeking sponsors. I also heard about him from people in France who were taking hold of the new ideas and proselytizing on behalf of them. Through my connections, I was able to acquire some books which were, as you know, forbidden – *very* vocally condemned by Cardinal Wolsey - and of course, Lady Anne, it should come as no surprise to you that I was not a great favourite of Wolsey's?"

We met each other's glance and started giggling at the understatement about what had been an awful time, but was now so far in the past that it seemed almost humorous.

At this point in the story, I picked up the narration. I was glad that Lady Anne and I were alone, and Henry in another chamber with Sir John so that I could speak frankly. Nevertheless, I still lowered my voice to a near whisper.

"You may know that Tyndale, in his reckless but committed way, wrote against Henry's pursuit of a divorce from Katherine?"

"I do, Your Highness. That must have been difficult for you," she said with obvious regret.

"It was. But strangely, I found that I was less angered by that action of his than those by others who just spoke against us with no basis for their argument. There has always been something about Tyndale, for me, which prompts me to cheer for him. I firmly believe that what he is doing will change the world. I was given my own copy of his English translation shortly after Henry and I became betrothed. It remains one of my greatest treasures. In fact, I have it with me. Would you like to see it?"

Her eyes shone as she nodded in silent affirmation.

I went to my chamber and brought the dark leather-bound book to her. As she leafed through its pages, her lashes became wet with tears.

"It is incredibly moving, is it not, Lady Anne?" I commented softly after a long while. "I feel the same way whenever I read it, or even touch it. What a brilliant, incredible, crazy man! And what a gift he has given us all. I have no doubt that, although you and I will fade into lost memory once we are gone from this earth, the name and the work of William Tyndale will live on. As well it should. And thank you for the part you have played in nurturing his life and his works."

She reached out to touch my hand in silent gratitude for my comment. I saw that she was overwhelmed, and I returned her grasp to let her know how much I valued our truthful conversation, and the privilege I felt at visiting their home.

I ventured, "Master Cromwell and I hope to discuss Tyndale's fate with Henry. Even though he still holds resentment from William's foolish publication about Henry's first marriage, there is no question Henry still considers Tyndale to be a great mind. His earlier work *Obedience of a Christian Man* was what truly enabled Henry's thinking about his supreme authority as a King – his divine right to rule. So we owe much to Master Tyndale. And, if you and Sir John will join the conversation, together I think we can convince His Majesty to offer a stronghold for William, and perhaps have him return to England to continue his work."

"You know, Madame, that he is now imprisoned somewhere in Brussels? We have just received word of this through our sources abroad."

"I had heard the same thing, Milady. It is terribly wrong. We are obligated to do whatever we can to allow him to continue his work. Do you agree? Will you join us in discussing it with the King?"

And, just as I expected from this brave and intelligent woman, she nodded her agreement.

So it was that we sat and talked, long into the night: Henry, Cromwell, Sir John, Lady Anne and me. I led the discussion, fervently making a case for the need to match our ideology with action. Henry listened to me speak, giving me his full attention, and allowing the others to present then their views. At the conclusion of our impassioned plea, recognizing that Tyndale and his work formed a core of our new religion, Henry conceded that he would do what he could to have Tyndale released from prison, returned to England, and allowed to complete his work on the biblical translation.

The very next day, Cromwell composed a letter on behalf of the King of England which would be forwarded to Flanders, seeking Tyndale's release. Only time would tell if this tactic would prove effective.

Once the letter was composed and completed, we raised a toast to its hoped-for success. As we did so, Master Cromwell studied me intently, both in appreciation of my achievement and in a sudden comprehension of the sway I now held over His Grace, the King.

… studied me *very* intently indeed.

•

August gave way to summer's end and, this year, I fully indulged in its rich golden beauty. How I loved the season – I always had – and marveled at the difference a year had made. Although I was stabbed with the sharp pain of profound sorrow whenever I thought about the loss of our baby girl, I believed that I had never been happier than I was on that cusp of September. If it had been possible to achieve the good fortune of such contentment in these months past, how much more might Henry and I gain in the years to come? I could not help but smile in happy anticipation thereof. We had travelled miles, stayed in wonderful houses, ridden though marvelous great swathes of the English countryside and, perhaps best of all, we had garnered approval from the many, many people we had met along the way. I had been accepted: I was the King's partner, and it was known to all who saw us.

And now the time had come for us to look forward to yet another significant event – the consecration of three illustrious bishops who had advanced the cause of the reform in England. The ceremony was to take place at Winchester Cathedral on 19 September, and it would be a blessed, meaningful hallmark in the chronicle of reformation – not only for England but also for the other European countries whose numbers of evangelicals increased every day.

Before then, though, we arrived at Wulfhall, the home of Sir John Seymour, on 3 September for a several day visit. Sir John was the father of my maid of honour, Jane. Sir John's wife, Margery, was soft spoken, a seemingly kind woman and one who very warmly welcomed us into her home. Wulfhall was located near Marlborough, in Wiltshire. The property, which lay on the edge of the thick Savernake Forest, consisted of an attractive manor house – certainly not lavish – but the surrounding gardens had been well cultivated and were lovely, the lands extensive, and the house had a private chapel.

It was within this chapel that Henry, Cromwell, Archbishop Cranmer - who had joined the progress - and several others of Henry's Privy Council convened to sign official documents confirming appointments of Edward Fox, John Hilsey, and Hugh Latimer as Bishops in the new Church of England.

After this memorable rite, all the guests adjourned to the broad chamber to celebrate with a feast. When we entered the hall, however, I was momentarily surprised to encounter the Seymour's daughter, who – of course, I well knew her – was my maid of honor. I had forgotten that Jane had sought permission to spend part of the summer with her parents at Wulfhall while the rest of the court was on progress. Immediately she approached and smiled, curtseying respectfully.

"I welcome you, Your Highness! Welcome to Wulfhall. I hope you and His Majesty will be comfortable and feel at home here."

I nodded to her in return. "Well, thank you, Jane. That is very kind of you. I feel certain we will enjoy our stay. Your family's estate is lovely, and we greatly appreciate your father's hospitality."

It was strange. As I turned from her to be seated at the table I suddenly felt uneasy. Admittedly I had never taken a liking to Mistress Seymour. Not that she had done anything which was offensive. But nevertheless, there was *something* about the young woman.

We all took our places at the long table which had been carefully placed and beautifully set for our repast. Rhenish wine was poured, along with a strong ale imported from Holland. Henry stood at the head of the table and raised his glass.

In his deep voice, he pronounced: "My gentle friends - on this quietly momentous day – one which has clearly marked the legitimacy and the authority of the English Church – I would like to thank those who have worked tirelessly to enact it. Of course, we give all good recognition to Doctors Latimer, Foxe, and Hilsey, for their enlightened ideology and beliefs that have guided them and which will now, thankfully, guide us as well. Also, though, we must be grateful for the determined efforts of Master Cromwell, and of my entirely beloved wife, Queen Anne. Without their foresight and inspiration, we would not have in place the firm foundation for a Church, which will serve our Almighty Father and the people of England." Then, as he lifted his arm holding his goblet aloft, Henry looked down at me with pride and love. "So now I bid you all to raise your glasses and let us honour them for their contribution."

Oh, so many dishes covered the table. The ale was potent, and talk and laughter grew ever louder. I sat to the right of Henry, and we spoke animatedly with our hosts and the others, but also often with each other. His constant smile was a joy to my soul. As the guests ate and conversed, I happened to glance down the length of the table and caught sight of Mistress Seymour. She had no idea I watched her. But how could she? Her gaze was solely fixed on Henry. She never took her eyes from him, and her countenance was one of pure adulation. Occasionally she glanced down, and I saw a blush flood her cheeks. But it was not long before her adoring attention returned only to him and she followed his every word and every nuance.

Henry, on the other hand, had no idea of her absorption with him. Observing this, I was confused. But in a mere moment's time, I realized what I was witnessing, and a knot of white-hot anger was kindled in my gut. I stared at the wretched creature until somehow she must have sensed my glare and looked up from her worship of my husband to catch my expression. At first, she was taken aback and grew quite red, eyes darting about the room as if she were innocent. I kept my unblinking watch on her, never wavering. Then, though, instead of becoming ever more flustered, she looked back at me. She looked me directly in the eye. I saw her draw in her breath, sit straight, and raise her chin at me in defiance.

Oh, I recognized that challenging gesture.

It was the same cold stare I had levelled at Katherine, years ago.

We remained at Wulfhall for several days and during that time, I kept my distance from Jane. Henry, who very clearly had noticed nothing during the meal, or after that, was constantly busy hunting, reviewing documents, meeting with Cranmer and Cromwell in preparation for the upcoming ceremony. I knew of his whereabouts every minute of each day. By the time we were packed and ready to ride on, some of my raw anger had subsided. How impudent of that young woman - I *knew* there had been a reason why I had disliked her from the start! But I resolved not to allow her simple behavior to affect me overmuch: it was absurd to fear that that a man like Henry would ever notice a girl like Jane, much less take an interest in her. For a start, she was exceedingly plain, poorly dressed unless she wore one of the costumes I provided at court, and unintelligent. She had not spoken up once at dinner, nor did she when my household was convened. She hardly read, and spoke no languages other than English – and that, not artfully. In fact, more than not, she quite faded into the background altogether. Henry would never take heed of her – nor would any other man, sadly for her, I concluded.

But I …? I still determined to keep a watch on the unpleasant little strumpet.

The liturgy and appointment of the Bishops was a beautiful and gratifying event. A great and happy surprise arrived at the appearance of the French ambassador Jean de Dinteville, who had come to Winchester to attend the consecration. I had always been fond of Monsieur Dinteville, and this time he brought me an esteemed message. Marguerite, sister of François, that lady whom I respected above most all other women, had sent her gracious compliments and admiration to Henry and me. She was pleased with the news of the consecration, and of the great strides we had made for reform in England. In exchange, I returned a message to say that, other than the blessing of having a son, my greatest wish was to see her once again. And perhaps I would be able to if Henry and I were to travel to France one day.

The end of our progress was in view. But while we still had the freedom it offered, we hawked and hunted in the harvest fields, and I absorbed every aspect of that marvelous time Henry and I shared.

By mid-October we arrived at The Vyne, a house already familiar to me, imbued with good memories from a visit Henry and I had made to Lord Sandys' estate about four years previously. And what a gorgeous residence it truly was! Massive, imposing, with every comfort available, and I had my own large suite of chambers on the first floor, which adjoined Henry's apartments. The fittings in my chambers were of the finest quality – silk and satin drapery, velvet bed coverings, plush padded chairs and benches, and a warm fire constantly burning in the hearth. Even the bed was enormous and invitingly soft. I hoped Henry and I would make good use of it!

Once the entire party had been settled in their respective chambers, bags and trunks unpacked, we attended a service of thanksgiving in The Vyne's breathtaking chapel. A lovely, ethereal light streamed through the tall leaded glass windows, each of which bore a coat of arms of the Sandys dynasty. Its panelled walls and choir stalls were of highly polished oak, intricately carved, while, most astonishing of all, were its floors. They were lined with colourful tiles, each remarkably depicting a different image: portraits, birds, animals, and occasionally, a reminder of our mortality and the consequence of living a lawless life – human skulls. As we admired them, Lord Sandys told us they had been specially commissioned in Antwerp and shipped to the house for laying in the chapel, and other areas of the manor.

The service was most moving, especially since we had just been favoured with the raising of three good men to bishoprics, men who were staunch defenders of my title and position. In addition to giving thanks to God for the many blessings we had been granted on our journey, I made a point of praying fervently that the refreshed bond my husband and I shared would result in a conception. Dear Lord, I beseeched: this time of a son. Perhaps my prayer would be heard, and my request granted. I had great hope.

The days we spent at The Vyne were idyllic. We were able to enjoy repose since, while in residence, there was no need for evangelisation; the consecration ceremony being behind us now, and which had been carried out without flaw. Indeed, I had only one regret: an awareness that we were coming to the end of a glorious time.

Henry came to my chamber each night, exclaiming that not only was he there to lie with his beautiful wife but because he believed it to be the best bed in the house! Our lovemaking was tender and very satisfying, and each dawn following I sighed with gladness and relief.There had been earlier periods, in the past months and at the start of our travels, when he had come to my bed yet the act of love had proved impossible for him. I worried terribly when this first happened. What had gone wrong? In the past, he had always been greatly aroused when we lay together. I had to admit to myself that he was almost 45 years of age. Though I knew of men who fathered children past that point, it was not a common occurrence. Perhaps they, too, suffered the same difficulty. It was a subject I was unable to discuss with anyone, though … or anyone except my brother George, perhaps? Might he be able to advise me - and either way, he would certainly be discreet! I resolved to ask him when I next had a chance.

Our visit to The Vyne drew to a close but instead of following the intended schedule, with our final destination being the city of Bristol, we diverted our path because we had been informed that cases of plague had broken out within that city's confines. Instead, we rode a short distance to the home of Sir William Paulet, Henry's Comptroller.

Basing House was large, quite formally laid out, and fastidiously appointed. It was so luxurious that I felt as if I were back at court. No longer did I have the blithe sense of freedom

I had come to delight in riding most of the day and roaming from place to place like a nomad. I savoured those final days at Sir William's estate but knew a return to the full conventions of court lay just ahead.

We returned to Windsor as October waned and the trees' leaves turned brown and crisp. The air had settled into a steady chill, but we had certainly been favoured with remarkably fine weather for the almost four months of our passage. Now, at the close of the progress, I was tranquil and in good spirits. The invigorating exercise, exhilarating sights, and the accomplishment of our intentions for the mission all had acted as a soothing balm for me and, of even greater importance, I could see that they had done the same for Henry. He looked fitter than he had in many a month: his strength had increased, his face showed a high and healthful colour, and once more he laughed easily and often.

We prepared to hold a merry Christmastide at Greenwich, where I planned to give my King an early gift.

My joy knew no bounds, for once again, I was pregnant.

Greenwich Late Autumn Christmastide and New Year 1535

I DO NOT KNOW who was more elated at the news: Henry or me.

I had recognized the early symptoms of this, my third pregnancy right away, and had a strong suspicion of the happy truth by late November. By mid-December, as we readied the palace and the court for an especially merry Christmas and New Year, my notion was confirmed.

Strangely, those early days did not cause me bouts of nausea such as I had endured during my previous two pregnancies. Instead, the most difficult challenge was trying to quell the fears which were so natural: that I would carry this baby almost to term, then lose it yet again. But my midwives were wonderful in their reassurances, telling me it often happened that a too-early delivery would result in the death of an infant, yet the next pregnancy produced a robust, healthy baby delivered at full term.

So I did my best to keep my attention on my activities, banish pessimistic thoughts, and busy myself with a myriad of duties both domestic and official.

Since we had returned from progress, there had been much talk about how and when – even *if* - the many monasteries scattered about the kingdom should be dissolved. Cromwell was working diligently on a report which would collate findings as they poured in from his assistants across the realm who had been assigned to visit the large monastic houses: each charged with conducting full audits, and providing their details to the secretary.

From the beginning, the early dispatches were distressing, recounting a litany of corruption, embezzlement, limited attention to their holy purposes, and even depravity. The decision whether or not to allow them to remain in place looked as if it would be an easy one to take. Master Cromwell and I had numerous talks about the subject during which I made quite clear to him my preference - that if all the houses were to be dissolved, the riches therein, their lands, and any other potential income would be gathered and used to endow educational pursuits – perhaps a new college? – or supporting education in the smaller villages and towns, in addition to providing significant alms for the poor. I was firm about this and wanted to devise a way to distribute these monies in an organized and highly effective manner.

In one of my regular meetings with Secretary Cromwell, I expressed these intentions about the funds which would be released.

He listened carefully, head slightly cocked to one side, as he had a habit of doing. I told him that it was my wish - no, my *expectation*! - that he would support me in my aim to underwrite charitable pursuits with the money.

Cromwell pursed his lips at that, but the rest of his features remained impassive. He was a true master at disguising his reactions.

"Madame," he began deferentially, "your motives are noble and denote what a refined and benevolent Queen you are. I am truly privileged to serve you - and of course your husband, His Grace the King ..."

"Thank you, Thomas," I interrupted sweetly, "But proceed if you will. I know quite well that there is more to follow your pretty compliments. Just tell me what you think!"

He cleared his throat. "I believe, Your Highness, that there is a way for us to contribute to some educational endeavours, yet still pay much-needed attention to the significant deficits that exist in the treasury. It is an inescapable truth that there is a desperate need to shore up those assets. I expect you know this?"

"I am well aware my husband the King is of such a generous nature that he will spend largely on items to give pleasure to people he cares about. I also know he has embarked on much building and improving of his properties. But that has been needed for many years, Thomas, otherwise those buildings will fail entirely. What, then, are you suggesting?"

"Madame, this is a unique opportunity – one which we may never again have in our lifetime. Here is a trove of funds ready not only to make your husband the richest prince in Christendom – which he well deserves, by the way – but also to enhance our army. We may even be able to afford to build several new ships – warships and cargo carriers, which we need perilously."

"I understand those requirements, Thomas. But I do not agree with using these monies for those purposes. These are riches acquired from what were once holy sources. It is money which has been *donated* by our subjects – the churchgoers - for the intent of paying tithes. We cannot use it to pad the pockets of the Crown! Even if we were to build ships for war those people who gave their life's earnings for a place in heaven would not want that. No – we absolutely *must* use it to help the poor and indigent, and to educate the subjects of this realm! You *know* this to be the right thing, Thomas!"

I felt my annoyance beginning to slide toward outrage. I would NOT allow that man to overrule me!

Maintaining an absolute composure which exasperated me even further, he replied calmly, "Your Royal Highness, with nothing but the greatest respect, I must make you aware that the King has discussed my plan with me, reviewed it with his councillors, and seems to be in full agreement that any funds which come from the monasteries should, and will, supply the coffers of the Crown. Once invested, it will be determined exactly how the money will be used, but I would signal now that he is much in favour of reinforcing the country's defences. At present, were we to be attacked, we have little confidence that we could overcome an enemy, and that is not an acceptable position for our Kingdom to be in. I am certain you can understand that."

In his voice, I detected a slight tone of condescension. As if I, a woman, might have a hard time comprehending the need for a strong defence. And I could not bear it.

"I am very well aware of the discussions the King has had on this subject. He is my husband, and always keeps me well apprised. However, that does not mean my wishes will not be honoured. And I *ask* you, Thomas, to be wise and to know that your great approval with the King is in good part due to my endorsement of your many merits. His Majesty listens to me above *all* others; I would remind you - therefore I suggest that you do whatever you can to sustain that positive endorsement!"

Without awaiting his response I stood, lifted the hem of my gown and abruptly marched from the chamber: a queen prescribing her royal entitlement.

Why was it, then, that I felt such unease from sensing that his eyes bore into my back every single step of the way?

•

As Christmas approached, Henry could not have been more kind or considerate of me. He ensured I had anything I desired to eat and was always solicitous of my becoming overtired. But I was once again in the vulnerable position of not being able to provide my husband with lovemaking, which concerned me. And rightly so, it appeared.

One afternoon I sat sewing with my ladies. We'd been busy making shirts and smocks for the poor villagers. I intended we would have a good number ready to be delivered by Christmas, so we had been at our activity steadily since dinnertime. Having sat way too long, I had risen, stretched, and walked stiffly to the window embrasure to gaze out over the gardens when I felt someone touch my arm. It was Jane, my sister-in-law. She steered me to a small adjacent closet and, once out of sight, lowered her voice.

"Madame, may I speak with you?"

"What is it, Jane?" The insistent tone and her knitted brow gave me concern.

"Truly, I hesitate to talk of this, but I feel you must be made aware. And – you are my sister, so that makes it even more important."

"Then speak. Tell me what you have to convey." I liked Jane, but I was impatient. She really could be so cloying.

"It concerns Madge - Madge Shelton, Your Highness. She … she has been seen slipping into private chambers with the King. Just Madge and His Grace. Alone. And on more than one occasion. Of course, I know not what happens behind the closed doors, but I thought you might want to be apprised."

She eyed me hesitantly then, as if I might strike her, but instead, I felt as if I had just been punched in the belly. Even the breath left me, but I did not want Jane to see such reaction so, with a mighty effort, I maintained my composure and replied courteously, "I am sure they are simply partaking in some courtly flirtation, Jane. I am not concerned. But thank you. I know you only mean well."

"Indeed, Madame. Your well-being is of the utmost importance to me."

She curtseyed when I motioned to dismiss her, but then I quickly added, "Oh - and Jane? I would greatly appreciate it if you keep this information strictly to yourself. Please do not fan gossip by spreading the account. I depend on you for this. Do you understand?"

"Of course, Madame. Implicitly."

And she left me standing there in silence.

I did not say anything to Henry. I knew it would have been folly. But I did, very generously, offer Mistress Shelton the chance to depart immediately and spend Christmastide, as well as a goodly time thereafter, at her family home in Norfolk. She hesitated when the offer was made, but when she saw my face, she quickly curtseyed her appreciation and blurted that she was grateful for the opportunity to be with her parents for Christmas.

Before she took her leave, however, I followed with, "Madge, are you not betrothed to Sir Henry Norreys? Or am I wrong in thinking that?"

"No, Madame, you are not. I am indeed promised to Henry."

"Then may I make a suggestion? I recommend you use this time to make plans for your wedding, and you carry them out with all haste. You should not delay and let a man like Norreys remain unattached, Madge. You never know when he might set his sights on another young woman - and unfortunate things can happen, so I would like to see you married before *you* meet such a fate. As soon as possible!"

A flush suffused Madge's pale neck as our eyes met. It was enough. She understood that I knew of her trysts with my husband.

Fearfully she quickly dropped her gaze, sank into a deep curtsey and, upon rising, whispered, "Please do excuse me, Your Highness. I will take great heed of your advice." Whereupon she backed from the room.

Our Christmas, New Year and Twelfth Night festivities were filled with cheer. Or at least, that was the appearance they gave for there were times, too many times, when I was flooded with misgiving. But then I remembered that I carried the King's child, and my spirits were restored.

This time, I was certain, it would be a boy.

Hampton Court Palace
January 1536

THE NEW YEAR gift-giving and feasting over, we would remain at Hampton Court through Twelfth Night. But events moved on, even though we, ourselves, did not.

Immediately after Christmas came a report from Kimbolton that Katherine was ailing terribly and might not last through the next day - yet again! Shortly after that, however, we heard that she had revived, and I recognized that, as had happened so many times in the past, it had merely been a further device to gain Henry's attention and sympathy. If so, it did not work. To my complete satisfaction, Henry remained indifferent to the news. I also thought about how Mary must have felt, not being permitted to be by her mother's bedside but though I felt a twinge of pity – especially since I had little Elizabeth at court with me – I had no choice but to put it out of mind. Over and over the girl had refused to make things so much easier for herself and her mother simply by acknowledging me. She had had been offered every chance, and never acted on it. Therefore, there was nothing else to be done.

The King, George, Norreys, Anne Zouche and I were having supper on the early evening of 8 January when a crier announced the delivery of a message by the hand of Ralph Sadler, Cromwell's secretary. He entered the chamber, bowed and offered the King a folded letter and then the unexpected happened. Henry broke its seal, read it - and slumped back in his chair with a peculiar expression.

He remained motionless for some time while we all sat wondering, not without some trepidation, as to its import. Only eventually did the King announce that Katherine was dead. She had, it seemed, succumbed during the early morning hours in the presence of Sir Edward Bedingfield, who had been her steward, and Sir Edward Chamberlain, her lord chamberlain.

Paradoxically, I felt numb at the news. It was not unexpected for all her devious pretences, and I would be wrong not to admit there were times when I had wished the woman dead and out of our lives forever. But now that she was well and truly gone, I was reflective. Rivalry apart, as a woman she and I had shared the same man, had suffered a common grief, had daughters whom we loved. There was something universal about those experiences and, because of that, in my heart I silently wished her well on her spiritual journey.

On the positive side: having regard to the reality of my place as Queen and my daughter's as heir to the throne, I was relieved that she no longer posed any threat.

Henry remained inscrutable. I could not ascertain how he felt about Katherine's demise. I think he had so long been frustrated by her that he'd become devoid of any personal feeling although I knew he would have liked, in the early days of their separation, to treat her kindly if she had only obeyed his wishes. Instead, his relief at never having to worry about her again was evident.

The next morning, he summoned me to accompany him to a dinner in the Great Hall, requesting that I ready Elizabeth in beautiful attire as he wished to show her off to his court. I knew that it was his way of closing the book on the story of

Katherine, which had too long been untidily open. So I dressed in a beautiful spring green gown, had Elizabeth gowned in a sweet golden robe, and went to meet my husband in the Hall. I was a bit surprised when I saw him: no sombre mourning clothes for Henry, attired as he was in a sunny yellow jerkin over a fine white silk doublet while wearing a gold bonnet from which a white feather waved.

He was in great form and had ordered up an excellent feast for himself and his guests. He came to me immediately, encircled Elizabeth and me with his arm and gave me a resounding kiss, upon which he took Elizabeth and, holding her in his strong grasp, carried her proudly about the room, bouncing her and lifting her aloft so all could see his beautiful, red-haired daughter. Elizabeth, of course, adored the attention of her father, and laughed and giggled delightedly, which pleased Henry to no end. I will admit I enjoyed the time immensely myself. It was not often that we were able to present ourselves as a true family so I, too, smiled and laughed, and had a grand time.

In retrospect perhaps it was not the most prudent display. I know there were some, observing our behavior, who felt affronted by our seeming lack of respect for Katherine's death. But it was my husband's choice, and I followed his lead.

It wasn't difficult. And rather more fun than mourning.

Henry's good humour persisted, matched with the equally good weather. So good, in fact, that he planned a tournament at the tiltyard as January began its third week. He made a certain statement by the planning of the joust since it was to be held on the very day of Katherine's interment at Peterborough Cathedral.

I knew of his plans, albeit my private view was that Henry was well beyond the age where jousting was wise. But after hunting strenuously for the duration of autumn, he had experienced a resurgence in his physical stamina. He'd been playing tennis, had spent time on the archery field, and in general felt well and strong: so much so that he determined he was able to joust again, with the same level of skill he had displayed throughout his youth and, of course, I said nothing to him about my disapproval.

Henry was right jolly in his preparations. His armourer had been diligently working to create an outstanding suit which he looked forward to showing off. He had recently acquired a new stallion – an enormous horse of Belgian breeding, which Henry and Carew tested in the riding rings near the stables. By then, as the day of the joust approached, Henry had become almost giddy with excitement.

For my part, I planned to remain indoors with my ladies, having no interest in watching the spectacle.

As we worked, we enjoyed the breeze which wafted through the open casement: the day being unusually warm. The number of spectators was great enough that we could detect the distant bellow of the crowd when one jouster took down another. We stitched and gossiped, and then I noticed that it had been some time since we had heard any noise at all from the tiltyard. At that exact moment, my Uncle Norfolk appeared at the door to the chamber, his face ashen.

"Milady!" his eyes sought mine. My heart stopped.

"What *is* it, Uncle? What, has something happened? TELL me!"

"Madame, 'tis your husband, the King! He was galloping toward his opponent …"

His usually resonant voice failed momentarily; then he regained control.

"… but as they closed, his horse lurched, slipped and fell - directly on top of His Majesty! The horse was injured, and they had to pull it off the King. Lady, the King did not move. I fear he is dead!"

My ladies gasped, and some started immediately to cry. I felt the blood drain from my head and became so faint I believed I would swoon. Anne Zouche rushed to me, removed the fabric and needle clutched frozen in my hand, and had me lie flat on a bench. She fanned me with a swatch of cloth and cried for someone to pour ale. I felt as if I would vomit from fear. Anne held my head forward and had me sip the weak brew, but it helped little. My hands trembled violently, and my thoughts were jumbled. Henry *dead*? It could not be! He was so hugely alive and robust mere minutes ago!

Eventually, feeling terribly unwell, the ladies and a steward helped me to my bedchamber where I lay dry-mouthed, shivering with fright and covered with a blanket while Bess Holland scurried to seek further information. It seemed hours that I waited, and while I did, all I was able to think of was what I would ever do should Henry be gone? What if his death was confirmed and I now should bear him a son? The cruelty of that possibility caused me to weep. I prayed that somehow a mistake had been made, and he still lived.

When I thought I could bear it no longer, Bess returned with my blessed brother. I gazed at him wild-eyed. "George, tell me the truth - what has happened to Henry?"

George sat on the edge of the bed and took my ice-cold hand in his. "Anne, he lives. Thank God Almighty, he has been restored to us!"

With a little cry, I sat up and George hugged me close while I sobbed with a mix of fright and relief. When I, at last, could compose myself, he told me that the Henry's huge steed had taken a heavy fall after losing its footing and that my dearest had been trapped beneath it. But even when the horse was lifted, a Herculean task which required eight men, the King had remained pale and unmoving. When he did not respond to being called - and because, due to his armour, no one could tell if he still drew breath - it was first assumed that he had perished. It took many more men to carry him to his chamber on a strong litter, whence he was laid upon the bed. With great difficulty, his armour was removed, yet *still* he did not wake!

Only once his breastplate could be removed did his doctor listen to his chest and declare that the King still breathed. Those in attendance gave great thanks, but it was yet many minutes before Henry opened his eyes. He seemed not to know what had happened to him, George told me, but he was now resting, attended by several doctors administering many potent remedies: all known to be the most efficacious available in the Kingdom, and because of their skilled interventions, Dr Butts felt that the King would recover.

My prayers of thanksgiving were fervent: my relief immeasurable.

But I felt very unwell.

I did not see my husband for several days after his fall. He convalesced in his privy chambers with the assistance of Henry Norreys and his doctors. Only eventually was I given a report that his strength was returning and that he would be hale once again. In the meantime, I too kept to my chambers, resting and taking little activity. Something was not right. I felt unusually tired and drawn. I had no appetite. My ladies fussed over me. What I did not tell them - what, in fact, I was reluctant to admit even unto myself - was a dawning awareness that the infant in my womb, once again, had ceased moving.

I felt as if I floated outside my body. Looking back, I believe my heart was not able to grasp such a bitter possibility, my mind being shrouded in such a fog of confusion. This was how I fought for survival in the face of such a dreadful truth. Until that truth, itself, became inescapable.

Just five days after Henry's accident, I began to bleed. The midwife was called and quietly and quickly I was delivered of an infant so small it was as yet only partially formed. Such a tiny, defenseless soul! I did not look upon it, but brave Nan Cobham, who was with me as ever, told me how it seemed as if it would have been a healthy child, had it lived and grown in my womb as it was supposed to.

Through my sorrow, I posed the question which had to be asked. She hung her head, and I saw her tears glint in the candlelight as she answered.

"It was a male child, my dearest Madame."

Whitehall
Eastertide 1536

THERE WAS NOTHING to do but recover.

I had no other choice.

I could hardly lie in melancholy on my bed until I died there while my ladies anguished for me. It was bad enough they crept about like sad mice, pulling handkerchiefs from their girdles to mop quietly shed tears. I watched them for some days until finally calling them together.

"My ladies, you are dear to me beyond words. Truly, I know not what I would do without every one of you. Your distress is a comfort to me because it means I am loved, and love is the salve that heals all wounds. But I want you all to know this - although I sorrow deeply for my poor unborn child, I will survive this tragedy. Already I am feeling increasingly well. Every day I regain strength, so much so that I can tell you I *will* conceive again, and that it will be soon. And this time it will surely be the son the King and I both long for. Weep for me no longer for I have deep faith in God, and truly believe He will grant this to me, and to our noble and much-loved monarch. So, please, dry your tears: let us put smiles on our faces and make ready for the Lenten season, and for Easter. Meanwhile, I ask you to pray for me and my petition, while I, in turn, will pray for each and every one of you."

With just a few more sniffles, they gathered themselves and went about their business. It had helped me, too, giving that speech.

I, myself, had even started to believe what I'd just said to them.

More than a week had passed before I saw Henry while, in the interim, I both craved the comfort of his presence and dreaded the sight of him. After all, I had failed my King yet again. Failed just like his first wife, who now lay dead and mouldering. But there was no putting it off further. He entered my chamber in complete privacy one morning in the middle of February as I sat awaiting him in great trepidation. He crossed the room and heavily lowered himself into a chair facing me while I, for my part, felt the sweated palms of my hands slide from the arms of my seat. We gazed at each other, and I was struck speechless. When I peered into his face, a countenance so familiar to me I knew it better than my own, it did not belong to the man I knew and loved. I was so bewildered I swallowed convulsively, whereupon my words stuck in my throat. The more I gazed at him, the less recognizable he seemed! What had happened? His return stare was cold in a way I had never – not *once* in all the time I had known him – encountered. It was as if he knew me not at all, either.

"Henry...?" I began, though not at all sure of what next to say.

He stopped me with a curt retort. "I see, Madame, that neither you nor God will give me a male child."

"That is not *true*, Henry! We have conceived three children in three years! You must surely realize that our baby was lost only due to my great shock at hearing about your accident." I fought desperately to gather myself before continuing, "Husband, I feared you were *dead*! And I could not have borne that anguish.

You have said it yourself - we can again conceive, and this time it *will* be a boy. I … I shall take great care of my health. You will see!"

He stared deep into my soul with those cold, glassy, alien eyes, all the while with that peculiar look on his face. It gave me a chill such as I had never before experienced.

With nary another word, he scraped his chair back, stood, and left the room.

Greenwich
April 1536

FOR DAYS HE avoided me, leaving the disconcerting feeling that my once greatly beloved husband was no longer the man I had known. I made mention of it to no one, but it seemed that hurtful news was the order of the day when, shortly after that, I was hesitantly informed by my very dear Nan Zouche that Henry had been seen with Mistress Jane Seymour, her arms wound about his neck and her bottom perched upon his lap. At first, my fury threatened to take over, and I was ready to find her, slap her face, then send the ugly wench packing back home, never to return to court. But Nan restrained me, wisely counselling that if I were so to do, it might well give the King all that much more cause to defy me and pursue my rival even more avidly. She convinced me, with great difficulty, to allow any potential assignation to run its course.

Most reluctantly I agreed, though I could not look upon the harlot, and kept her as far from me as possible.

But that was not the end of my travails. I then discovered that Cromwell had been diverting revenue which had been gleaned from monastery closures to an account of indeterminate nature: one which he had taken complete control of. It meant he had purposely contravened the instructions I had given him when we'd discussed this matter on numerous occasions. And of even greater concern: I was certain he had garnered Henry's complete agreement.

I decided to fight the battle in a way other than by confrontation.

I met with John Skypp, one of my three chaplains, and my almoner, who was to assist me in the distribution of aid to the needy. It was arranged that Skypp would give the sermon on the Sunday before Easter, the Passion service, at which the entire court would be in attendance, to include Master Cromwell. I outlined for Master Skypp what I wished him to convey, and left him to what he did best – create an eloquent sermon.

On Sunday 2 April, every stall in the Chapel Royal was filled. As soon as Skypp stood to deliver his homily, he had the full attention of the congregation. He began, cleverly using the allegory of scripture, to accuse the high and mighty of the court as promoters of false intent simply to please the King, and to advance their personal interests. He went on to relay an Old Testament tale: the story of Esther. Skillfully weaving this before the congregants, he drew a very obvious comparison to Thomas Cromwell - he being the Deceiver - while alluding to me, the noble Queen, as Esther: the representative of Good who was ignored, but who triumphed in the end. He summarized by making it clear to all that Cromwell's intentions, backed by members of Parliament, was to enrich themselves with the money they collected, and not to do good throughout the land as intended.

There arose very audible discord within the chapel, and, once the service had concluded, the courtiers and their wives filed out while whispering intently behind their hands. It was clear Skypp's sermon had had quite an impact.

It was not long after that that I was approached by Cromwell, his features rigid with annoyance. When he addressed me, it was only in short, clipped sentences. Within the confines of propriety which he was bound to obey, he let me know in no uncertain terms that he had been humiliated by Skypp's sermon; that he held me accountable, and that I was completely wrong in my assessment. He ended by stating that he no longer held any trust for me.

I said, "Thomas! Your statements are unkind."

Most sharply he replied, "No Madame. I am merely direct!"

… and with that, our meeting concluded.

But the rising tide of bad news did not.

It was during that very week - Easter week - that I discovered Henry had appointed Edward Seymour, the despicable Jane's brother, to his Privy Chamber. This knowledge, too, made me extremely unhappy. But I held no recourse.

On Good Friday, Henry and I attended mass during which I performed the Queen's tradition of washing and presenting the blessed crampe-rings, after creeping to the cross. And on Easter Sunday, we attended mass with Elizabeth, sitting next to one another in the Chapel, and then processed to the grand banquet held in the Great Hall as was the custom every year. Our interactions were awkward, though. There was no closeness between us. And my heart ached because of it.

Early in the week after Easter, I attended an early service with Henry. I felt buoyant that morning because, upon greeting my husband, his demeanor had considerably warmed toward me, and he seemed to have lost that strange and unaccustomed look. Perhaps there might be a *rapprochement* between us, after all? I could only pray so. To encourage our good relations, I was cheerful and very accommodating indeed to him.

As we walked to our pew, I passed Ambassador Chapuys. I turned to him, gave him a cordial smile and nodded in greeting. It would have been appropriate had he kissed my hand then, but pointedly he did not. However, I refused to allow his rude conduct to ruin what had been an exceptionally good start to the day.

Mass concluded, we returned to the presence chamber and dined with George and two other French ambassadors. I thought it strange that Ambassador Chapuys was not present, but, curiously, as soon as dinner was ended, and I stood to depart, he miraculously appeared. I noticed that Henry motioned for Chapuys to join him at one side of the chamber for discussion. I also espied Cromwell, nervously pacing at the opposite end of the room. He kept glancing at Chapuys, and it seemed quite obvious to me that they were involved in some collusion which was not going as planned. It struck me as exceedingly strange and gave me yet more reason to mistrust entirely Secretary Cromwell.

Later, George told me that, at the conclusion of Chapuys' audience with the King, Cromwell had been summoned and, as he and the King conversed, their discourse became heated. George said that discussion soon escalated into an argument, and Cromwell had to step out, shaking with ire. Through further, discreet investigation, George found that, in part, the argument had concerned Chapuys' continuing and adamant refusal to recognize me as Queen.

So I had been right in my suspicions, then. Cromwell *had* turned against me, and in some underhanded way was aligning himself with Eustace Chapuys: long my enemy!

At this stark realization, my blood ran like cold water. This was no child's game. It was now an open rivalry, and it was deadly serious. I had no choice now but to try and convince Henry that his dedicated servant Cromwell was a sneak and a plotter.

But how to go about this? I hoped to build upon the good will I had shared with Henry on that Easter Tuesday. In this way, I might shore up our relationship, and also convince him that he must be wary of Cromwell and his nefarious intentions. I pondered my approach. And what better way to restore normalcy than to affect merriment, I thought? So that was what I set out to do, in the hope of settling the uneasiness of recent months. As in the past, I held evening *soirées* in my chambers, including members of Henry's close retinue - always taking great care to invite him, of course. Most often we played cards or entertained ourselves with music and dance. I had taken a liking to the young musician Mark Smeaton, who had played lute for Henry and me on a number of occasions. I found him equally able to play lilting tunes which were perfect for dancing. My ladies enjoyed themselves on these evenings, and I deliberately promoted an air of relaxed pleasure. I will readily admit that after the withdrawal of Henry's approval, I had suffered greatly, and it had caused me to lose confidence. Suddenly I found myself craving the confirmation that men still found me attractive, and that my skill at courtly flirtation had not abated.

It was in this setting toward the end of April, on an evening when His Grace the King was not in attendance, that I found myself somewhat unwillingly engaged in discussion with Henry Norreys. Norreys had had too much to drink and proved loud and bawdy from the onset. His betrothed, Madge Shelton, was not present, which inhibited him even less: and when he took me aside to converse, he stood too close. I had my back to a corner, and as he leaned in, I asked him quite pointedly when, if ever, he intended to marry Mistress Shelton? He laughed dismissively before moving even closer. By then I was becoming seriously alarmed but didn't intend to show it, so I challenged him directly, asking if he were not man enough to take a wife?

I was confounded by his reply, for he said that he had delayed his marriage in the event, though unlikely, that the King would cease to exist, and then *he* might have me! I was struck silent, because the risky nature of his comment was astounding beyond belief, and the lecherous implication of his rude behavior entirely unacceptable. I wished to reach out and slap him, but that was impossible, so under my breath so as not to be overheard, I hissed, "How *DARE* you, Henry Norreys! You presume to fill a dead man's shoes with *ME*? While the dead man you speak of is your *King*? You best rethink your offensive and traitorous words! I demand that you leave my chamber immediately."

He stepped back, abashed, and lurched toward the door. By this time, others who had been in earshot stared aghast at what had just taken place. I thought it best to say no more about the unpleasant incident.

The next day, however, it became apparent that someone had informed Henry – if not the exact words of that distressing confrontation, certainly the scenario of Norreys leaning in as if to kiss me had been recounted with, no doubt, considerable relish!

Henry was *furious.* He confronted me at dinner - but stalked off before I had any chance to explain. This was a setback I neither wanted nor needed, so I hurried to the nursery and gathered Elizabeth. Holding her in my arms, I carried her to his Privy Chambers and found him stalking agitatedly to and fro. Calling to him, I approached and waved away the esquires who were in attendance. Henry stared fixedly through the window, refusing to face me as I implored him to hear me and understand that I had had no part in soliciting Norreys' highly inappropriate actions.

For most of that time I spoke while his back was to me until, at last, he whirled around and spat that he could no longer TRUST me! That I had deceived him time after time and had not kept my promises to him. How could he ever feel hopeful about us again, he snarled? He did not know.

I had to make him understand, and so I talked and talked until I was hoarse and Elizabeth grew restless in my arms. I believe at the end he was slightly mollified, but I feared it was not to be the same between us. Perhaps ever again.

There were loyal friends who provided me with dire inside information. They warned that there were enemies including Nicholas Carew, my own uncle Norfolk and the vindictive Seymours, all followers of the Pope and the Roman Church, who conspired to capitalize upon the distance which had become apparent between Henry and myself in order to supplant me, and place the Catholic princess, Mary, firmly back in the line of succession. In their view, if I were to be abandoned by Henry and supplanted by a new queen, it would offer the ideal opportunity to restore the one true church in England. It just might also pave the way for the powerful rise of a new familial dynasty.

And who did they want as *their* new Queen?

Jane Seymour, of course.

Tower of London
May 1536

I WAS NO STRANGER to threat or confrontation. This time, though, I had not only myself to think of. So, feeling very uneasy following the distressingly strange setting of that last week in April, I sought out Matthew Parker, another of my chaplains whom I held in high regard. Parker was a learned and kindly man, and I had always found his perspective to be heartening.

Quite baldly, I asked Matthew, with great earnestness, that should anything happen to me – were I to be deposed, for example - would he provide protection for Princess Elizabeth? He was clearly taken aback by the question, and seemed quite ill at ease with it, but when I insisted, he agreed and gave me his word that he would be her benefactor. His commitment allowed me some relief.

My moods veered wildly from fear and despair to hope that my marriage with Henry might still be saved and, in fact, revived. Then I learned that a visit to Calais was in the offing and that I was to go with Henry. Delighted, and indeed surprised, I suddenly felt I could breathe freely again and immediately began to prepare for what I hoped would be this chance to renew fully our broken relationship. Surely this was a very positive indication that he was willing to consider renewing his faith in me: in *us*. After all, we had always been at our closest during our travels. Undoubtedly this diversion was just what we desperately required.

Feeling jubilant for a change, I looked forward to May Day; always a lighthearted celebration. Better still, the very next morning, 2 May, Henry and I and our company of travellers were scheduled to depart for Rochester on the first leg of our journey to Calais.

This year the May Day revels were to be marked by a jousting tourney. I took my place in the *berfrois* with the ladies to watch the competition from the seats closest to the riders and near to the King and his men.

Henry, thankfully, was not competing in this event, and because I did not have to watch and worry about his safety, I felt a greater sense of calm than I had in some days. We cheered and waved to the crowd and competitors, and I was enjoying myself, so I did not take notice immediately when a messenger arrived to speak privately in the King's ear. Maggie, sitting next to me, nudged my arm, however, and I looked up in time to see Henry and several of his courtiers stand and hurriedly abandon their seats. I caught only a glimpse of Henry's expression – it was not reassuring: set hard with displeasure.

They disappeared from view while the rest of the court present were left whispering and wondering what had occurred to cause the King to leave in such haste. Maggie and I exchanged glances of concern: Henry had not looked my way; he had not passed me a message explaining his departure – I had no idea where he had gone and was bewildered. Something did not feel right.

Mind in a whirl I stayed for the remainder of the tournament, yet comprehended little of its outcomes. But how could I? As each moment passed my instincts screamed ever louder that something was terribly amiss. The evening was spent in my chambers, alone. I had no appetite, ate little, and slept even less.

Henry did not make a return appearance in the following day's tennis matches. I had planned to attend, and so I did: sitting in the stands with several ladies, pretending – but not knowing - who played or who won. At its conclusion, as I left my seat, I was met by a royal messenger. He very stiffly told me that I was to present myself to the Privy Council of the King, by the King's orders, immediately.

My heart pounded, and a cold sweat broke out on my forehead. A guard accompanied me to the council chamber. Upon entering I saw three men - the Duke of Norfolk, the brother of my beloved mother, Sir William FitzWilliam, and Sir William Paulet - awaiting me, their countenances most solemn.

I felt the bile rise in my throat but summoned all my courage, took a deep breath, and greeted coldly, "Good day, gentlemen. Please explain what purpose have you to summon me in such a way?"

Their response was beyond anything even a madwoman could have anticipated.

Norfolk - my own *uncle* - replied, "Madame, we are here to inform you that you are charged with evil behavior. You are accused of having intimate relations with several men, including the musician Mark Smeaton and the Groom of the Stool, Sir Henry Norreys. What say you to these charges?"

I stood unblinkingly while I tried to understand what had just been said. How could this possibly be? My hand flew to my throat, willing it to speak. My voice, thankfully, remained strong despite my inner terror.

"Sirs, you make of me accusations which are of the most preposterous and repugnant nature. In no way, and at no time, did I *ever* conduct myself but with the utmost respect and love toward my husband, the King. *Never* have I strayed – neither in thought nor in deed! Release me immediately!"

Norfolk made little attempt to conceal a smug smile.

"Nay, we shall not, Madame. You have already been fully implicated. Two of the men named in this vile scheme have already admitted their guilt, the fact of which His Grace the King has been informed. You will not be released: instead, you will only be permitted to return to your chambers, where you will be watched."

Ashen-faced I was escorted in stony silence by the three nobles to my Privy Chamber, where they left me under the eyes of a royal guard. Laughably, the servants had provided lavish food and drink for my repast - indeed, a dinner fit for a queen! - but I touched nothing and paced about the room doing my best to control my horror. Before very long had passed, Norfolk returned, along with a group of the King's esquires, with a writ – the warrant for my arrest!

They were to take me to the Tower ...

Here, the turmoil of those hours – nay, day after endless day – becomes so distressing that it is difficult to maintain a concise telling of what happened. My mind swirled incessantly – sometimes it remained sharp, well-functioning: at others I might well have been that madwoman, indeed. Throughout it all, I endeavored to maintain my dignity although I could never, for one blessed moment, rid my thoughts of those poor men who had been accused – so unjustly … so falsely! - just to serve the purpose of tumbling me from the throne.

With pathetically few belongings thrown hastily together in a leather satchel, I was placed on a barge and rowed to the Tower. I remember little of that journey other than how chilled I became, with the wind-torn sheets of spray adding to my misery. Finally, we disembarked, and I was met in the Tower grounds by Sir William Kingston – a man whom I had always been friendly with: the man who had assisted me so pleasantly during my coronation, and whose wife was one of my ladies in waiting. His face was sombre, and I sensed his pity.

Struggling to keep my composure, I asked, "Mister Kingston, shall I go into a dungeon?"

Gently he placed his hand on my arm, "No Madame, you will go to the lodging you lay in at your coronation."

His eyes were kind, and I just broke down at that small mercy. I cried, and through my tears and near hysteria, reflected, "It is too good for me!" after which we began walking toward the Queen's apartments. I called out, "Jesu, have mercy on me!"

So distraught did I become that they had to stop momentarily so I could gather myself.

When we arrived at the Queen's chambers, I feverishly stalked the rooms while Kingston remained, awkward and silent. I then found, to my even greater discomfiture, that I was to be served by Mary Scrope, Lady Kingston, and two other ladies with whom I had never been close ... an aunt, Elizabeth Boleyn, and Lady Shelton, Madge's mother. I also had at my service Margaret Stonor, and a former lady in waiting who had pretended to be my ally but whom I had always suspected was not - Margaret Dymoke, Lady Coffin.

All of these women had questionable allegiances, as I was well aware. Even more so when I discovered they had been appointed to their duty by Master Secretary Cromwell himself – who had instructed them to record anything, and everything, I did and said.

That evening, as I sat at the table with Constable Kingston, I still could not eat, and so I talked instead. I told him with no uncertainty that I was completely clear from the company of any man except my husband. I asked him where my father was since he had not been in the tiltyard – whereupon Kingston replied he had seen him earlier in the day, at court. I thought then of my lady mother, and that recall alone was almost enough to bring me to my knees.

Then an abhorrent concern came to me, and I asked tremulously, "... and Master Kingston, where is my sweet brother? Please tell me?"

Kingston hesitated a moment, then informed me that he had left George at York Place earlier in the day. I was relieved, but not entirely reassured.

After a short period of most agonizing silence, during which I again lost control and began weeping, I found myself musing aloud how Norreys, who was now imprisoned in the Tower as well, had unwittingly implicated me in such an awful plot – all stemming, I realized, from his drunken, foolhardy behavior that night in my chambers. And then, of all unlikely alleged lovers, there was poor young Mark Smeaton? How *utterly* absurd – that I would make the King a fool for a poor, uneducated and unworldly musician!

Finally, I pleaded, "Mr Kingston, pray tell me, will I die without justice?"

I asked, yet I knew …

Gently he responded. "Madame, even the poorest of subjects hath justice."

Really, I thought?

It was laughable.

In the several days which followed my arrest, I made a mighty effort to balance myself. At times, I experienced a modicum of peace – usually when deep in prayer; but mostly because the pain of my circumstance was nigh to overwhelming, made yet more excruciating when I was told by Kingston that, along with Smeaton and Norreys, Sir Frances Weston and poor William Brereton had *also* been accused of adultery with me, and were now imprisoned.

God's tears - they were Henry's closest *friends*!

It was horrifying. Did even my enemies think I had no respectability at *all*? Had they not known me since I was first at court: a girl of 22 years? Had I ever been reputed to be morally loose in my behavior?

But in moments of clarity I came to know what it was about. All too well. I would be conveniently removed, making way for another Queen, another faction – another wife more malleable. More fertile. And I knew who was behind the stratagem. For uncharacteristically he made no appearance; instead visits to receive Kingston's reports were handled either through his secretary, Sadler, or in an even more cowardly manner – secretively - so I would be denied any chance to confront him in person.

Thomas Cromwell.

Only finally did Master Kingston muster courage enough to tell me what I believe I already anticipated - that my brother George, my blood, my dearest friend and constant defender, had been arrested after being accused of knowing me, his sister, carnally. When I heard of this, I ran for a basin and heaved and heaved until my insides had no more to relinquish.

Therefore, my fate was predestined, and brutally clear. Yes, there would be a trial. Would it exonerate me? Of course not. How foolish I would have been to have harboured that vain hope for even a second. I was well aware of how these situations were contrived. I was considered a traitor, and therefore, I would die, and along with me five innocent men - Smeaton, Weston, Norreys, Brereton, and my beloved sibling, George Boleyn. Surely not even God would forgive my accusers for what they intended to do.

And what about Henry? Was my sense of betrayal worse than his must have been when persuaded of these odious lies? I knew very well that he was a man whose need for absolute loyalty was almost childlike. I had watched him be hurt before, only to strike back without mercy upon even the slightest suspicion that he had been forsaken. So, I could well imagine his pain and resentment, his great willingness to believe even the most outrageous of untruths, when informed that he had been cuckolded beneath his very roof, and by his best friends - even by his own brother-in-law! His frenzy would have been uncontrollable.

But then, as I had been the idealized object of his veneration for so long, and we had loved so deeply – that could not be denied – I wondered, if only I were able to see him, to *speak* with him, might I just be able to convince him that he was being deceived into believing such accusations?

So I insisted upon an audience with the King. That demand, passed through Kingston, to Ralph Sadler, Cromwell's devoted personal assistant, and thence to Cromwell – the master conspirator - was flatly and quickly denied. I doubted whether Henry was even consulted, the decision being made for him.

Left with no recourse, I asked if I might at least compose a letter to my husband and have it passed to him. Surely this could not be denied me? After all, I was imprisoned but not convicted. And I *was* still Queen.

To my surprise, I was told by Kingston- although undoubtedly the instruction came from Cromwell - that I would be permitted to dictate a short letter, but that it would be scribed for me and then sent on to the King.

Left with no alternative, I agreed.

I knew precisely what I wished to say to Henry. It was not to be a letter from an anguished prisoner begging for her life from her King. No – instead it would contain the words of a dearly beloved wife to her cherished husband. For that is what I still considered us to be.

The writing of the letter, on 6 May, four days into my imprisonment, proved a sombre, but momentous event. Constable Kingston was present, along with other witnesses: Lady Boleyn, Lady Coffin, Lady Kingston, and the scribe, Master Ralph Sadler - of course, it had to be he: Cromwell having sent his most devoted henchman to record my words.

I sighed. So be it, they would each hear what I knew, in my heart, to be the last words I would ever convey to the man who had been my life's love, my King, and my second self.

As Sadler sat with quill poised, I began:

> *"Sir, your Grace's displeasure, and my Imprisonment are Things so strange unto me, as what to Write, or what to Excuse, I am altogether ignorant; whereas you sent unto me (willing me to confess a Truth, and so obtain your Favour) by such a one, whom you know to be my ancient and professed Enemy; I no sooner received the Message by him, than I rightly conceived your Meaning; and if, as you say, confessing Truth indeed may procure my safety, I shall with all Willingness and Duty perform your Command.*

But let not your Grace ever imagine that your poor Wife will ever be brought to acknowledge a Fault, where not so much as Thought thereof proceeded. And to speak a truth, never Prince had Wife more Loyal in all Duty, and in all true Affection, than you have found in Anne Boleyn, with which Name and Place could willingly have contented my self, as if God, and your Grace's Pleasure had been so pleased. Neither did I at any time so far forge my self in my Exaltation, or received Queenship, but that I always looked for such an Alteration as now I find; for the ground of my preferment being on no surer Foundation than your Grace's Fancy, the least Alteration, I knew, was fit and sufficient to draw that Fancy to some other subject.

You have chosen me, from a low Estate, to be your Queen and Companion, far beyond my Desert or Desire. If then you found me worthy of such Honour, Good your Grace, let not any light Fancy, or bad Counsel of mine Enemies, withdraw your Princely Favour from me; neither let that Stain, that unworthy Stain of a Disloyal Heart towards your good Grace, ever cast so foul a Blot on your most Dutiful Wife, and the Infant Princess your Daughter:

Try me, good King, but let me have a Lawful Trial, and let not my sworn Enemies sit as my Accusers and Judges; yes, let me receive an open Trial, for my Truth shall fear no open shame; then shall you see, either mine Innocency cleared, your Suspicion and Conscience satisfied, the Ignominy and Slander of the World stopped, or my Guilt openly declared. So that whatsoever God or you may determine of me, your Grace may be freed from an open Censure; and mine Offence being so lawfully proved, your Grace is at liberty, both before God and Man, not only to execute worthy Punishment on me as an unlawful Wife, but to follow your Affection already settled on that party, for whose sake I am now as I am, whose Name I could some good while since have pointed unto: Your Grace being not ignorant of my Suspicion therein.

But if you have already determined of me, and that not only my Death, but an Infamous Slander must bring you the enjoying of your desired Happiness; then I desire of God, that he will pardon your great Sin therein, and likewise mine Enemies, the Instruments thereof; that he will not call you to a strict Account for your unprincely and cruel usage of me, at his General Judgement-Seat, where both you and my self must shortly appear, and in whose Judgement, I doubt not, (whatsoever the World may think of me) mine Innocence shall be openly known, and sufficiently cleared.

My last and only Request shall be, That my self may only bear the Burthen of your Grace's Displeasure, and that it may not touch the Innocent Souls of those poor Gentlemen, who (as I understand) are likewise in strait Imprisonment for my sake. If ever I have found favour in your Sight; if ever the Name of Anne Boleyn hath been pleasing to your Ears, then let me obtain this Request; and I will so leave to trouble your Grace any further, with mine earnest Prayers to the Trinity to have your Grace in his good keeping, and to direct you in all your Actions.

Your most Loyal and ever Faithful Wife, Anne Bullen

From my doleful Prison the Tower, this 6th of May."

Sadler frowned uncertainly at that, then asked did I not wish the signatory to read, '*Anne the Queen*' instead? Emphatically I said no. I wanted Henry to hear the words of the woman he met, fell in love with, pursued and married just as she had been then … *Anne Bullen*.

Sadler shrugged, shook the sand pot, briefly showed me the resulting page, then meticulously rolled it for transport to his master. I asked him when he believed it might be delivered to the King. His gaze would not meet mine as he replied, "I believe soonest, Madame. I will ensure that Mister Cromwell receives it today and am certain he will deliver it to the King with haste."

I did not share his assurance. In fact, I doubted whether Henry's eyes would ever light upon my words. I was consoled only by the knowledge that at least they *were* committed to paper, and perhaps if he did not witness them today, or tomorrow, or months or even years from now, they would remain as a testament to my innocence and, more importantly, to my abiding love for him.

After Sadler had departed, I slumped, deeply lost in thought. The ghosts of those who had fallen victim to deception and the perjury of others did a macabre dance before my closed eyes … Thomas More, John Fisher, the Carthusian monks, the crazy Nun of Kent, and even Katherine of Aragon. And now I, too, would number amongst them, for I had no illusion about my fate.

Weeping copiously at the thought of leaving her, I prayed fervently that God would care for my sweet daughter Elizabeth, allow her to grow and reach womanhood, and fulfill her bright promise.

Eventually, I opened my Bible and sought one of my favourite passages.

I read. And was comforted:

'Be sure that the Lord is God: it is he that hath made us, and not we ourselves: we are his people and the sheep of his pasture.

O go your way into his gates with thanksgiving, and into his courts with praise: be thankful unto him, and speak good of His name.

For the Lord is gracious, his mercy everlasting and his truth endures forever ...'

Finis

Epilogue and Afterword

WHEN ANNE CAUGHT a glimpse of Henry hurriedly departing the jousting tournament on May Day, 1536, she had no way of knowing it was the last time she would ever see him. During the weeks leading to that date, murmurings had abounded predicting an ill-fated end to her marriage. Anne must nevertheless have been shocked and utterly horrified when, on the following morning, she was charged with adultery, and hence high treason. Well-documented accounts of her attempts to maintain her presence of mind throughout her imprisonment and trial are poignant.

Her friend and confessor Thomas Cranmer, Archbishop of Canterbury, was equally aghast when informed of Anne's arrest, and the substance of the charges levelled against her. Even though he had been denied an audience with the King, he still attempted to argue for Anne's innocence and release in a letter which still exists today. Again, Cranmer's intervention proved unsuccessful, although the Archbishop was permitted to visit her in the Tower and to hear her confession – one in which she swore her innocence before God in advance of her impending demise.

On 15 May, a trial was held within the confines of the Tower to hear the cases for and against Anne and her brother, George. Separately they were indicted, and each responded to the charges, proclaiming their innocence with clear and cogent arguments but, compelling as those pleas may have been, both were found guilty and sentenced to death. Although their trials took place on the same day, consecutively, and in the same chamber, they were not permitted to see each other. Anne never encountered her brother again.

She was led back to her apartment then, to await beheading. Anne would certainly have been aware of the moment when her five implicated male companions, one being her beloved brother, were executed on Tower Hill on 17 May. She was not witness to their ends, but within the walls of her prison she mourned the loss of those innocent pawns: all falling victim to false accusations of having had a carnal association with her.

Anne was led to meet her death on Tower Green on 19 May 1536. In a short valedictory speech, she called for the people, '*always to pray to God for the King, for he was a good, gentle, gracious, and amiable prince.*' Then her head was sliced from her body: not by a traditional English axe but by a French executioner's sword. By all accounts, both parts were then placed inside a modest wooden box and interred in the adjacent Chapel of St Peter ad Vincula, where she rests today.

The letter which is dated 6 May, '*from my doleful prison in the Tower*', has been much discussed, written about, copied, and debated over the centuries. I have included its full text in my narrative because I believe it to be crucial to any study of the life of Anne Boleyn. In fact, I found it so compelling that I spent almost a year researching it exclusively. I published my findings and opinions in a book entitled *Anne Boleyn's Letter from the Tower*.

My investigation of that letter, linked with what I have come to know about Anne and her life, has led me to believe, with deep conviction, that the composition is indeed Anne's. I feel its content indicates Anne was not only very much aware of her impending doom but had also concluded that those written words would be the last she would express to her husband, and that, perhaps, they would exist in perpetuity as a final record of her sentiments. The fact that the handwriting is known not to be Anne's, but that the message is resoundingly commensurate with what we have come to know about Anne and her temperament, allows me to determine that the actual letter was transcribed for her - probably while closely overseen. I surmise that the architect of those restrictions was Thomas Cromwell: it being widely accepted, due to notations on later copies of the letter, that the original draft had been found hidden among Cromwell's private papers after his execution - also at the hands of his master, Henry VIII - four years later. I do not believe that Henry ever saw the letter which Anne had composed for him.

Anne's story is one of profound highs and lows: a key reason why we remain so enthralled with her *persona* and her life. Many accomplished biographers, historians, and novelists have documented the rise and fall of Anne Boleyn, but I wanted, in writing this two-book work, to explore Anne's relationship with Henry Tudor from the fictional viewpoint: narrated from her perspective. And on completing much thorough research before writing, I did come to believe firmly that Anne and Henry had, indeed, been truly in love: a well-matched pair – 'soul mates' in today's parlance. Clearly something went terribly wrong: a perfect storm of events and emotions ultimately leading to Anne's downfall. The exploration of that particular aspect of their lives has been undertaken by many antiquarians and historians, but in truth will never be satisfied, for we will never really know what went on in their minds and hearts.

In the creation of a novel which has at its basis significant historical fact, I referred to primary sources – contemporary to Anne and Henry's time – whenever they were available. In preparation for Book I, *Struck With the Dart of Love - Je Anne Boleyn*, I was permitted to study the original love letters which Henry wrote to Anne over a period of several years. That study fostered my belief that his adoration, at first hesitant and hopeful, soon was well returned. The evidence presented by his handwriting, his increasingly casual application of pen to paper and his familiarity with using terms of endearment all contribute to this conviction. I also viewed the *Book of Hours* in which Anne and Henry inscribed lovers' messages to each other. This, too, was a moving experience and informed my thinking greatly. For Book II, *Truth Endures - Je Anne Boleyn*, I viewed many documents held within the archives of the British Library including the letter which Anne wrote to Cardinal Wolsey in which she insisted upon a postscript added by Henry. I also viewed documents authored and signed by Thomas Cromwell, Thomas Cranmer, William Kingston and the scribe, Ralph Sadler, as well as very old editorial documents written by early antiquarians who have remarked upon the life events of Henry VIII and his second wife. The ability and the permission to view each and every document have been a blessing and an immeasurable advantage, and I am enormously appreciative to the staff at the British Library, and also to the officials at the Papal Library, where Henry's love letters are kept.

The people and places recounted in the two books are based on historical fact. The way in which the story unfolds - the characters' thinking and their reactions as events take place - is, of course, a work of fiction. Each book includes a cast of players who had a real part in Anne's life. Those strictly created by me include Anne's maids - Charity, followed by Lucy, Emma and Simonette - and the seamstress, Mistress Joan Clerke. Anne's documented deep friendship with the real person Margaret Wyatt, Lady Lee, is characterized in the novels by Anne's use of the affectionate nickname Maggie, although there are no records of Lady Lee being called by that name. It is widely believed, though, that Margaret accompanied Anne to the scaffold, fulfilling her fictional promise to remain Anne's stalwart companion until their death. Anne's greyhound - and we do know from primary documents that she had one - is, in my tale, called Jolie. Though many people believe her hound was named Urian, it seems clear from the writings that Anne's pet, and the one belonging to William Brereton's brother, Urian Brereton, did indeed get into some mischief together, thereby causing confusion regarding their names.

I have been unbelievably fortunate to have come to know and be supported by many truly wonderful people. To the authors and historians who have informed my work and inspired me, I offer my deepest regard and thanks. I would be remiss if I did not mention my indebtedness to the brilliant composer, Mr Trevor Morris. His radiant soundtrack for the TV series *The Tudors* has fuelled my imagination over and over again. And for the members of my beloved Tudor community – your friendship and encouragement mean everything: Claire Ridgway, Beth von Staats, Natalie Grueninger, Adrienne Dillard, Deb Hunter, Catherine Brooks, James Peacock, Sarah Bryson, Janet Wertman, Gina Clark, Philippa Vincent-Connolly, and Debbie Brown. I could not have crafted the scenes in which Anne, a great horsewoman, rode and hunted without knowledge and inspiration provided me by a dear friend, Patricia Schreck. To my friends and family who have allowed me to talk endlessly about Anne for many years, I thank you and love you: my mother Marie Corry, my sister Beth Corry, Maria Maneos, Donna Bolno, Terri Gasbarra, Bob Ketterlinus, Sue Wilson, Cathy Howell, Warren Miller ... you have all been crucial to my efforts.

It is difficult to find the words to thank sufficiently my wonderful, kind and generous editor who has provided me so much guidance and confidence over the years: Brian Callison. Thank you from the bottom of my heart. And Tim Ridgway, the CEO of my publisher MadeGlobal – you are simply marvellous: wise, gracious, considerate, and very skilled. I am delighted to have the chance to work with you.

To my husband Tom Vasoli, my most loving and capable proponent, critic and guide, whose patience and encouragement are without measure: thank you.

And to my daughter, to whom the book is dedicated ... you inspire me every day.

SOURCES

Contemporary Accounts

Brewer, J., ed., *Letters and Papers, Foreign and Domestic, of the Reign of Henry VIII,* Volume 4, 1875

Brown, R., *Calendar of State Papers*, Venice, 1867

Camden Miscellany XXX Vol 39 *William Latymer's Cronickille of Anne Bulleyne* , Offices of the Royal Historical Society, University College London, London 1990

Cotsgrave, R.,ed., *A Dictionarie of the French and English Tongues*, London: Adam Islip, 1611

Gairdner, J., ed., *Letters and Papers, Foreign and Domestic, of the Reign of Henry VIII*, Volumes 5 through 10, 1880 – 1887

Gayangos, P.ed., *Calendar of State Papers, Spain*, Vols. 3 and 4, 1873-1879

Grose, F. Esq and Astle, T. Esq., ed., *The Antiquarian Repertory: A Miscellaneous Assemblage of Topography, History, Customs and Manners,* London: Edward Jeffrey, 1809

Hall, E., *Chronicle Containing the History of England During the Reign of Henry the Fourth and the Succeeding Monarchs to the End of the Reign of Henry the Eighth,* London, 1809

Hinds, A., ed. *Calendar of State Papers and Manuscripts in the Archives and Collections of Milan* - 1385-1618, 1912

Mayhew, A. ,ed., *A Glossary of Tudor and Stuart Words*, London: Oxford Press, 1914

Nichols, J.G. ed., *Chronicle of Calais*, London: Camden Society, 1846

Nicolas, N.H. Esq. ed., *The Privy Purse Expences of Henry the Eighth*, London: Wm Pickering, 1828

Phillips, J., ed., *The Love Letters of Henry VIII to Anne Boleyn, With Notes*, Watchmaker Publishing, 2009

St Claire Byrne, M. ed., *The Lisle Letters , An Abridgement*, Chicago: University of Chicago Press, 1983

Wriothesley, Charles, *A Chronicle of England During the Reign of the Tudors*, London: Camden Society, 1875

Secondary sources

Carley, J., *The Books of King Henry and His Wives*, London: The British Library, 2004

Cherry, C. and Ridgway, C., *George Boleyn Tudor Poet, Courtier & Diplomat*, MadeGlobal Publishing 2014

Cressy, D., *Birth, Marriage, and Death – Ritual, Religion and the Life-Cycle in Tudor and Stuart England,* New York: Oxford University Press 1997

Drummond, J., and Wilbraham, A., *The Englishman's Food – A History of Five Centuries Of English Diet,* London: Readers Union, 1959

Emerson, K., www.kateemersonhistoricals.com/TudorWomenIndex.htm, 2008 – 2013

Fletcher, C., *Our Man in Rome, Henry VIII and his Italian Ambassador*, London: The Bodley Head, 2012

Fraser, A., *The Wives of Henry VIII*, New York: Vintage Books, 1994

Ives, Eric, *The Life and Death of Anne Boleyn 'The Most Happy'*, Blackwell Publishing, 2004

Jokinen, A., www.Luminarium.org, 1996

Morris, S. and Grueninger, N., *In the Footsteps of Anne Boleyn*, Amberley Publishing, 2013
Mikhaila, N. and Malcolm-Davies, J., *The Tudor Tailor – Reconstructing 16th century dress*, Hollywood: Costume and Fashion Press 2006
Ridgway, C. TheAnneBoleynFiles.com
Ridgway, C. TheTudorSociety.com
Ridgway, C., *Tudor Places of Great Britain*, MadeGlobal Publishing, 2015
Starkey, D., Six Wives, *The Queens of Henry VIII*, New York: HarperCollins, 2003
Thurley, S., *The Royal Palaces of Tudor England - Architecture and Court Life 1460 – 1547*, New Haven and London: Yale University Press, 1993
Weir, A., *The Six Wives of Henry VIII*, Grove Press, 2007

Sandra Vasoli, author of *Anne Boleyn's Letter from the Tower*, *Struck with the Dart of Love* and *Truth Endures*, earned a Bachelor's degree in English and biology from Villanova University before embarking on a thirty-five-year career in human resources for a large international company.

Having written essays, stories, and articles all her life, Vasoli was prompted by her overwhelming fascination with the Tudor dynasty to try her hand at writing both historical fiction and non-fiction. While researching what eventually became the *Je Anne Boleyn* series, Vasoli was granted unprecedented access to the Papal Library. There, she was able to read the original love letters from Henry VIII to Anne Boleyn—an event that contributed greatly to her research and writing.

Vasoli currently lives in Gwynedd Valley, Pennsylvania, with her husband and two greyhounds.

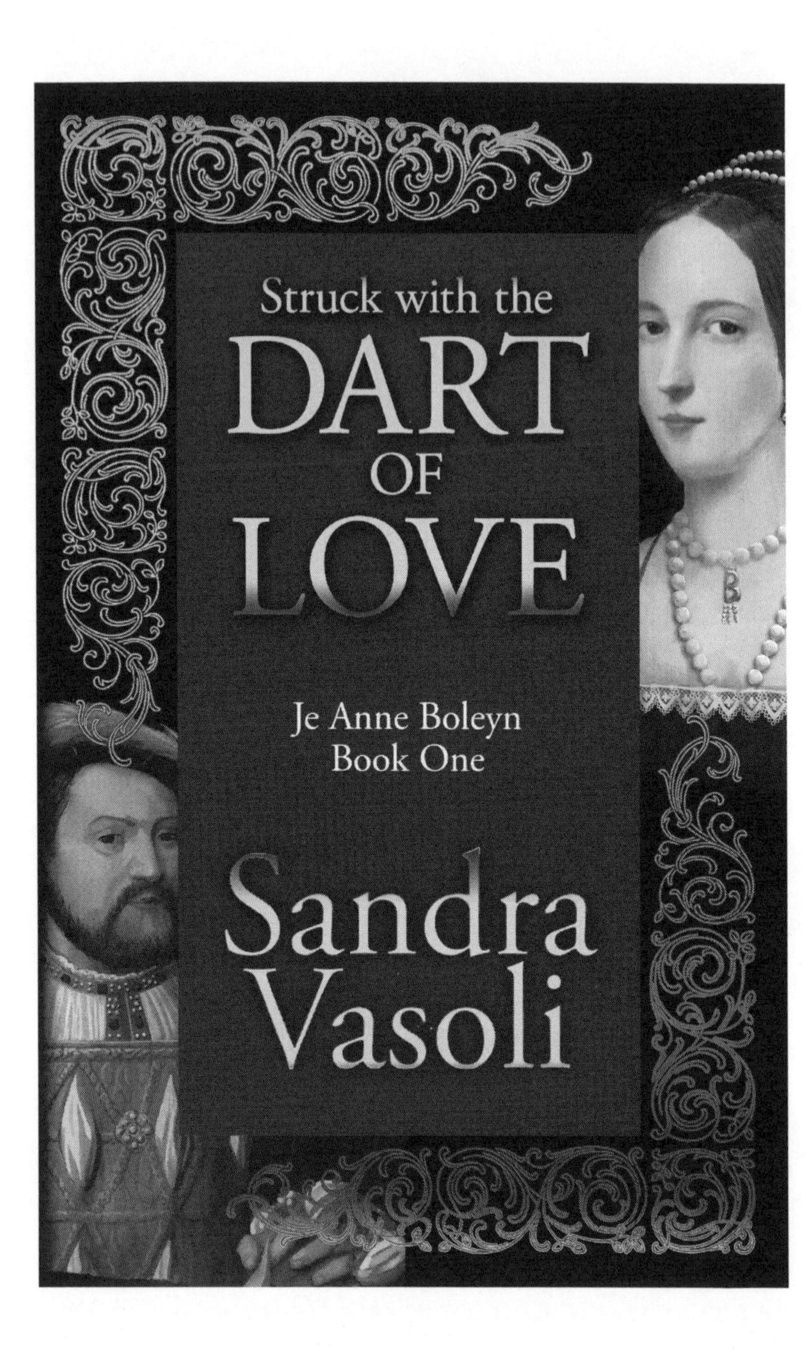
Struck with the
DART
OF
LOVE
Je Anne Boleyn
Book One
Sandra
Vasoli

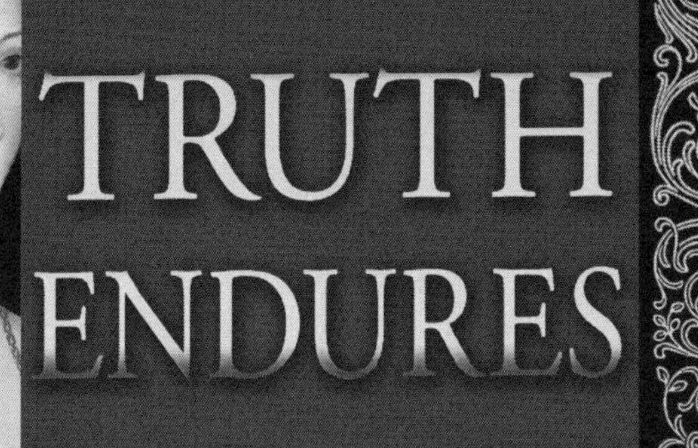

Je Anne Boleyn
Book Two

Sandra
Vasoli

Sandra Vasoli

ISBN: 978-84-943721-5-5

"Sir, Your Grace's Displeasure and my Imprisonment are Things so strange unto me, as what to Write, or what to Excuse, I am altogether ignorant."

Thus opens a burned fragment of a letter dated 6 May 1536 and signed "Anne Boleyn", a letter in which the imprisoned queen fervently proclaims her innocence to her husband, King Henry VIII.

ISBN: 978-84-944574-9-4

Anne Boleyn is accused of adultery and imprisoned in the Tower. The very next day she is due to be executed at the hand of a swordsman. Nothing can change the tragic outcome. England will have a new queen before the month is out. And yet...

What if events conspired against Henry VIII and his plans to take a new wife? What if there were things that even Thomas Cromwell couldn't control, things which would make it impossible for history to go to plan?

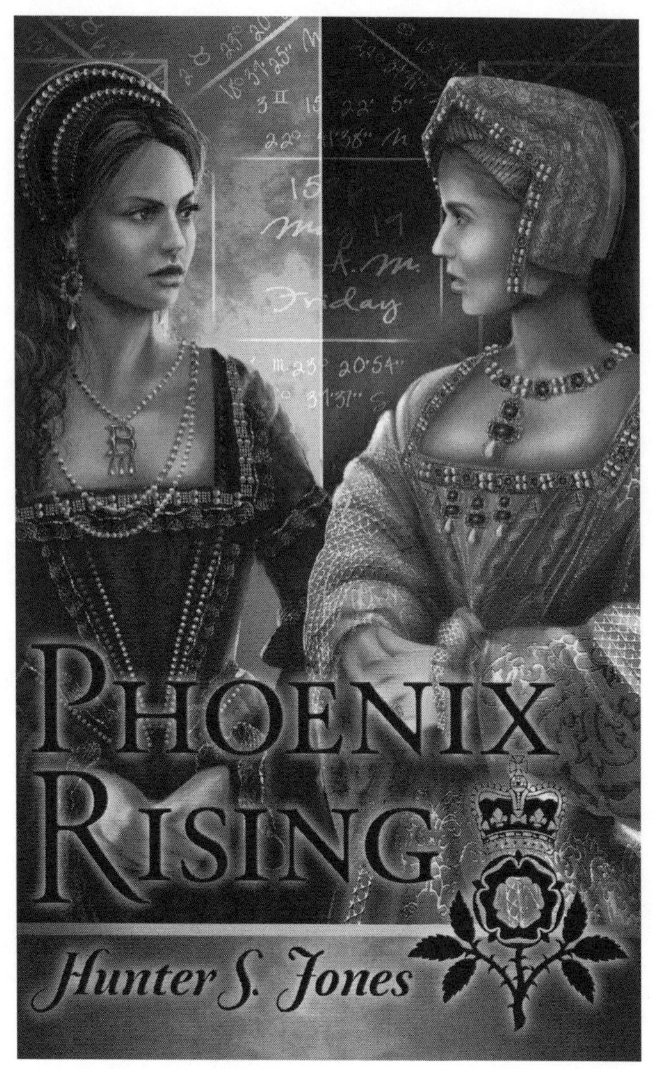

ISBN: 978-84-943721-4-8

The last hour of Anne Boleyn's life...

Court intrigue, revenge and all the secrets of the last hour are revealed as one queen falls and another rises to take her place on destiny's stage.

A young Anne Boleyn arrives at the court of King Henry VIII. She is to be presented at the Shrovetide pageant, le Château Vert. The young and ambitious Anne has no idea that a chance encounter before the pageant will lead to her capturing the heart of the king. What begins as a distraction becomes his obsession and leads to her destruction.

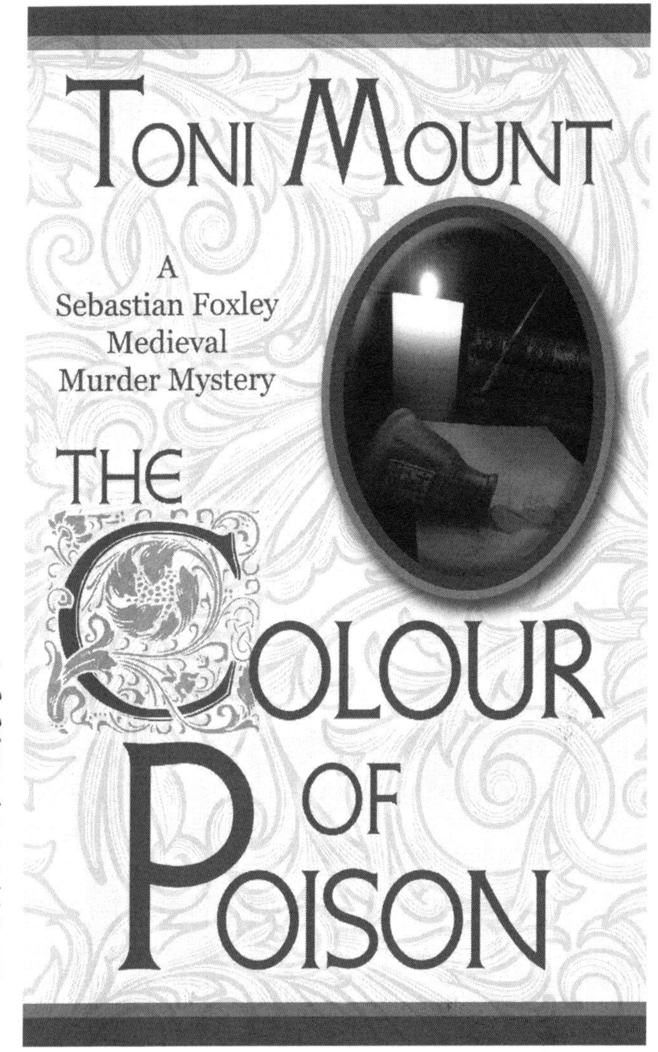

The narrow, stinking streets of medieval London can sometimes be a dark place. Burglary, arson, kidnapping and murder are every-day events. The streets even echo with rumours of the mysterious art of alchemy being used to make gold for the King.

Join Seb, a talented but crippled artist, as he is drawn into a web of lies to save his handsome brother from the hangman's rope. Will he find an inner strength in these, the darkest of times, or will events outside his control overwhelm him?

If Seb can't save his brother, nobody can.

Non Fiction History

Anne Boleyn's Letter from the Tower - **Sandra Vasoli**
Jasper Tudor - **Debra Bayani**
Tudor Places of Great Britain - **Claire Ridgway**
Illustrated Kings and Queens of England - **Claire Ridgway**
A History of the English Monarchy - **Gareth Russell**
The Fall of Anne Boleyn - **Claire Ridgway**
George Boleyn: Tudor Poet, Courtier & Diplomat - **Ridgway & Cherry**
The Anne Boleyn Collection - **Claire Ridgway**
The Anne Boleyn Collection II - **Claire Ridgway**
Two Gentleman Poets at the Court of Henry VIII - **Edmond Bapst**
A Mountain Road - **Douglas Weddell Thompson**

"History in a Nutshell Series"

Sweating Sickness in a Nutshell - **Claire Ridgway**
Mary Boleyn in a Nutshell - **Sarah Bryson**
Thomas Cranmer in a Nutshell - **Beth von Staats**
Henry VIII's Health in a Nutshell - **Kyra Kramer**
Catherine Carey in a Nutshell - **Adrienne Dillard**
The Pyramids in a Nutshell - **Charlotte Booth**

Historical Fiction

Struck with the Dart of Love: Je Anne Boleyn 1 - **Sandra Vasoli**
Truth Endures: Je Anne Boleyn 2 - **Sandra Vasoli**
The Colour of Poison - **Toni Mount**
Between Two Kings: A Novel of Anne Boleyn - **Olivia Longueville**
Phoenix Rising - **Hunter S. Jones**
Cor Rotto - **Adrienne Dillard**
The Claimant - **Simon Anderson**
The Truth of the Line - **Melanie V. Taylor**

Children's Books

All about Richard III - **Amy Licence**
All about Henry VII - **Amy Licence**
All about Henry VIII - **Amy Licence**
Tudor Tales William at Hampton Court - **Alan Wybrow**

PLEASE LEAVE A REVIEW

If you enjoyed this book, *please* leave a review at the book seller where you purchased it. There is no better way to thank the author and it really does make a huge difference!
Thank you in advance.

16371969R00132

Printed in Great Britain
by Amazon